Best wishes

WHAT WOULD TOM DO?

CAROL J. BOROWIAK

authorHOUSE®

AuthorHouse™ UK
1663 Liberty Drive
Bloomington, IN 47403 USA
www.authorhouse.co.uk
Phone: 0800 047 8203 (Domestic TFN)
    +44 1908 723714 (International)

Published by AuthorHouse 09/19/2019

ISBN: 978-1-7283-9366-7 (sc)
ISBN: 978-1-7283-9367-4 (e)

Library of Congress Control Number: 2019914366

Print information available on the last page.

Any people depicted in stock imagery provided by Getty Images are models,
and such images are being used for illustrative purposes only.
Certain stock imagery © *Getty Images.*

This book is printed on acid-free paper.

DEDICATION

I would like to celebrate this novel in memory of my father.
FOR MY DAD, THE GREATEST
MAN I HAVE EVER KNOWN.

ACKNOWLEDGEMENT

My thanks go to Helen Andrew, Dee Wild Kearney, and Erica Fox, for being by my side as I have walked through this amazing process and for making my life bearable at times of sadness. My sisters as I would have them known in and out of this novel. My characters in 'WHAT WOULD TOM HARDY DO?' will also bear a resemblance to these fabulous girls. Big thanks to David Meredydd Parry for being at the end of the phone in regards to my lack of computer skills.

PART ONE

CHAPTER ONE

LAURA

J ust like me not to have a jacket or cardigan in my car for emergencies. I wasn't expecting to finish work at 2am though- that's my excuse. We are only just hitting autumn, but it seems like mid-summer. Just a little chill in the air (hence needing the jacket). Usually I'd have been heading home around six. Finishing this late? I am a little pissed off to say the least, as I was looking forward to a group chat catch up with friends that I have neglected recently, accompanied by a king size kebab with all the trimmings. Marmite on toast and a cuppa it is then. Not an unusual day.

My adorable little pussy cat comes to greet me and stretches up for a kiss as I enter my home. (More affection than I ever got from my husband or children.) We go straight to the 'treat cupboard' and her little purring engine starts. That's her sorted for now! I notice the neglected pile of mail, bloody hell- looks like more than I can cope with in one sitting. I think about making a start, but in fact, sod it! Leave it where it is. I hate opening mail! It cannot be important anyway, having just recently moved in, so it's probably companies fighting to feed my home with gas and electric. No time for junk mail!

Under my covers with my mug of tea and a plate of toast, Pud curling up next to me, her engine still vibrating. As if my day has not been scary enough, I switch over to the horror channel. At least I don't have to set the alarm! Nothing important awaits my attention in the morning so I can make the most of the scary film. After an hour, I drifted off, the television shuts itself down. Like most people after a long day's work, it usually takes me a couple of hours of 'me-time' to start to relax and get into chill mode. I crashed as soon as comfort and tiredness overtook me.

I woke with what felt like the worst hangover. Did I miss something? The clock on my bedroom wall says 5:45, but the sun is streaming through the window (Batteries must have gone.) My phone, along with my reading glasses remain in my work bag, wherever it landed when I came home some hours ago. How many hours ago? I arrive at the conclusion that I have overslept, which usually makes me feel a bit groggy and somewhat miserable. "Okay Pud: brew, meds, mail." She understands and speeds down the stairs with ease, while my bones creak their way down. I pick up the mail as I follow my terror into the kitchen, where she is already sat next to her cupboard. Kitchen clock says 7:50. "7.50? Why are we up this early on my day off, Pud?" The sun is already warming up my extremely bare kitchen, which is now finished after handyman Dave has excelled himself again with his tiling and decorating.

This afternoon has me visiting my favourite shop to buy whatever it takes to make my little cookhouse beautiful. Not that I will use the kitchen much- only really when I have visitors. After the kids flew the nest and since my divorce, my culinary expertise has come to an end.

I hear a loud bang in the distance.

Another car door slams. "What's going on Pud?" It's just so unusual to hear three door slams in as many minutes. Then raised voices. Followed by more door slams. It's no use looking out of the downstairs windows because you cannot see onto the road, or even into the neighbour's gardens. We are all hidden behind some sort of coverage, be it fences, walls or in my case, trees and fencing. That was one of the things that endeared me to this almost reclusive place. My privacy is of utmost importance now, as I age.

"Come on Pud, back to bobos for a few hours, Mummies still tired." We get back into bed, having forgotten the noises we are yet to identify. Usually, not a sound could be heard beyond my grounds. Too late now anyway, back in bed with my Puddles cuddling up. The truth is, I can't be arsed going into one of the front bedrooms to be nosey.

"Oh God, what the hell's going on?"

Out of my pit again! I have got to go and see what is happening. We (Pud and I) run to the front bedroom window knowing something is not right and are faced with what seems to be a crime scene across the road. Well, I know it's a crime scene, what with it being written all over the tape! It's a little overwhelming though, seeing it right outside your own house. We all know what happens at a crime scene, being involved in many through my work over the years, but not on my front door!

I am not really familiar with any of the residents on this lane, with having only lived here for the last month, but I know the occupants of that house are quite an elderly couple. Jeez- I thought I'd escaped this kind of reality moving here! Maybe this place isn't as quiet as it seems? As a criminal psychologist, I have dealt with the worst types of crimes imaginable, so nothing fazes me anymore, but I did not expect to be looking out of my bedroom window at a crime scene.

Fortunately, I do have a barmy sense of humour and a silly side. Out of the workplace of course! Apparently, my ability at bringing out the best in people works wonders though when I'm assessing clients, contributing to my rather good success rate. (If I may say so myself!)

I watch for another ten minutes at the comings and goings, then realise there will probably be a knock on my door at some point.

Quick shower, and as I'm just getting dressed, my intercom buzzes. I listen to the police woman's voice on the other end introduce herself. I buzz her in to enter my gates and explain my appearance (as if I give a damn anyway), but I will always be polite- if the situation requires it! I lead the young lady into my dining room-the nearest door.

I tell her to take a seat and excuse myself, telling her, "I'm putting the kettle on- it's my first brew of the day- I'm gagging! I didn't get home from work 'til two am this morning, and I have obviously been woken by the commotion across the road. I gave up trying to sleep and got in the shower in the end. Won't be long." She seemed quite surprised that I hadn't immediately tried to find out what had happened. She probably wasn't expecting me to tell her about my attempt to get some shut-eye, and as for describing the police presence and cordoned-off house as merely a 'commotion'! A serious crime has happened just feet away, and here I am sounding like I don't care, by the look on her face.

She accepted my offer of a coffee and within five minutes I returned with two cups and a plate of pastries.

Before this pretty young blonde could thank me, I got into it: "Right. Let's have it-what's happened? I take it there has been foul play?" She looked bemused by my callousness. I'm generally known for my forwardness and lack of shock, regardless of the circumstances or offense.

"Yes. Mrs?" she starts to enquire.

"I'm Laura Timmings, but Laura is just fine." I inform her. She is Police Constable Sarah Parish. My phone starts ringing. It's in my work bag, but still loud enough to be annoying. I take my bag and put it in the living room. It carries on ringing. "I think that may be a friend ringing me to find out what's going on, as I see that the media are already in situ." I comment.

"This is just routine Laura. There has been a homicide."

My lack of any real concern takes her interest. I feel the need to explain: "I think you might wonder why I don't seem to be shocked or horrified, but if I tell you that sixteen hours of my day yesterday and leading into the early hours of this morning were taken up with attaining information about the two young men that are alleged to have committed the Blake murders in Manchester, you'll understand why. I'm a Criminal Psychologist Sarah." I use her first name and she smiles. "You're too pretty to be a policewoman." Another smile.

"I was not told that you worked for us, you know what I mean, and I have not met you before." she says quite shyly.

"I only moved here four weeks ago, mainly because it's out of the city, quiet, off the main track and peaceful and as you saw when you arrived were well-secured. But that is all in question now?" I am asking.

"Yeah, very sad. Do you know the occupants of number seven?" she asks.

"So there has not been a death then? You said do, instead of did." I say.

"Yes, there has been a death in the house." she says sadly.

"But it wasn't the old couple who live there? I have seen the old man at the gates a few times, but with us all sort of being barricaded in, we don't get to see each other. I have yet to meet them." I reply. "They had a guest living with them for a while and its this person that has been killed." She enlightens me.

We eventually get my interview over, the usual questions one is asked living in the vicinity of a crime. The perpetrator may have been on their premises when I arrived home last night. Now that is a scary thought.

I did not ask, and she did not give me any information as to who it actually was who had met their demise. We talk more about the area I was now living in, then I walk her to the door. We shake hands and I say: "Until we meet again." She reaches the gate.

"It was nice meeting you Laura, and thank you for the coffee." She turns and says. "You too Sweetie and you're welcome. Take care and good luck with the case." Once the door closed, I say "Christ Pud, that's really fucked up." to my gorgeous little house mate, as she follows me into the kitchen. I make another brew and finish the snack size pastries. I say snack size because I ate four.

"Errrrr....you called?" Rae was my last buddy to have phoned me, so I connected straight to her. "Do you not know what's going on right outside your front door?" She near enough shouts.

"No what?" I enquire. Rae, listening to the news, probably knew more than I did. She then goes on to tell me what the media is saying, and I had either brought back some rookie and been at it all night, or as usual, my music was too loud. I then tell her the truth. Brought back some rookie, cheeky beggar!

I go into detail of what I have been told, which is not much. I ask her if she speaks to anyone who wants to know what has happened here today, then she can tell them that I am fine, and they were sure to find out more by listening to the news. I have gone through the events once informing Rae and I know I am going to have to repeat it several times anyway to my annoyance, I am positive about that. I hate having to repeat the same scenario, over and over again. I tell her my plans for the day and vice versa, then we disconnect. I do have little tolerance regarding reiteration. Hence my putting my phone on silent. I will remind myself to ring my son Benjamin and my friends Livvi and Daisy later. I just wanted to get on with the day.

Obviously, there was still plenty going on in the Lane as I drove away, in the small space I had to pass through with my rather large jeep. A present to me from me. Moving to the countryside, I needed a 4WD to explore my hilly surroundings. I thought about my earlier return home. Did anything stand out as unusual or was it an inside job?

I drove twenty-five miles to the nearest retail park and secured my car in front of the DIY shop B&Q. I needed light fittings, blinds and other bits and bobs for the house. Dave was coming to put all the final purchases in place next week while I'm working, so I don't need to spend my days off with a workman in the new home I was still getting to know. Least of all listening to drills and hammering!

I was quite pleased that I was able to attain everything

on my list, along with a stunning chandelier for my living room. I put the goods into the car and made my way to my absolute favourite shop- TK Maxx. Apart from some new bedding and cushions, the world was my oyster, and I knew there would also be several items of clothing and maybe some ornaments that are not on my list that would find their way home with me.

As I reached the entrance of my Aladdin's cave, and before the doors could open, I heard my name called from behind me. I recognised the lady, in her mid- thirties, with a sorrowful expression on her face, as a neighbour. I was terrible at remembering names, even though this young woman was the first to introduce herself and her children to me on the day I arrived. I just smiled and said hello. I already understood why she looked so sad, as she along with the people living around today's crime scene, had known each other for many years. What she had to tell me would now put a slight downer on the rest of my shopping expedition.

I remembered her name as she opened her mouth to speak. Rosie, how could I forget? Her name suited her as any other name would not. Rosie by name, 'Rosie by nature'. Everything about her seemed to be impeccable. From her hair and nails, to her lovely clothes and accent. I would not usually listen to hearsay, but Rosie's other half just so happens to be a Sergeant in the local police force. I will meet him at some stage through my work or as my neighbour, but as of this time I have not seen anyone in the vicinity of my home that would resemble a person whom works for the Criminal Justice System (in this role anyway).

The house under investigation. As it turns out, had been broken into, and the son of Mr and Mrs Graham, Robert (their only child, aged forty-five), was the victim of a homicide. Robert had been living with his parents for the last six months. By the change in Rosie's tone (as she started to tell me about him), I became suspicious.

He had only recently come home, after a long term in prison. I could feel her distaste at the mention of Mr Graham and she held her stomach when she spoke. I assumed this reaction meant that his crime or crimes that put him in prison still made her feel sickly. Yes, people everywhere, no matter in what location you live, there will always be someone who has done a stint in jail. From trivial offences to hard crime. Robert's crime so obviously was not trivial, and from Rosie's vibes I sensed it may have something to do with a child, though she was not about to reveal it. Good on her.

"Robert was found in a terrible state, blood everywhere. They cut his throat and wrists, he was nearly beheaded. Poor Elizabeth and Ivor." Rosie said. Not poor Robert. Making my first assumptions seem more plausible. Well, well, well; maybe now I am a little more interested in what has occurred with my neighbour, as initially I was not. We spoke a little further, but nothing of any real importance was to be gathered. I felt my usual slight empathy for Rosie, who was so upset about the older couple she had obviously come to love. I stroked her back and she walked away after our farewells, with tears in her eyes. I'll give her that, she obviously knew what she could and could not say. I applaud her for not being a gossip and will go out of my way to be a little friendlier to her in the future. Bless her. I was a little intrigued but decided that this was not going to stop me from shopping.

It had changed my totally relaxed mood, and now I found myself thinking more and more about what had gone on. I purchased quite a few items of clothing, ready for my autumn and winter walks, around my new country of Wales.

Living on the verge of the Snowdonia mountains, with the sea in view and a hundred yards away from my house is the reason I moved here. I purchased several more items (mostly decorative for the house) and once I had left the store, decided to go into Sports World to pick up a couple of pairs of walking boots.

Rather than stay out for lunch, I had now decided to make my way home. My intentions had changed, and I just felt I wanted to spend some time with Pud and put my feet up. I was feeling a bit shit to be honest and somewhat tired. A feeling of disappointment about the location of Robert's homicide. How selfish of me. Am I ever going to escape from crime unscathed? As I get older I tend to worry more about the levels that severe crime has peaked to in recent years. I am actually quite a cold arse, if you ask anyone who does not matter to me. I am tough and big enough to look after myself, but as the years pass I am afraid that this is not going to be the case. My tolerance levels are already showing a sign of change, even though my passion for my job still remains the same.

Boots acquired and thrown into the back of my Jeep, I make my way back to Penmaenmawr, knowing I have at least three phone calls to make, before I can settle down to my day off. It is feeling more like a nuisance day, rather than a day off to enjoy my own bloody space. I popped into the bakery in the village and picked up something for lunch. I had a bit of banter with the owner, who is a bit of a comic, then made the one-minute drive home.

I was parked in my drive minutes later, making sure the gate was definitely locked before I put the key in my front door. I didn't even glance over at the crime scene when I'd passed. I felt really tired once inside. I picked up my little friend, took her to the Dreamie cupboard and fed them to her by hand. She was so cute. I am definitely a big softie with animals. All animals. If I ever do decide to cut my hours, I would love to buy a pedigree German Shepherd pup.

When in the kitchen, I didn't feel hungry anymore. I put the bakery items in the fridge to save for later. I wanted to make three phone calls, just in case I succumbed to a long sleep, as I decided maybe a nap would lighten my mood. In order, I chose to ring Rae, then Daisy and finishing off with my son Ben.

CHAPTER TWO

RAE

"Hello you, so what have you found out?" I asked Laura when she rang. I had phoned her this morning regarding a report on Sky news. There had been the murder of a gentleman. The crime that was reported had been committed across the road from Laura's new home. Obviously, I was distressed greatly as I had not received the call from her which she had promised last night. I put it down to her workload, as she always worked till much later than she intended.

Laura went on then to tell me what she had learnt, knowing that anything she said would remain between ourselves. Not that there was anything that you could not find out on-line. We chatted for an hour or so, catching up on a week without speaking to each other, which was virtually unheard of. Our conclusion to the crime was the same after she had repeated her discussion with her neighbour Rosie.

If the victim had recently returned home from a long prison sentence then it might be a vengeful killing, which is more understandable if Laura was right and Robert Graham had caused some injury or abuse of some kind to a child.

I immediately started up my computer, as I said I would look up Mr Graham for Laura. She felt weary and was going to take a nap. I told her I would ring her again later in the evening, to see if she felt any better, and inform her of what I have learnt, that is if I had gathered any information? In a way, I hoped Laura was right. It would be safer for her if this was the victim's identity that was at threat, rather than anyone else in the community.

I found many articles on Robert Graham. From accounts on his past abuse on puberty-aged children, to the latest articles referring to his last atrocity which saw him with what I and the majority of people would think to be such a short sentence, for a nauseate and repugnant crime. My instant reaction was he got what he deserved, and how good Laura was at her job that she could tell by a women's body language the depth of another person's depravity.

I am working too many hours myself at the moment and have decided that when I next speak to Laura, Livvi and Daisy, I am going to make sure we have a four-way conversation and book a break together. We will put it into our diaries as we speak. My job as a producer on issue-based documentaries kept me busy at the workplace, also slaving at home. I have some free time coming up now for the next few months and I will make sure my friends take some time out too. We have all worked bloody hard over our lifetimes and brought up our children single-handedly. It would do us all good to think about semi-retirement.

Clucey is guiding her lead towards my chair, so I guess that means we are going out for a walk. Why not, it is a beautiful autumn day. Hot enough to apply sun cream. After enduring two surgeries for skin cancer, I am not going to inspire a third bout. "I think we will walk into the village Cluce and pop in at the bakers." I lock the door and we head in the direction of our little nest of shops. Forrest, my husband is working in the neighbourhood today so he will be returning home a little earlier than usual. His job takes him over many boroughs, working as an environmental officer. It's quite nice when he works in the vicinity of our home, we can eat an early dinner together and maybe take in a show or visit the cinema which is unique on a weekday.

CHAPTER THREE

DAISY

"Well it has taken you long enough….. Where the hell have you been?... "I don't really care, I have been worried sick. As soon as I heard it on the news I have been constantly ringing you. I have left several voice mails. Good God Laura, you should have let me know you were okay. You're so inconsiderate at times." I replace the handset as my conversation with Laura comes to an end. "Oh God she is infuriating." I say to my youngest son Mark, whom has just walked in through the front door looking hassled and catching the end of my rant at Laura. "What's eating you?" I growl.

"I should ask you the same question?" Mark replies. "There was a murder across the road from Laura's house this morning, or last night. I have been ringing her from early morning, since I saw it on the news. You know what Laura's like for not answering her phone. I'll let you know how it turns out when I know more. She's not feeling so good. Just tired like myself. Now why the long face and why are you home so early?" Mark goes on to tell me that he has just given in his notice at work. No explanation as he wanders off into the kitchen and into the fridge. I follow him. "Oh God, so you're just going to leave it like that?" I growl at him.

"Errrrr…Yes." Is all he manages to say. I am not in the mood for this today. In fact I am livid.

"Fucking Hell Mark, what would happen if I just decided to give up work and sell the practice?" No answer, just grunts and he starts filling his face. I was going to walk away but my anger made me stay and resolve this. "Mark, answer me God damn it." I do not even get an obliging response.

Grrrr…. I could hit him. This was the third time he had walked out of a job this year. 'Mummy makes lots of money with her vets practice, so it does not matter whether I work or not' was his attitude. Does not give a fuck.

I squared up to him. If I had to resort to intimidating him, then so be it. I could see he had become uneasy with my stance. "I'm sick of being given all the shit jobs. I work the hardest in there and Bob still gives all the best jobs to the smelly cow. I've had enough and told him to shove his job up his rectum." Mark replies, then starts to walk away.

"Excuse me I have not finished with you yet." I shout at him.

"She stinks, I can't work with her anymore, she's knocking me sick." He says this like he doesn't have a care in the world.

"God give me strength. If you had done like I said and had a word with her. You don't have to be rude Mark. You just politely say: 'I am sorry Lucy, but the deodorant you are using is not working and I am…'" I stopped talking. He was not listening.

"Have you turned to religion today? Coz that's all I've heard since I came in. God this, God that. Anyway it's not BO she stinks of, it's her vagina." he says, looking at me scoffing a pork pie. I thought did he just say what I thought he said. I'm going to get out of his eyeline before he sees me crease over with laughter, especially as I am so annoyed at him

"I am going to have a lie down. You get looking through the paper. GET A JOB." I screamed the last bit at him and then got out of his sight before I fell over laughing. I didn't want him to see I was amused by his comment. Can you imagine going for an interview and being asked why you left your last job, and Mark answering, 'Well the girl I was working with had a smelly vagina.' I lay on top of my bed giggling from within. I was fucking annoyed at him; he didn't even think his behaviour warranted questioning. Here was I suffering from the bloody menopause, depressed, hot flushes, fucked off with work and pissed off with a husband who didn't even know his family existed. At least I have my other son Damien's bedroom now that my eldest child has flown the nest, so I do not even have to see him. Bollocks to everyone and everything. I do not even have to get under any covers, I was always hot and sweaty. I put on my favourite tunes with headphones in place and whether I sleep or not, I do not bloody care. Bollocks to myself as well.

CHAPTER FOUR

LAURA

When I slowly came to consciousness, I was astonished to find that I had slept for four hours. I had not expected to plunge straight into a deep dreamless state. But even just the thought of it made me feel restored. I was also famished and Pud was now licking my hand, hinting at me to feed her, her favourite 'Dreamies' (which I always do when I wake). "It's not really treat time Pud." But the cuddles and love I receive from her are so delightful that I always give in. I still had to retrieve my buys from this morning out of my car, and there was still plenty of time to arrange my goodies around the house.

It was still a beautiful day and reaching dinner time, so I took my drink and two items that I should have had for lunch into the rear garden. When I looked at my phone, I had received several voicemails from Ben. 'Mum this, Mum that, Mum, Mum, Mum…'. That was Ben. I was still recovering from the shock when he announced that he was going back to university to study Dentistry, just a few short months ago, and now he was settled into his apartment over two hundred and fifty miles away. This time, I knew he was ready. The last time, (four years ago) I was not so sure when he chose to do the same; unfortunately I was right. He mentioned something about an early Christmas present. I just hope it is something I am going to agree with.

Just as I was about to ring Ben, he rang me, through a face to face on WhatsApp. There he was, sat in front of his laptop with his customary sunglasses in place. He always wore them when he spoke to me: for a reason. I can read his body language with ease-especially his eyes. A great actor he is, receiving awards in drama, but he is also a bloody bad liar. I have no idea how that works! "Hello Mummy, how are you?" he says, smiling widely.

"I feel as great as you look son." I say in answer to his question. I know Ben had only been away from home for several weeks, but I missed him terribly; just being around, constantly happy and full of life. "How have the last few days gone?" I asked him.

"Perfect. I know it is early days but I already feel at home. I am much chummier with my flat mates now and we get on famously, so that's one element I am happy with," he responds.

"Fabulous Ben, I am really pleased." I say with a lump in my throat. We then go on to discuss the topic of the day: the murder of my neighbour, which Ben had no idea about. The first words out of his mouth are of no surprise.

"Your work load is ample enough so do not get involved. I know you." He says with concern in his voice.

"I have absolutely no reason for doing so." I tell him. At

times, I have no intention of getting tied up in crimes that are not related to my work, but I do do so, often.

"Right, this early Christmas present? Enlighten me Ben, and from your perspective out of ten, how likely am I to say yes?" I ask him. "Erm…perhaps three… but hopefully ten." He says.

I got an "Oh God" in before he starts his 'the reason why I need this is because…' trying to convince me. Ben has always had the confidence to get up and perform either comedy routines or theatrical productions since he was very young, drama being his second love to what now is his choice of profession. I think I will need a tissue to wipe away either the tears of laughter or of financial ruin.

"Here we go. Are you ready?" he says.

"No." I reply. I am going to need that tissue.

"Well, you know how atrocious I am at organising myself, how forgetful I am when shopping for food and being able to prepare lunch for Uni, as well as washing and ironing clothes. I am lousy at living on my own Mummy." He carries on demeaning himself for another five minutes. "Right, right! I get it. I am not moving nearer to you so that I can still play Mummy for you at the age of twenty- four. I have only just moved here, and may I add that if I'd have had my way, I would have relocated to Wales many years ago. But my darling, I had two sons that cried and did not want to leave their school or friends." I say in a condescending manner.

"Mum- stop! I am not asking anything like that. Promise not to say anything till you have heard me out; please?" I conceded with his request. In fact, he was building this so far up that I felt a little bit relieved, thinking it was not going to be so bad. He has done this since he was a little boy and then requested money for an ice-cream! Fingers crossed.

If we had not been face to face, I am sure I would have keeled over with laughter and dread. Not only from his comical request for a present, but the absolute absurdity of it. I was sat here now wondering whether my previous thoughts of his internship at university were now fading quickly and my confusion at deciding whether to laugh or cry was shown by an open-mouthed numbness.

Ben wanted an extension of his Mummy. Someone to do all his organising, from alarm-setting to food shopping. In fact, he gave me a list of approximately thirty reasons why he needed this figure so life could be made much simpler for him. I comply with the fact that having dyslexia can cause some upheaval in regard to his organisational skills, needing more time for his written work and exams. I thought maybe what I have always thought of as his laziness, is perhaps more to do with the disability. "Are you asking me to hire you an au pair?" I asked him.

"No, just someone like Lynne who looks after Alan Partridge." My mind said, 'what the fuck', my answer was a bloody long pause. I did not laugh, as I was unsure of his seriousness. Lynne from Alan Partridge! One of our cherished past-times, was me introducing Ben to some of my best-loved comedians- Partridge being one of them. Alan became one of his icons, often taking him off at various times. One of our major bonds was the parallels in our humour. I told him I would figure something out, and if he was taking the piss I would gladly do the same to him on some other occasion. He assured me he was not, and, in my heart, I knew his failings, and what seemed like a riotous request now turned into a serious quest.

I would have to think earnestly on this one. We spoke for a further twenty minutes without mentioning his needs again. The apple does not fall far from the tree with

Benjamin and me. It must have hit him harder than the apple that fell from my wonderful father onto me. Saul was the same, we had the identical amazing relationship, until his true colours came through. Ben was on his way out so big loves and goodbyes were said at the end of our conversation. My youngest child was the one that found it the hardest to let go of his Mummies apron strings. Saul was independent from a young age.

I spent the next few hours placing all my colourful ornaments around my kitchen and up on my walls, which I enjoyed doing, brightening the place up beautifully. TK Maxx never lets me down, and at bargain prices, I had done well!

My working schedule at the moment was hectic, so I elected to take a brand-new file relating to a recently-committed massacre of a family of three by two brothers into the conservatory. Just as I seat myself and take out my laptop for notes, the phone rings. It is Rea. She is educating me on the life of Mr Robert Graham, and any sympathy I might have had for the victim or his parents was waning. I sure as hell would not have let the bastard (my son or not), enter my home again. No surprise now as to why he was butchered. There are children living around the home of this couple, and they bring their son to live in this place. It would literally be his play ground. I did think of sending a sympathy card, but I have none. That is one off the streets. Criminals whom abuse children, especially for sexual gratification are a 'no-no' on my work plan.

Before Rea had cut the call short, she mentioned a little break away for Livvi, Daisy, herself and me. Daisy was going through a bad spell, as we women always do at certain ages. A get-together will do her the world of good. It will do us all the same. We would arrange that in the next few days. Rea and her husband Forrest were on their way to see a movie.

That is one of the things I miss, not being in a relationship anymore (going out in male company).

After I feel I have done all I have to do to get my house to be more my home, I make myself another brew, and get down to some work. I might decide to take one of the guys I have met through work up on their offer of an evening out. It is time to get back on the dating scene.

I start reading about the slaughter of the Blakes, beginning with the scene at their home, as it was found by Sasha Blake's sister, Patricia Knowles. Mrs Knowles had not yet been questioned by the police. As can be imagined, the young woman was in shock and sedated. At the time of the report she remained in hospital. This lady's life will never be the same.

Sasha and Michael Blake were both found in their bedroom. This was described as a scene from a slaughterhouse. Besides the blood splatter, bone fragmentation and brain matter that covered walls and ceiling. The report stated that every sharp instrument that lived in that house was used on both bodies, and just lay casually where the perpetrators had left them. A hammer was also used on the victims.

I read about the wounds to the bodies and then went on to acknowledge the scene in the second bedroom. Like every normal human being, I am repulsed by any kind of cruelty to a child; this was Melissa, an eighteen- month-old baby girl. Melissa had been beaten to death. I pause; this is my work. I cannot become emotionally involved, but in cases like this it is so fucking hard to do.

The executioners of this vilest of acts, are two brothers: Brian and Eric Ward. This is where I come in.

Brian, fifteen, being the youngest of the two by twenty months is diagnosed as being autistic and of having three arrests. All crimes are committed whilst in Eric's company. Eric is the leader and has a record of fifteen arrests. I read on, then phone the place of incarceration to confirm my separate appointments with the two. I have another day off tomorrow, so I will visit the boys within the week (as long as the investigating officers are ready for me to do that). From what I can deduct from scanning through the evidence left at the scene, a scrap of paper with the words 'Brian and Eric did this' was found under the body of Mrs Blake- only just legible, owing to the victim's blood. I consider this was possibly composed by Brian and if this was so, it would be plausible to assume this was written whilst Eric was still committing the atrocity, maybe on the baby. The note was hidden, not intended for his older brother's observation. The words written were an acknowledgement of their guilt and were intended to point officers to themselves. Again, assuming Brian wrote that note, going off his arrest history compared with his brother's, he may not have actually participated. If this was the case, then Brian would be entitled to some form of counselling depending on his mental state.

This worried me, even more so with him having traits of Autism. It does not say in the report the extent of his disability; I will have to make sure his medical records are obtained. If Eric is not a participant and was bullied into joining his brother at the home where they forced their way into through the conservatory window, then he should not be confined in a cell without support.

Returning the files to my case, I took a cold drink and some fruit into the lounge and switched on the television. Something I never did at this time of the day and did not know what to expect on the TV. The only time I watch television is when 'The Voice' is on its once-yearly sequence. Later on in the evening, I occasionally watch the crime channel. As if I did not have enough fucking crime in my life! Pud cuddles up on my knee, but within minutes she shoots away from her resting place with a fright. My reaction in disgust at the TV would have caused anyone to jump! How many times do I scream 'Oh my God!' at the screen when Claudia Winkleman pops up on her shampoo commercial! The woman is worse than an 'annoying personality vacuum'. She is more a comparable to Jenny Éclair's commercial for 'Vagisan'. In fact, I would compare her more to a 'bothersome vagina'. I just cannot tolerate her.

I phoned Sian, a lovely young friend and colleague from work. She assisted me more like a PA. I wanted to give her the heads up on the next workload. I went through the day's scenarios. Like with the majority of my friends, we would end up in hysterics on certain subjects, but commonly it would be a person's blunders that prompted the giggles. I told Sian about my earlier chat with Ben and his request. I must admit how when I revealed the object of our discussion, it did sound humorous. She laughed as was expected. In fact, she nearly choked! When she realised I was being genuine, she laughed more hysterically. "Please tell me you told him to piss off?" she said sincerely.

"Well…" I just about said, and she continued.

"All joking aside, Laura, it is about fucking time you let him grow up and be responsible for himself. You're stopping him from becoming independent and before you start with 'he has this problem and that problem'… what do we do when we have problems? We solve them. Just like Ben should be doing. He is twenty-four for God's sake." I knew every word she said was true and I became a little more accepting of her criticism. "With your working history you should be able to make alternative suggestions, like notes, alarms on his phone. You're so good at your job and you can read a stranger from fifty feet away, but when it's something personal, you're bloody hopeless." she told me with such sincerity. Actually, I totally agree with her. What would he do if I died tomorrow? Sian had neglected to say, as I would have done in her shoes. We chatted for another ten minutes then she had to leave to pick up her young son from his football training. I turned on the crime channel and watched the television 'til I fell asleep, after saying 'Oh my God' again several times to the bothersome vagina.

I woke in the same position I had fallen asleep in, with my glasses sliding down my face. Pud was just stretching herself into wakefulness, then the realisation on waking that it was 'dreamie time'. She jumped off the sofa and headed to the kitchen. Amazingly, I stood without the aches I would have expected in a sat-up position sleeping on the sofa. I had had a good night's sleep. It was nearing eight and the morning sky was a deep blue. It would imply another beautiful day was beginning.

Once Pud was fed, watered and treated, it did not take long before I was ready to hit the road and head to Llandudno. An hour or so looking around the many shops that were at one's disposal. My appointment at 'Top Notch Tattoo' with Lou was at ten-thirty. I had been coming to Llandudno for two years on breaks, mainly to visit this parlour, as it was 'on the map' for being one of the best. There was no doubt there- it has a talented group of professionals. I was to be stationed here for the day whilst Luci branded me with a watercolour portrait of Pud on the back of my right shoulder.

I have acquired many beauteous tattoos since coming to Top Notch, including a recent one by Luke who did me the most breath-taking portrait of my hero of forty plus years, David Bowie. On previous visits, Luke proved himself to be a master of his craft. The man who has kept me grounded throughout my life with his words and song- Leonard Cohen, secure on my leg forever: a beautiful portrait! Then there's my first, the biggest legend of them all, my Daddy, whom I lost just over a year ago. Lou had excelled herself at doing several cover-ups which were quite a challenge, in addition to other wonderful designs. Craig had applied some multi-religious tats on my leg, and Daisy, the trainee, did a couple of Indian religious icons.

Tattoos had become a craving, my addiction to having everything that has been beautiful in my life memorised in ink by stunningly-gifted artisans. Owing to my profession, I have nearly run out of space to adorn that can be hidden from my clientele.

I thoroughly savour my time spent here, and while Lou prepares her station, I watch Luke work on a gentleman whom is sitting having a portrait of his lost child. The way I talk about the talents that these lovely people have to the guy, generates blushing to the young artist's face.

We always giggle in our conversations and swap comical stories. For example, the last time I was here Craig was working on my biblical characters and Lucille was covering a friend's shin with a pussy cat with numerous accessories. There were many comments from observers that came either as friends or to book an appointment. The 'pussy on the leg' joke had gone on that long that Laura (me) opened her big mouth and informed all, that women's 'pussies' as they called them, were absolutely nothing like or cannot be compared to a cat. If you tried to do anything sexual with my pussy, she would bite your fucking hand off. It's an insult to these gorgeous little animals. "I suppose my pussy being worked on now will cause hilarity?" Did I really just say that? Obviously, an inaccurate statement, causing a group cackle. "You all know what I meant." You see, these young folks were not just my tattooists, we had become friends through respect and humour. Lou had offered to look after Puddles if I decided I needed a break. I had said I could not put her in a cattery and would not be able to saunter off on holidays, and Sian lived too far away to look after her now. Maybe I was hinting. It worked anyway.

My new addition is astounding without doubt. Leaving the shop at five o' clock I headed to Subway to pick up a foot-long spicy Italian sandwich with the hottest of everything possible, encased in tasty Italian bread. I had a stash of Magnums for afters in my freezer. I got to my car and headed home, past the sea and the glorious mountains, listening to a CD of Echo and the Bunnymen I had bought at HMV this morning. 'Hee Hee', I thought to myself and looked back to make sure I had not forgotten the bag with my newly gotten DVDs I had decided to buy- every film that they had in the shop on Blue Ray that had Tom Hardy in the cast! I was having a teenage crush in my mid-fifties! I could not stop saying 'Phwoar' to the screen every time he appeared, and as he was the lead in all but one or two, I would be hoarse at the end of these viewings! A series of eight episodes called Taboo. Eight hours; I was in my element.

After I had entered my home, and before I settled down in front of the TV, I gave Pud a bit of attention, with the obligatory 'Dreamies' being swallowed rather than chewed. I got all the things that would be needed for my working day tomorrow ready, made some notes, then listened to my answerphone messages on my landline and mobile. I added some more notes following the messages, then headed to my bedroom to put my jimmies on. "Come on Pud, let's get letching and munching." As if I needed to tell her to follow me!

Maybe I should make a transition from my bedroom to the lounge? I repeated what happened the evening before, only this time, four hours of Tom Hardy made a deviation from the previous night's true crime. I slept healthily and felt fully refreshed for the day ahead.

I met Sian Knight heading to the same area from a different path as myself. We always greeted with a 'good to see you' hug. Coffee was always first on the agenda, to be accompanied by my favourite pastries that Sian had picked up fresh from the Deli on her way in. I could eat them every day and they would still be a treat! The first hour was taken up by a case we were assigned to several weeks earlier: two sixteen-year-old girls that had been on police and social services radar since they were very young. We call the behaviour of these girls 'environmental' due to the circumstances of their growth, with parents that are handicapped from a substance misuse point of view. These kids never had a chance. Taken away from their creators on numerous occasions and then being let down by the system and committed into their parents guidance yet again where they were left to decline.

Their alleged crime was to enter Alice Acres' home by an unlocked door at three o'clock in the afternoon on a sunny day in August. Alice (aged seventy-nine) had left the door unlocked after her home help had departed. Janine Cross and Emily Hill were sat on a wall across the road from Alice's small terraced house when they witnessed the help leaving. On the spur of the moment, the girls decided to enter the premises and immediately eyed Mrs Acres (a widow of seven years), sat in an armchair facing a television set that was switched on. The alarm on the aged woman's face became a stimulus for what was next to develop.

Emily held Alice down forcefully while Janine ransacked all the rooms. On her return she held out a bag that she had retrieved from a closet to show Emily what she had acquired on her search. Instead of vacating the property after their pillage, Janine elected to punch Alice in the face. Two amiable females carried on to beat Alice around her face, arms and legs, take some biscuits from her food cupboard and left. They were seen by a neighbour whom recognised one of the girls.

Alice died on the way to hospital, after the neighbour accessed the house and found Mrs Acres unconscious. In quick response, she phoned the police emergency line. Ambulance and officers arrived on the scene approximately five minutes later. The paramedics did try to revive the frail old lady, but to no avail.

Janine and Emily were arrested just a few hours later and taken to the station without their parents; both sets being under the influence and using derogative language and swearing at the officers (whom had witnessed this on many occasions, including from children being questioned over many types of crime.) I have spoken to both girls at length and have just about put the finishing touches to my report. Sian will deliver this to the lawyers of both girls whilst I make my way to attend my interviews with the two boys in relation to the Blake murders later.

I go through this most recent crime with Sian, after I tell her what I know about Robert Graham's demise. We both agree that he is better off beneath ground, and it might even be a relief for his parents. It certainly would be if my child had committed an atrocity of the worst description there could possibly be. "Did they deserve to have their son's horrific slaughter on their doorstep though?" Sian asks, meaning the choice of scene to end his life, from the perpetrator's perspective. "Well that is where he was living and I suppose his probation does not let him leave the house, as his release date was still quite recent." I answered.

"Right, now to Brian and Eric Ward." I announce to Sian. She is already aware of the case, but I bring her up to date on the boys themselves and what I had concluded from reading their report. Once we were through, still giving me an hour to spare before I set off for Manchester prison, we meet up with Livvi (my long-time buddy), who has been a police sergeant for some years in this area, and we head off to the nearest café.

To say we had moments ago been discussing such horrific subjects, the tone was now definitely lowered! Livvi is coming to stay with me over the weekend and expects to go out and do some letching and maybe join up with some fellas. "Copping off with guys does not do anything for me anymore." I tell Livvi while young Sian looks on with amusement.

"Well it is about time you got back into it, especially when I am around. You're an attractive, funny, intelligent woman. Surely to God you still need a shag?" she replies.

"Why don't you say it loud enough for the whole café to here!" I say.

"She is having a fantasy love relationship with Tom Hardy at the moment, so a good seeing to might do her some good." Sian announces.

"Fucking hell Sian, who put a coin in your slot?" I can't help but butt in on Sian's comment. "Do you remember when we were kiddies and our Mums told us about the 'birds and the bees' and we were repulsed at the thought of a man putting what he wees with inside the place where us girlies wee- a wee pipe in your wee tunnel! Ooooooh..." I finish saying as we all burst into laughter. I carry on with "When I was going through the menopause, nothing revolted me more. Oh my God, did I really let all them men put their piss pipe into my piss tunnel? How the hell did I enjoy that?"

We were laughing hysterically. I do not think my facial expressions helped.

"You do not think like that anymore. You've not long since separated from Steve." Livvi says.

"Steve did not have a willy pipe! I am not kidding either-I am serious. That is why I did not have a sexual relationship with him; we were just friends that went out. I promise you he had no idea in that direction, not a flicker of… Right, I have got to go, I cannot carry on talking trash with you two reprobates! I have got to get back into professional mode." We hug and say our 'laters' and we all head for our vehicles.

I arrive at the prison ten minutes early to find that both boys are in interview with homicide officers. So instead of filling myself up with more coffee, I head to a vacant room, take out my laptop and carry on making notes on another pending case, where I will be a witness in court. I might as well get in front, then when I have four days off over the weekend there won't be a backlog when I return to work.

I had not realised 'til a young man came to greet me, how long I had just sat there happily working away. It was now three-thirty. My initial appointment was at one o'clock. I went through the usual palaver before you enter prison: hand over all personal items, fore finger print, sign in then I was taken to an office holding three members of the homicide team and the prison doctor.

Nothing that was said between us was really news to all: the same scenario, another day, different culprits. I brought up my concerns regarding Brian. Peter Sanders (the prison doctor looking after the young boy) agreed with the deliverance of my diagnosis. The homicide officer in-charge was not as agreeable. This is the norm generally, as police officers are not educated in psychology or the challenges of mental health faced by a suspect. Brian was not talking, and Eric was putting all the blame onto his brother: denying he had ever been on the premises, even though the evidence (without the note being considered), said differently. The boys did not use gloves, so there were finger and palm prints everywhere. When the brothers were arrested and their house searched, their bloody clothes were found in the washing machine. A few items that were believed to have been taken from the Blake residence were located in Eric's room.

We talk for a further ten minutes by which time I divulge, that I have now been here for three hours and I had yet to be offered a drink. I am led down to the interview rooms and enter with a half-smile. I had chosen to speak to Brian first as this would be the greatest challenge and I wanted to acknowledge the depth of his personality.

"Hello Brian, my name is Laura Timmings. If it is okay with you, I would like to have a little chat. I am a psychiatrist, which is a type of doctor. I am here to make sure that you are being looked after." A prison officer enters with my coffee. I ask the young boy if he wants to join me in having some refreshment. No answer. No eye contact. As still as a statue. He had not even slightly changed position since I had walked into the room. I tell the officer to bring a soft drink as I take a seat. I notice Brian has many cuts and bruises, some old, some new.

"It looks like you have been in the wars young man." I say with sympathy. He was listening, which was a good sign and taking note, because he looked over his hands and arms. "You do not have to talk to me today. I am here to assess you. Do you understand what that means?" No acknowledgement. "Do you have any hobbies Brian? Anything you like to do when you're not at school that you get enjoyment from? Do you like to draw?" There was a flinch. I took this as an affirmative. "Would you like me to have some sketching material brought in for you?" Another affirmative. "I think you do like to draw, don't you?" A nod of the head. This was going to be less complicated as I initially thought. "I will make sure that you are given some materials for etching." Brian took a quick glance at me. He relieved himself of some tension and turned a little towards me. This child looked so young and inoffensive; the more I conversed with him, the less awkward he became. Twenty minutes, later Brian was sat facing me. He was now open to our meeting.

By the end of our session, I knew that he would be letting me see more of the natural Brian the next time I would visit. Eye contact was made for just a second on several occasions, and either nods or shakes of the head were used by him. I hoped that he would look forward to our next appointment. He had nodded before I left, to my request that he draw me a picture.

I had what I needed for my initial report. On to brother number two

Eric Ward was a different kettle of fish. His demeanour as I entered his cell was intimidating; from the look on his face to his posture. "Hello Eric, my name is Laura Timmings."

I was interrupted with "I know who you fucking are ya' stupid bitch. Them dick heads told me. Now fuck off and go see someone who gives a fuck." He growls.

"Let's get this straight from the start Eric. I would really like to leave this room and help someone who does give a fuck. Unfortunately, you're stuck with me just as much as I am stuck with you." I cut off his reply by hovering over him. Now I am intimidating. "Shut up and listen to what I have to say, or I will ask an officer whom is a very good friend of mine, to come in and shut you up. I would do it myself but I have just had my nails done!" This kid had more than adolescent angst, and the sheer frenzied violence that he inflicted on such innocent victims, told of his state of mind. Only people in the profession will understand that. He is punishing himself also. At the time he was executing the bloodshed, he was losing his life in an alternative way. A choice he made. I felt nothing but abomination towards him. Then I go into my detaching mode. "I am sure we are going to find some level ground, so we can work together without such profanity." He stayed quiet. Now he was assessing me. The young ones were always the worst. He has the blood of a beloved family on his hands without doubt, yet he is perched in front of me like the world owes him a favour. I take my seat whilst he turns away with nothing but revulsion on his face.

"I ain't fucking talking to you." he spits out.

"Okay, but you're going to listen to what I have to say, like it or not." Silence. "Eric, my aim over the next few visits is to build up some kind of rapport with you so we can at least try and get to some sort of conclusion as to why you thought it okay to take the lives of a young family. I am not asking you to become my best friend, but as of right now, I am all you have got besides your lawyer to talk to. I am actually here for you." I speak to him on a level that he positively understands.

"I haven't even bin in that 'ouse." he replies; more comfortably now. "That being so Eric, why have your fingerprints been found all around the house and on all the weapons that were used in the crime? You had the blood of the victims on your clothes. The list goes on Eric. This is not 'let's play dumb time'. I can see you are a clever young man and you know you have been caught fair and square."

The swearing and the hard man image collapsed after ten minutes into my interview with him. Eric was harbouring such hate for his elders. What I had gathered from reading records, the brothers' upbringing had been tumultuous to say the least. I have dealings with many perpetrators of crime, but not all have had horrific childhoods. The amount of crime committed by those that have is sometimes excused slightly by the judicial system because of the impact of the environment of the offender on their rearing. How many hero celebrities do we have that have had difficult and abusive upbringings, yet they make something of their lives? Through art, writing, gymnastics; the list goes on and on. How few of those that suffer from such neglect or abuse through their young years go into any genre of crime? Thank God only a small minority. We all have a path to choose and these boys certainly did pick a bloody wrong one. Getting back at society is not granting their parents the punishment the boy's might hope for.

It is not the parents who go to prison.

Eric did not deny towards the end of the visit that he had executed these assassinations. In fact, he became much more amenable. My heavy-handedness when I first entered worked with the majority of clients. After I asked him to stop swearing, he complied. We talked about his likes and dislikes and how he was being treated within the walls. He knew that he was open to injury due to his harm to a child. Did Eric have a death wish? Was this his attempt at self-harm, to have it administered by others? I was fortunate to have him tell me that Brian was innocent and that before they left for the Blake's residence, he had held a knife to his younger brother's throat as enforcement for him to comply with his own wishes. The lad was an imbecile. Deranged, cretinous and should never step foot on the outside again. My own personal view, which I cannot put into my report.

Although we came to a compromise, this evil soul had absolutely no remorse for what he had undertaken, in anger.

Although I have a lengthy drive home, I decide to go back into the office so I could get my reports on the two typed up immediately. I had learnt so much on the background of the Wards and certainly of Brian's innocence (another reason for my severity towards Eric). Forcing his autistic younger brother to conform to his own depravity. Sian's car was still in the car park, which meant I could go through some details with her rather than later, by email or phone- at least some time would be saved. We were without our own private secretary at the moment, and Sian was working that post as well as her own. I was trying not to let the stress of the situation show, as it affected both myself as well as my amazing partner in crime. I was lightening some of Sian's load, by doing more of my own admin. I just wanted her back for me, too. I miss her at my side. Me being selfish again.

"You saw me coming in. You beauty! Have we any biscuits to go with it?" I asked as she handed me a latte.

"I am afraid my dear I could only offer you Jaffa cakes, which I know you would decline." She is happy to say, having them to herself. I hate Jaffa cakes! I do not like chocolate and orange together, and I am repulsed by jelly. "Take-out on the way home then, me thinks." I say, giving her a peevish stare.

After revealing Pud, my new tattoo, we get down to business. Sian helps with this workload. Reading Brian's medical records gives me the energy to get his report done and be sent to the right people first thing in the morning.

He should be placed in hospital for monitoring and assessing.

CHAPTER FIVE

DAISY

"Daisy, are you alright?" asks Jordan, obviously worried.

"Yeah, I am just tired and before you start being nosey, I have slept well, the boys are looking after me and John is still leaving me to stew in my own misery." I tell her.

"Excuse me for being concerned; you looked like you were going to keel over." Jordan says in that squeaky little voice she puts on when she is unsure of me and the mood swings I have lately.

"I will be in the office. While Pam's here, I might as well make full use of her. If I do not feel any better and it stays quiet, I am going to piss off home. No questions asked." I say. No answer. Good- she is annoying at the best of times. I have been to see the doctor at least eight times over the last twelve months: HRT, Anti-Depressants. There is no healing for the bleeding menopause. God, I could be having hot sweats and going on like this for years. There are words for how I feel: anger, resentment, frustration, aggression…hot and fucking bothered, all the bastard time.

I sit in my chair and ring Rea. She usually has a calming effect on me. If I would have phoned Laura, I would get a professional view and we would end up being sarcastic with each other, and not always in our jolly way.

"Hiya… not really, no." I say in answer to her question. "I am getting worse day by day. No aches or pains anywhere, just horrendous agitation." Rea is sympathetic without masquerading as a preacher on how to make my woes disappear. We chatted about Laura's repulsive neighbour who got what he had coming to him. I hope he felt every slash. Then we get onto the subject of her moving so far away. "I can't blame her; she has wanted to move to Wales for years. We even talked about doing it together some decades ago." Rea had to cut me off when one of the directors on the show she was working on decided to ring her at my inconvenience.

I have to go home. I am of no use here, just a 'Daisy-hindrance' to anyone that steps into my path today. I do not like being disliked. I am totally the opposite, but what can you do when your hormones turn you into a monster? Even I do not, like me! I just pick up my bag and make my way to the back door. If no-one misses me by the time I get home, I will ring in and tell them. I think I have given them justification to fear and loath me. Laura and Rea have suggested a few days away together and Livvi will also be asked to join us. I think I need to take them up on the chance of a rest away from here. It will do me the world of good.

CHAPTER SIX

RAE

"Sorry about that Lawrence, I was talking to a friend about a break away now this series is coming to its finale. I need a good old break." Lawrence is the director on the series of documentaries I have been working on. To say he is an absolute arse is putting it mildly. He is a pompous snob that literally looks down his nose at you. Apparently, he met the Queen and Prince Phillip at an opening ceremony and was as rude to them as he is to everyone else. Fortunately, I just giggle inside to myself when he is on set. Nobody cares for his attitude towards good-looking young men either. He has (as usual) a few requests. I note them, tell him I will comply and have them at his convenience as soon as possible. In fact, what he was requiring from me was already in place. 'Obstacles' he called them when I had first suggested them to him, but now he has had some innovation, my ideas have become his own.

Lawrence likes to show his superiority at any given occasion, especially with the younger males that work as crew. In fact, any young person would get his attention, even if it was their criminal record that was under review, as was the case in these latest productions.

Concerned about her wellbeing, I rang Daisy back. I do not like what age is doing to my dear friend, and we are all aghast at her deterioration in her mind, though not her body. I did think when Laura announced she was finally relocating, that it would not be long before Daisy followed. The two were always glued at the hip. It would be good for her to open a small veterinary surgery in Wales, as her first love is horses. In the city there is not really a call for such stunning animals. Daisy did not answer her landline so I ring her mobile and she eventually picks up the call on my second try. I tell her my trivial conversation regarding Sir Lawrence and then get on to the subject she is so hostile about: her issues. "We would not love you so much if we ignored how you were feeling." I told her.

By the time our conversation had come to an end, we were laughing about some of the antics that we had both been a part of during our times away together, most of the time with Laura, who is a demented mentalist at any other time than when she is working. How can anybody as professional as she is in her work place be so maniacal when away from it is beyond me! It is incredible how she can detach herself from the career she has. Lately, Livvi (whom Laura has known for thirty years) has been joining us on our little excursions and we have become a considerable force. The four of us.

I am going to take a little nap if possible, (mind running overtime), as I have a long journey ahead of me this evening. I would rather travel on motorway journeys at night when the roads are clearer. I don't know, we move away to these remote places, then moan when we have to travel so far to visit our friends and family. Unfortunately, this time, it is a funeral.

CHAPTER SEVEN

LAURA

I have not needed to travel into Manchester for the last two days as all the work I have needed to do is mainly typing up reports and talking on the phone. All my main concerns have been dealt with, and tomorrow will be spent doing more in-depth interviews with three of my clients. Then I have four days off. I will be gallivanting around Wales with Livvi, and now Daisy has decided to join us, which I am very happy about. I am sure we will find much to do. I cannot blooming' wait!

As today is the first day I have let Pud go into the garden to explore her surroundings, I am seated on a lounger watching her. I keep letting out little chuckles at her excitement and giddiness. I hear a voice shouting 'Mrs Timmings' through the trees. I ask who it is, and he explains he is Joseph Keil, Rosie's husband. I tell him to stay put for a few seconds whilst I nip into the kitchen and select the garden gate key. When he enters, we shake hands and make a more informal exchange of names. "I thought you had company as I heard you laughing, so I was not sure whether to interrupt." he says.

"No it is fine." I tell him that Pud is my only company and explain why I am out here on watch. Pud, as always has to come and sniff around the stranger. I offer Joe a cold drink, which he accepts. We chat about our little village, and then he gets on to the subject of the Lanes homicide.

He had already mentioned that he knew what I did for employment, so I think his trust in my confidence was indeed planted. The investigation is no further on than it was when Robert's body was found. I inform him that I had done my own bit of investigating and now knew of the victim's ugly past. I did pass a few comments, but nothing in regard to the bastard getting what he deserved. I cannot even try to imagine what it must be like to have a child taken from you at the hands of a very ill person, whom sought to commit his crime rather than seek help. I think I would want to kill him. Joe held his hands up and said. "Everyone hates a nonce, so it is not just the victim's family that would hold an obvious grudge." I agreed wholeheartedly and nearly spewed out what I would do to anyone that would harm my child, especially in the despicable way Robert Graham had done. If anything, Joseph would be happy about the loss of the victim, having two children of his own living adjacent to the child molester, or nonce, as he had put it.

"It looks like the perpetrator has either struck again, or another very similar case was called in this morning." Joe tells me. The look on my face and his reaction, then my intake of breath tells me he has been doing his homework about me.

"It's not that I'm just so nonchalant, I have been in

this work for that long that absolutely nothing shocks me anymore." I inform him. He just nods his head as he tells me if anyone can tolerate having to establish a rapport with someone that has committed such evil atrocities; then that individual would be myself.

"It is the only way of going forward and I dissociate with the offence at hand, so I can get results. If I was to become emotional or horrified, I would get nowhere." Joe went on to tell me that after evaluating this morning's crime scene, it would seem that the injuries and the weapon used were of the exact same as Robert Graham's. I admitted that that was a little more than coincidence and asked whether the victim of this crime had been a child abuser. 'There was no likeness in his last crime, but it is still in relation to a younger person, and he did have a history of sexual abuse as the perpetrator previously', was all I was going to get from him.

Miles Taylor lived in Sheffield. Out of Joseph's jurisdiction and quite a distance away, but with the growth in technology within the services now a crime relation report would be gathered immediately. Miles was thirty-one years old and had just been released from prison after serving seven years for the manslaughter of a young man.

"Is there any connection between the two men? Did they do time in the same establishment?" I ask.

"Too early to tell, and as far as I am aware, up to now we have absolutely no evidence. Yes- just as over the road." was his reply.

"Mmmm." I thought aloud. "Quite a similarity, I agree." He understood my logical process by conceding: "Well, I will leave you to enjoy the rest of your day and I am sorry if I have ruined it in any way. Nice to meet you at last and thank you for the drink- it was very nice actually." Cheeky sod, did he not expect it to be? "Why thank you kind sir. No, not ruined at all. I have been typing-up reports on several homicides over the last few days, hence not needing to go into the office. Just another added to the list. I am pleased to have finally met you too. It makes one feel a little safer knowing we have someone of your standing close by." He let himself out and pulled the gate shut. I wandered over to lock it. I did not mind him calling to update me about the Robert Graham case as it was too close for comfort, but in regards of any other case- my day off and my personal space- I do not even want to think about criminality, never mind discuss it.

Murder, bloody murder! I think no more of it after I lock the gate and play chase with Pud. She is more like a dog than a cat. At seven years old, she is still as cheeky and as playful as she was as a kitten. I get so much pleasure from her! She is like my shadow- even sits on my knee when I am on the loo! (Not that I think that a pleasant endearment.) "I am going to have to leave you for a short time Puddles whilst I go shopping. Aunties Daisy and Livvi are coming to stay for a few days. How exciting is that for us?" I ask myself, not Pud really.

The supermarket carpark was full. Silly time to choose to shop, but I will not feel like it tomorrow after work. I wander around the aisles in Asda in a dream like state. I felt so much more relaxed living here and I was so happy that I had finally found the exact place I wanted to be. The only nuisance was the ninety-minute drive to Manchester.

I am thinking of taking on fewer clients, so at least I can explore my new surroundings before I get too old. Mind you, thinking about it, joking apart, I will be fifty-seven on my next birthday. I fill up my trolley 'til I can put no more items in and make my way to the till. That was easy! It is the putting of it away when I get home that I do not like! I realise as the store's so busy I am not asked if I need help with my packing. Actually I do not think I have been offered that service at this store. "Looks like you're struggling, here, let me help." As I am about to reply with "No, but thank you", I look up into the most gorgeous pair of brown eyes, which turned out to be equivalent to the rest of him. "Thank you, that is very kind of you." I reply instead.

"No problem. Errr?" He is asking me my name.

"Laura, and you are?" I ask.

"Pleasure to meet you Laura, my name is Tony." he answers. We shake hands and start packing up the shopping whilst the young man at the till tries hard to hide the smirk he has on his face. He does not try hard enough- it is obvious!

I am impressed that he is separating the items into the right bags. After I pay, we walk away, with Tony carrying the two bags that would not fit into the trolley. "You must have a large family?" he enquires with his eyes on my goods and obviously wanting to know more about me.

"Yes, a large family of friends" I inform him.

Tony carries the bags and walks with me to the car. We stand chatting for what seems like minutes until I realise the sun is going down. He asks for my phone number and I oblige, surprising myself. I am also shocked that I leaned over to kiss his cheek, for thanks before we say our goodbyes, only he catches my lips instead. I couldn't attain whether that was accidental or not, but I give him the benefit of doubt. Not like me at all to be so blatantly transparent when it comes to guys chatting me up-even a little kittenish! I had already determined he was too young for me. We did not discuss age but I imagined him to be early forties. Very attractive, tall, eloquent. Even though he was quite tanned, it did not represent the beautiful hot summer that we have had- maybe Greek or Italian ancestors? I did not feel comfortable now, thinking about it. It really was not like me to hand out my personal mobile number so eagerly. 'I need to make friends in my new locality though', I thought, then thought no more about it.

After I had put all my shopping away, I got comfy on the sofa with Pud and my phone. Rea answered almost immediately. She was fine, I was fine, she's looking forward to our time together in a few weeks and is envious that she would miss out on our break together this weekend. I told her about meeting Tony, and Rea being Rea was already administering the "Watch it" prognostic.

I revealed the conversation I had with Sergeant Joseph Keil. Rea was establishing herself as a warrior of women's rights regarding the government's betrayal to the females born in the fifties-the rise of retirement age, and loss of their monies. The 'WASPI' platoon were growing in numbers daily and this morning Rea had recorded a radio interview for the cause. She tells me she is going to do an interview for an article regarding 'WASPI' for 'Women's Own' magazine. Rea was as passionate as I am when she got her teeth into something. She will leave her mark on this campaign.

Then we had our customary laughs. Tonight's victim was chiefly Lawrence. I could not stand the man and do not tolerate him when we are at the same party, production etc… Rea being Rea, I cannot apprehend her sufferance of the dick head that he is. She suffers no crap off anyone. The last time I was in his company and he made a derogative remark about a young woman on his crew, I told him to watch his 'pretentious-arse mouth'. Being the obnoxious prat that he was, I added that he was 'blessed to have anyone work for him when he was such a prick'. I finished with 'Thank you and goodnight' and left him stood there horrified. Two minutes later, he had no-one around him and you could see he was being cold-shouldered by the rest of the party!

When I worked as a crew member some years back (just for the experience), he asked me if I would like to join him at his home and he would make me a beautiful dinner and then He kissed his fingers. I was tired, and sick of his rudeness to the crew on set so I replied, "No thank you, I would rather eat my own vomit!", then trotted off. At least I know I can be rude, and would not aim it at an innocent party or with my staff.

My stomach was aching from laughing when the call ended. I make a brew before I face-timed my son.

I have two sons, Ben being the youngest with whom I have a fantastic relationship. Saul is twenty-nine years old and we have been estranged for many years. I brought up an imposter in Saul. Disloyal, sly and very selfish. He changed in his late teens and became plainly opinionated. My children were my life-the best part of it. The greatest thing I ever did. I more than loved them, I idolised the two. As we grew together, we were an invincible team-supported each other. If I'd have known, I would not have been able to live with the fact that years into the future, I would never see one of them again.

It happened out of the blue. His wrong doings could never be righted. Half my heart went with him and it is not something you can replace. I was in a bad way. As it happened, at the time I was going through the menopause- a very low moment in my life- the worst. I am very lucky and elated to be here. This is why I know what Daisy is going through. I only have one son now and I am very happy with that. I also have my closest friends' children that I love, it is as if I have adopted them and their children.

Ben answered his call immediately as he was sat at his

laptop. The familiar hellos were said. Just a short while ago, he had taken to educating himself in playing the piano, so every few days Ben would have a tune ready to play to me. We played 'Name that Tune', and today's music was Für Elise composed by Beethoven. I always wanted to learn to play the piano but for some reason it never happened, so I was thrilled to hear that Ben had taken it up. We tell each other our news from the last few days and end up watching Pud doing some of her dog-like antics. She loved playing fetch and today's item was a bobble I had taken from my hair. I mentioned that I might get a little puppy as a friend for Puddles. A big thumbs up, Ben being an animal lover like myself. We were to (over the next few days), start sending each other write-ups and pictures of different breeds of dogs. Our chat was over after our 'I love you's' and I headed to the kitchen to make some dinner. I was surprised to find myself actually cooking a meal, Bowie playing loud on my stereo.

Pud and I shared some tuna steak, but rather than cat biscuits, I had mine with salad and new potatoes! I got ready what I needed for work the next day, took a shower and was about to put on a few more hours of Thomas Hardy films when my mobile started to ring. I had the feeling it was going to be the guy I met at Asda tonight and blow me- it was! I opted to pick up the call. I have really bad judgement at what must be blinkered times.

"Hello beautiful lady, it is Tony your knight in shining armour from Asda." he says. I wanted to turn my phone off, as I do not like such familiarity from the 'get-go'. 'Knight in shining armour'! Who was he kidding?! I do not know why I did not go with my first instinct and not answer. I carried on, to have a long conversation with him. At first, I put his awkwardness down to him sounding a little bit slimy, but the conversation became more comfortable as

WHAT WOULD TOM DO?

time went on (except for the fact that was he was going a little overboard with compliments). He seemed intrigued by my profession, which we spoke about at length- not my choice. His occupation of quantity surveyor did not really warrant more than a few sentences. His choice, saying there was not really much he could tell me. He told me he did not have any kids, which I thought unusual when he told me he was forty-nine years of age. Oh well, not everyone wants children.

Tony was flying to Milan the next night to spend a month with his parents, whilst he did everything that needed doing around their home now they were elderly. It was up to their only son and heir to tend to the jobs. He did this twice a year. Well-I got the Italian heritage right! "Can I take you out for a meal on my return?" he asks.

"I don't know at the moment whether I can have a social life. I have made my move up here, ninety minutes away from my workplace where I spend many late hours. I did not have leisure time before I moved, so if we did go out to eat, it would have to be on a holiday." I reply." I need some friends in the area being a newbie here though, so some changes have to be made, me thinks." I continue, covering myself with the friendship idea. For some reason, I did not believe he was the age he told me. I am not great at guessing ages, but this guy looked forty-ish. But why would he lie? Unless perhaps he knew I was in my fifties and he thought it would be preferable to say he was older? Not sure, but I have a month to change my mind. Saying that, he does want to follow through with his offer. He was either a liar or a player. Something was not right with him. What the fuck do I know about men? You can see how little by my past! I did not have a great record. I got married in my early forties and was divorced by my mid-forties. I only obliged for my husband as he needed the security. It meant nothing except standing in front of a lady who tells us we are man and wife. The best day of my life: definitely not!

When Tom came on the screen, any other man went out of my mind! I started watching an eight-hour series called Taboo, and after the fifth episode, I had to watch another hour. I had previously watched episodes, so only two were left-deary me. Not only did he keep me mesmerised by his astonishingly good looks, excellent acting skills and sex appeal, the actual series was awesome and made in my favourite era-Gothic. I have always been associated with being gothic-looking with my black hair, make-up and choice of clothes. When the next hour was finished, I still wanted to carry on, but it was getting late and I wanted to sleep in my bed tonight.

I slept well and was in a giddy mood from waking up. I raced Pud down the stairs and played fetch with her whilst my breakfast was on the go. I let her out hoping she would want to come when I called her, so I could lock the cat flap before I set off for work. She actually popped in every five minutes just to check I was still here. When I was ready to leave, I called her name from the back door. At my request, she trotted in- just like a dog. A cat would never usually listen to her owner, but Pud always did. Everything in order, I set off towards Manchester.

There was a full office this morning and everyone was busy going about their work. We answered each-others questions, then all gathered in the kitchen to make brews and get snacks, before we set out to our destinations for the day. "Fucking Jaffa cakes again? Do you lot do this on purpose? Even if any of you brings sweets in to share, you make sure they're bloody Haribo and they are made from jelly as well. I think you are all tight sods and from now on

I will bring my own delicious treats in and you can all keep your fucking hands off them you bunch of fuckwits." I think that got through to them, or maybe not. I left the kitchen so obviously annoyed and their laughter followed me through to the office. As I was not having anything with my coffee I was the first to finish, so I picked up my bag and case and said to everyone, "Right, fuck off- the lot of you." More laughing followed me down the corridor.

Same prison- just another day.

My first interview was with Eric, and the mood I was in, I just hoped he was amenable today. As I entered the interview room, I could see a large amount of bruising and swelling around his hands and face. His mouth had stitches. The bulging from the beating around his mouth and face made it hard for him to talk normally. I was told by the prison officer who had walked me to meet this young man, that Eric had picked a couple of fights, but had come off worse. I hear that a lot. I really do not care how he got his injuries, after what he had delivered to the Blake family. However, I do have to show a little concern, after all, he is my client. I had brought a cold drink each into the room and he actually had the manners to stand up as I entered. Shock, horror! I sensed this leathering had been to more than just his face. I noticed there must be some affliction to his body by his stance and his facial expression. Eric held out his hand for me to shake. (he had some manners) I commented on the soreness of his hand and said it probably would not be a good idea to do so today. After my initial question of how he was being treated, he lied to me. He said everything was cool. "If everything is cool Eric, why do you stand before me looking like you have been in a car accident?" He looked down at the table but did not answer. We were then left alone after the officer witnessed the difference in Ward's behaviour.

This boy was severely lacking attention and he had already come to see me as an ally. "What do you want to say to me today, if anything? Any questions before I start requesting answers from you?"

"I don't know why I did it, so I can't answer no questions." he replies. "Well, something made you go into the home of a young couple with a baby. If your initial intention was to steal money or items, and not to harm them, why did you break into the house whilst the family were inside?" I enquired.

"I just wanted to nick some of their stuff, but I couldn't find anything worth 'avin' so I went upstairs and the woman woke up and screamed, and I didn't wanna get caught. I started stabbing them both with the knives I had in my hands, at the same time. I just went mental and I was mad for being caught. How else can I give me dad and mum money to let us live in their 'ouse if I don't go on the rob? Brian's ill in the brain and I've got to pay his up as well. That's why I make him help me. He d'int help me though, he was just shouting and crying, I 'ad to do it meself. That made me madder." I asked Eric all the questions that I needed answers to, and he interpreted them without dilemma. God, what I would do to the brother's parents. At least lock the bastards up. Knowing your children are out at midnight and aware they are up to no good, just so they could pay their way in a home that the boys got absolutely nothing from. They even had to supply their own food yet giving fifty pounds each a week for keep. Brian was still of school-age and this had been going on for three years.

Back at the office, I was starting my report on Eric Ward. I knew the narrative back to front. He had forced his brother Brian to follow him that night by knife point. With his younger brother being afraid of him, he pursued Eric.

I was told that he did not go out that night with the intent to commit any crime other than theft. Nonetheless, he was armed with a sharp kitchen knife, one of the many items used to kill the victims, adding some of the stab wounds, that would seem to be done more from pleasure. These wounds were committed after the victims were already dead. Just to add insult to injury. I pressed him further on his decision to take the life away from an eighteen month old baby. The child was too young to identify him and why choose a dissimilar exit for the baby than his parents? His answer was that "I didn't want to see a baby bleed so I punched it about twenty times coz it was crying loud and the neighbours would have heard it." Oh God! All I could think for a few seconds was, how do I do this job.

I then go on to try and make some kind of personal connection between him and this baby (other than murder) calling her by her name and telling him her age. But there was nothing and I felt nothing, but total sadness.

After my initial interview was over, I then asked him questions in regard to his fighting and the injuries he had acquired since being incarcerated. He told me that there were just two little scuffles because of his cockiness, but the rest of the wounds were down to self-infliction. He had used the cell walls to beat himself. I learnt that self-harm was something he did on many occasions. Why was he punishing himself? He denied this was what he was doing. To whom else was he paying penance for by beating himself up? This was not the norm for self-harmers. I have an appointment at the hospital shortly so I will finish my report later at home.

I nip into the Deli for some food, which I eat sat in the car. I arrive at the hospital at the appointed time, and I sit in a dining area that serves the patients in the psychiatric ward, and almost immediately, I am joined by Brian with a half-smile. He made glances towards me as we spoke, and he was much more at-ease than when I had last seen him. I had the report on his condition from a member of staff when I arrived. Today was really to see if he could add anything to what Eric had given me about that night. There really was not any need. His older brother said that Brian was not a witness to what he did; he stayed in the kitchen eating cookies and crying out 'No! No! No!' The hour passed quickly, and I was shown some of his sketches. They were fabulous. He certainly did have a good eye when it came to drawing animals- his favourites were horses. I would do everything I could to make sure this boy never went back into the company of his parents. His confidence had already grown in just the few days he had been committed to this place. I was pleased.

As I went back in the office to do what I could before my four days leave, I was giggling inside but did not show it. There was an array of cakes, sweets and biscuits stacked up on my desk! As the room was again full of its employees, I shouted my thanks with "I should fucking think so."

We had ten minutes of being daft, then we all got on with our reason for being there: the world and its scum. I actually got more than I intended done, including finishing my report on Eric Ward. Sometimes I wish they would bring back hanging and although I should not say, I would hang some perpetrators myself.

Sian, Mark and I went back to the Deli to have our tea. Well, it saves cooking when I get home. My phone rang and I noticed it was Tony before I pressed the red button. "He is too keen." I said out loud. Now I had to tell my work buddies about my admirer! Sian, I would have told anyway. I got the 'Go on, it is about time', plus other comments regarding my sex life. "There is something a little odd, maybe creepy about him." I voiced.

"Well, in our line of work it is hard to acquire new friends without being a little suspicious of them at first." Mark another Psychologist in our group says.

"A bit too eager." I reply. We finish our food and each head to our parking spaces. A ninety-minute drive home. More Echo and the Bunnymen. I did not think this long drive to and from work would start affecting me so soon.

Maybe I should think about having some fun, but the thought of someone younger did not appeal me at all. The last few sexual encounters I had had were horrific. Laughable really. It was with the same 'man'- if that is what I could call him. After suffering and getting to know his controlling ways, also tolerating his being absolutely inept in the bedroom department, I soon turned it into a platonic friendship. Not only did he not have the equipment, you could not even compare him to a fumbling teenage boy that we all have encounters with in our youth. My friends laughed when I told them that when I saw he did not have a willy. I told him that he should inform a woman that he has not got a penis before he tries to get her in bed! My buddies were horrified. Well, it was better getting to point from the get- go, they burst out laughing, then they agreed that was what they would do! I waited till he questioned me as to why I would not make love to him, before I brought it 'up' (pardon the pun!).

We stayed friends and went out a couple of nights a week (just for company). That was until he made me so nauseous that we just quit going out altogether. We called each other once in a while (for some unknown reason). When I moved to Wales though, he had so kindly offered to set up new email address and password, as I was struggling to sort it myself. It wasn't long before I started getting emails from my provider saying that someone was signing into my email account from various places over the last couple of weeks. Glossop in the morning, Macclesfield in the afternoon. A different location each time, but one place several times. The number of the phone used was shown, though I knew who it was. Only one person had my password. Fortunately, I had not been using it for anything important at that time. The main town of use was where Steve lived. I never let on-I just changed my email address. He was the type to deny it with the proof anyway.

I got home at eight o clock and Pud was waiting for me at the door. Lots of kisses and cuddles. 'Dreamies' first, then she headed to the door. Out she goes as I unlatch the cat flap Dave had fitted for me, well-for Pud. I had aired the two bedrooms the day before so I did not have much to do in awaiting the arrival of Daisy and Livvi tomorrow. Cup of tea, mail, then the last few hours of Taboo. I was loving the set and wardrobe, but if I walked out dressed like that I would definitely be committed! A therapist once told me she thought me a little eccentric.

Settled in front of the television with Pud's back inside, and on my knee, I'm about to press play, my phone begins to ring. If it had been one of my friends I would have answered, but the name Tony was on the screen again. For fucks sake this guy was starting to annoy me. I ignored it, along with the ping of a message a minute later. My four days off starts right now. Tom tonight, and the girls tomorrow. Now I had chilled a little I was really getting excited. I am planning nothing. I will just make sure they're comfortable in my home so we can 'go with the flow'.

I did not really want to stop watching Tom, but the series was now finished. It was truly excellent. I didn't fancy going to fetch another DVD. Brew and bed it was.

CHAPTER EIGHT

I was woken by the dreaded morning-paw, which usually means it's around eight o'clock. Lightly pawing my nose, and when that does not work, she nips at it, then paws my duvet away from me. I laugh, stroke and talk to her but she just wants her 'Dreamies'. She makes me laugh every single day. She is my little baby.

Shower done, make up slapped on my face, hair and nails done, and I am ready for breakfast. I take some pancakes, my brew and phone and go to sit at one of my outside tables. I am followed by you know who! I sit here on this beautiful day 'til the girls arrive. I was so chilled, and so looking forward to the next four days. I had been sat out here for over two hours. Pure bliss. I could never get fed up of looking at these stupendously beautiful mountains.

My besties arrived with lots of hugging and talking over each other. They have already visited previously, helping me empty boxes when I first arrived and made sure we sampled some of the good food on offer in these parts. They worked hard, bless them.

Kettle's the first thing on and I tell them not to tell me if they want a brew, and not to expect me to do it. If they are the first to announce that they need one, then they have got to make them for all of us. I get the usual 'lazy this and lazy that', so I tell them to 'fuck off'. "Just like in Manchester, the rules are the same." It is 'open house' to my best friends.

You would not believe how we chatted- as if we had not seen or spoken to each other in months. It was dinner time when I realised I was hungry. If I am hungry, then these two will be! I think they thought that the first person who mentioned food had to get up and prepare a meal for us all. I started laughing! I guessed right.

We decided to go to a pub a short drive away in the Snowdonia Mountains. The meals were lovely and everyone friendly as usual. We only just managed to get a seat after a lengthy wait. The hour passed at speed and we were still gassing away. Our meal at the Fairy Glen was spot on as per, and we took our drinks outside, to sit in awe at the most stunning views around us, watching a couple of Welsh mountain ponies trotting in freedom on the warm autumn evening.

"You are so lucky Laura having all this. We both think it won't be long before you retire, and rightly so." Livvi says with envy.

"That is next on the cards I think. Is it not?" Daisy enquires.

"Mmmm, the thought has crossed my mind. What is the use of having all this if I am still spending seventy per cent of my time still in Manchester?" I reply, basking in the glow of the ambience. A comfortable silence followed.

"Lucky Bitch." I knew it would not take long for Livvi (or most likely Daisy, thinking about it), to break that juncture.

"Thank you Livvi, I will take that as a compliment." I return.

"What are we doing now? Going back or a little drive around?" Livvi asks, as she is tonight's designated driver.

"No, we have plenty of time to do that, this is our first night- let's just head to Laura's." says Daisy in her authoritative voice.

We arrive home minutes later and the girls head upstairs to put their belongings in their rooms.

"Cups or glasses?" I shout to the upper floor.

"Glasses." Came the answer, twice in unison. I put some Leonard Cohen on in the background regardless of the tuts. Our chatting and laughter took us into the early hours of the next morning. Bedtime, and we hit the wooden hill to Bedfordshire. I had had a good night and went on to sleep merrily.

"Morning girlies, I thought I would be the last one up. I had an idea breakfast might be on the go." I enter the kitchen and announce.

"Lazy this and lazy that" I get from both guests.

"Yeah, yeah, yeah, gotcha'." I here that all the time, their talking about me-Miss Busy Bee. "Knock yourselves out girls; I will pay for breakfast in the village café tomorrow. I will just have a bacon butty please." I request of the two vegetarians. I settled for cereal and pastries, after getting a lecture from both (funnily annoying, if that is possible). My buddies tell me they have not been hired as servants for the weekend and remind me how well I am looked after when I pay return visits to their homes. Goes in one ear and out the other! I have learnt from Ben: I see what I can get away with by either charm, or what I think is being funny. It does work most times though, although I might get a little slap on my arm from Daisy every now and then!

The first item on the agenda was to take a walk on the beach that you can see from two of my top floor bedroom windows-literally a five-minute walk away, but only fifty yards from my back garden. We had done this walk twice before when they were here last. It was so hot today, but that has come to be the norm nearing the end of September and into October over the last few years. It was so lovely that we sat on the rocks and just talked and talked.

The second item on the agenda was forgotten when we realised it was one o' clock, and still too warm to wander round the shops in Llandudno. I think just the peace here was enough for us-we did not want to get involved with doing anything laborious. I was sure we would make up for that when the evening's entertainment was decided upon. Our walk into Conwy, to the best cake and pie bakery around, was slow and easy, as we were talking about all our childhood holidays to Wales. Some hysterical moments, obviously! On deciding to catch the bus back, we arrived home fifteen minutes later to Pud's delight, and headed straight into my back garden. "Hey, big girl. Did you miss your Mummy?" I baby talked to Pud in my usual way. I entered the house through the back door with the bakery parcels, then just brought them back out again with napkins and a bottle of white wine. On my second return I brought glasses and 'Dreamies'.

"More wine and we do not usually drink." says a disgusted Daisy.

"Just because your name's Daisy, stop being a cow." snarls Livvi.

"How is stating a fact being a cow?" Daisy makes a mooing sound after her reply then gets the bottle uncorked. "Have you got any lemonade to go with it?" There is no answer, so she goes in to have a look. "Do not worry about it Laura lazy arse." She says "Good." I tell Daisy to her little outburst.

This is where I bore my wonderful friends to death (whom I might add started the conversation) about looking forward to series five of 'Peaky Blinders'. "Right I have listened to what you have got to say about it with interest and due to binge-watching all four series on DVD in the first two weeks, when I first moved here, I wondered what the captivation was about. I found it quite boring, well at least fifty per cent so. There were some great entertaining scenes and great characters admittedly. I would, in editing the scenes myself, eliminate quite a number, and by that I include some of the actors! I would put more scenes with Alfie Solomon in and condense the whole lot into two series. Then, you would have a peaky blinding show. Before either of you interrupt me by saying 'I only wanted more Alfie Solomon because the role was played by Tom Hardy', then you're both very much mistaken.

The head of the Mafia supposedly the most chilling Mob in history was actually the most hilarious character in the production. Adrien Brody (alias Luca Changretta)-watch out for him! He acted as if he was educating himself on playing the role of Gino D'Campo in an auto-biography of the chef's life. Gino would have played the part of Changretta much more mafia-like. He performed just like the wop Alfie called him before he told this Godfather figure to 'Crack on.' Alfie's lines were slightly psychoneurotic to match his awesome persona. I think that the BBC should think on and do a prequel series of Alfie Solomon's life before the Peaky Blinders. Sorry Mr Changratta, you did not even enlighten yourself on how to chew a wooden toothpick- bloody ridiculous! Right, I have had my say, you can crack on now. I laughed. There was some disagreement, but on the whole they agreed. We sat in silence basking in the hot sun for another hour before dinner time had arrived.

A delicious buffet of salads, meats, cheeses, pickles and fish, with fresh crusty bread bought earlier at Conwy to have with dinner was prepared. I had put 'Lawless' on the DVD player as we ate the thoroughly enjoyable meal in the dining room. This was the true story of three brothers and their illegal alcohol business during the prohibition era. I had seen it twice before and loved the movie. The girls had not but were enjoying it. We settled on the sofa, still in the dining room, picking at the food on the table until the film ended. "Fucking hell Laura, that was good but have you got anything without Thomas bloody Hardy in it? You're obsessed woman! Fit as fuck though. Sian was right Laura you need a Welsh fuck buddy." Livvi was always one to say it like it was. (Just like Daisy!) "Thanks for that Livvi, I will consider it." I retort sarcastically yet thinking about how nice it would be to fill my lonely spaces.

"Yuck! Cannot think of anything more disgusting these days. John knows not to even think about it, he is frightened I might cut his dick off if he puts it anywhere near me, and he has got every right to be frightened! Right, are we getting ready?" Asks Daisy as we are laughing.

We decided to catch a bus into Bangor to test out the night life, and what a pretty good night out it proved to be. Everyone was enjoying our company in the pubs as we were theirs. In our defence, anything shameful that happened on this night was to be put down to the fact that none of us are drinkers, and that is exactly what we had been doing since dinner time! It was only two and a half hours in when the three of us went onto soft drinks, all feeling the same merry effect, but inhibitions already out of the window.

The three lovely gentlemen that had been entertaining us for the last few hours, requested our company for the next day. We welcomed the offer and gave details where to meet.

Kisses followed. Well for Daisy they did, Livvi and I got some good snogging in.

Oh my God did we get shit from Daisy all the way home! The taxi driver was eavesdropping and laughing with us. Daisy did not give up when we got in. "For fucking hell's sake, I am unhappily married, hate men and loathe sex and you pair of bloody tarts can piss off if you think I am coming out with you tomorrow, and stop fucking laughing, it is not funny." She pointed at each of us in turn. "I will toddle off by myself around Llandudno. I will enjoy that much more than being in your company anyway...oh fuck off laughing-I hate you both." Daisy had a smirk throughout that outburst. We had a brew each to take to bed, but I fell asleep without even touching mine.

As we gathered at the kitchen table whilst making grumping noises and sighing, there was the sound of laughter again. "Pair of hussies, suffering from self-commendation are you not?" The sound of laughter yet again. That is what life is about, being happy and laughing. No, we did not regret the decision we had made, and Daisy was sticking to her guns. She had explained her choice to her admirer so he was not to be meeting up with his friends. My guy was called Phil and Livvi's- Mike. They were seated at a table outside the café where we had elected to share our first latte of the day. As it was just the two of them, it proved Daisy was as good as her word. A boat trip followed a walk on the promenade, then a coach trip up and around the Great Orme, with some jovial tourist information spoken through the microphone of the driver. Again, fortunately for us, it was another strikingly sunny day. We were ready to eat now, and Phil drove us out to an old countryside pub with very tasty homemade food. I think I was talked into inviting the guys home with us. I say 'think' because I was not sure whether it was either a good idea, or a bad one. Daisy picked up on the first call. I thought it was only right that she knew we were having guests- male guests at that, on a girlie break. She was not bothered at all. "The more the merrier." she said. If she had not been as compliant, I would have made sure they did not stay too long. Livvi and myself had an exchange in the ladies, admitting to each other that we both liked our gentlemen friends and were having such fun with them, that we wanted to lengthen our date.

Once home, there was no awkwardness. These were two good-looking, intelligent guys. I put out nibbles and we all seemed to be getting on great. Fortunately, everyone drank wine. Daisy took her leave with a book around midnight; she was in good spirits though, so my guilt began to fade. How we ended up separated I am not quite sure, but Phil and I were settled on the sofa in the conservatory whilst Livvi and Mike had just gone up to her room. I was actually thinking this when I was suddenly encased in Phil's arms and had my lips firmly glued to his. Reality became clear: this is definitely what has been missing. It had been a few years, but it felt like I was about to make up for it. I just hoped Daisy had her 'matter-of-course earphones' in (her being in the middle room). To be blunt, after we made our way to my bedroom I was like a dog on heat, like Livvi always is and I used to be. A consummate intensity left us sleeping like babies.

Daisy was up first, and the darling she is had prepared drinks and pastries for our arrival downstairs. Enjoying our breakfast and an hour talking around the table, with each of us getting roped into playing with Pud, we parted ways with promises of phone calls from the guy's.

While in our rooms getting ready to have a trip out, I

answered my phone on its second ring. I saw it was Sian, so I picked up the call. Five minutes later, I pressed the off button and thought: 'I could see that coming'. Eric Ward had been killed in prison. Somebody got to him before he took his own life anyway. He's at peace with himself now.

Well, I was not going to concern myself with work on my last day off with two of my closest friends. I was to be driving into Manchester in convoy with them tomorrow on my way to the office, unless of course Daisy wanted to stay a little longer. Eric Ward would have to wait to another day.

Anglesey today: a little cloudy with a bit of drizzle, but not offensive enough to warrant us keeping indoors. The coolness after the last few weeks was gratifying. We walked along the beautiful beaches, both Benllech Bay and Treaddur Bay, then headed to an enormous pub to have a late lunch. Daisy decided that she needed to go home the next day, but wondered after she had got some jobs that needed her attention done, could she come back. "Absolutely my dear friend, you are always welcome and for as long as you want. You know you bloody well can, you fool." I tell her.

"What, even now you have unlocked the gate to your lady garden again?" she enquires.

"Trust you to lower the tone! Not that it is ever raised while you are around. "You're disgusting!" I reply.

"Well, now you have got yourself a fella I will be in the way, won't I? I mean, it's not like nobody knew what you were getting up to. I thought it was a full moon." she carries on.

"Stop encouraging her, Livvi." I say at her chuckling.

"Yeah, you were just as bad; I had to turn Rainbow up full blast to escape your howling!" Daisy directs at Livvi. I must admit, I still felt a little high after my night of passion and had suffered the girls' wrath at the breakfast table that morning regarding some chaffing. How unladylike we are! Livvi has been in a relationship with a fellow officer for several years now, but the man in question is unhappily married. We have all met the demon wife and nobody blames Stuart for taking on the sex-mad Livvi. Our lunch finished, we decided to go back to Penmaenmawr and 'chill the bill out'.

Just as we had settled round the living room TV Ben called, and all four of us were convulsed with laughter. Going over old ground, the girls were trying their hardest to humiliate my son. He was not perplexed at all and gave them equal degradation. I felt great when the call was over, my son was happy and that is all I ever wanted for him. The girls approved my choice of film and the three of us watched 'In Bruges'. The four days had flown past, and as I sat there with my eye's shutting; I knew I was really going to miss them tomorrow.

After the film ended, we each got up to get our belongings ready for 'back to work' the following day. We moaned somewhat, not being in the mood, but got on with it as responsible adults do- just for a change! We all had mouths like toilets, besides Rae and Forrest, but I think it was a release from the work that we did! Obviously we did not swear in public.

Gathered in the kitchen and preparing finger food between us, I realised how so much alike we were. Professional in our working lives and mad as a box of frogs in our social life. I was lucky to have such fantastic friends. Retiring early, I lay in bed talking to Phil on the phone, before I fell into a deep sleep, book still lying unopened on the bed.

CHAPTER NINE

I left for Manchester ten minutes after my comrades took leave, put on some Simon and Garfunkel, and sang all the way to our office carpark. A staff meeting was first on the agenda with my much favoured and appreciated pastries. Sian spoils me. I lectured for an hour, then listened to Mark go through the cases that had come into the office over the last four days. Then we had a visitor, a detective from the homicide division. Brian Wagner: the very handsome agent I had met at the prison. He wanted to discuss my interviews with Eric Ward as he was investigating his death. "Did Eric confide in you, anything to do with enemies he had made, whilst incarcerated?" he asks. I repeated what the young lad had said about the injuries he had sustained in the first week of his confinement; however there was nothing of any use. If there had been, it would have been my duty to report anything that could threaten his welfare.

Eric Ward was removed of his penis, had his throat slashed from ear to ear, causing near decapitation and his wrists were nearly severed from his hands. Gruesome. "And this all happened where?" I asked Brian with concern.

"He was found in his cell early yesterday morning. I know, it beggars belief." I agree with him. There was not very much I could say. All the questions would have no answers, as the detective was clueless himself. "Has Brian Ward been told of his death? If not, I think I would rather I informed him knowing his state of mind" I ask.

"Actually, that is another reason for me coming to see you, because I thought the same, and if you don't mind doing that then it will be much appreciated." he answers.

"I have an appointment with him this afternoon to discuss his leaving the hospital to proceed to supported housing, but depending on his reaction, he may need a few more days in the infirmary." I state. I walked Mr Wagner to the front of the building whilst we spoke more socially, than business. I requested he keep me in the picture. He concurred, we shook hands and I watched him leave. What was happening to me? I had just been informed of another horrific death and here I am, watching the attractive and quite sexy detective swagger as he left the building. I think Phil has roused my womanly wilds again. Fuck me, I thought I had lost my mojo.

Tomorrow, I was to attend court as a witness for the prosecution regarding Jannine Cross. Emily Hills case was to follow in two weeks. I went through my reports on the girls and added them to my case, as I would go straight to the court from home in the morning. It was an open and shut case. At the end of the day, the two girls were wicked. They were without any remorse and would in my opinion; go on to offend in years to come.

I was questioned at length once on the witness stand and chose to stay till I couldn't take anymore. It was so very sad to listen to. One of Emily's answers to the question. "After you left Mrs Acres home with her belongings and you were deciding what to do with the stolen items, how did you feel about what you had done, beating Mrs Acres to death to gain them?" was "We needed money to buy weed n other stuff, drink and that, so I was happy that we had some things to sell and the bit of her money, and we were hungry so we needed the biscuits." God help Alice Acres' family listening to this degenerate and her lack of contrition.

Reading up on a new case, and making an appointment to visit the perpetrator, then adding another new report to my work case, for studying at home, I left the office to head out for the hospital.

Brian was waiting for me at the locked door to the ward and as I pressed the bell and the door was released, Brian was smiling, but there was still just limited eye contact. I thought this was more to do with confidence rather than a trait of autism. I asked him where he wanted to hold our session- the now empty dining room, or his own room. He chose the latter as he wanted to show me some drawings he had done, adding he had done one for me to put on the wall in my house. I told him to wait in his room for me whilst I had a quick word with the ward manager. Mr Green agreed with my thoughts on Brian's reaction to his brother's murder, and the young man may have some more time in the ward if needed. He asked if he could be present at the start of the session so he himself could assess the affair.

As we entered Brian's room, the big smile had remained on his face, but I could see that he was a little agitated. I quickly realised this turned out to be related to the drawing he had done for me. As he handed it to me, he closely watched my response. He was worried I may not like it. I was overwhelmed; his drawing of a horse was stunning. Not only was the animal in a walking stance, the fields, trees, and cottage in the background were just as delicate and captivating. You could see the agitation leave the young boy and it was replaced with elation. I will put this beautiful picture on my dining room wall, once I have found an appropriate frame. He has a gift.

I asked Brian a few questions concerning his wellbeing and once that was over, I told him that I had some upsetting news. He sat on the edge of the bed while I took a chair. Mr Green placed himself next to Brian. There is never an easy way to announce the death of a loved-one to their family members. I told him of Eric's death, but not that it was murder. His response to my news was childlike. "He can't come back can he?". He is now free of his abuser. "No Brian, he cannot come back." I replied. I do not know what I expected, but this reaction was a response that did cross my mind, due to the drastic extent of his fright of his brother. He asked what would happen to Eric's body, but did not inquire as to how he had died. Mr Green and I talked to him about his moving into the new accommodation that would become his home until he was able to care for himself enough to satisfy his workers. To say Brian was excited was an under-statement.

Well, that is another case off my work load- one deceased and one free. I was now heading home to read up on my new cases. Going home from work, a ninety-minute drive to do some more work.

It was an easy drive home, managing to get on the motorway before peak time traffic. Only eighty minutes later I was in my village fish and chip shop. I was getting too used to having take-out food while I was on my own, or calling into a café, or the pub. I was getting lazy, but it meant the time I would have spent cooking, I could now do something more productive instead. If I spend a few hours focusing on the reports I have in my bag, then I can watch Dunkirk before I retire for the evening. I might even watch it in bed. It was getting darker earlier, so I was not missing any views from my windows. From downstairs you could see my lovely gardens and the tops of the mountains. From the upstairs rooms, the scenery was to die for.

Pud smelt the fish as soon as I walked in the door, my kiss was forgotten, and she was jumping up at the bag holding her favourite food. I took her little dish and my plate into the conservatory, and we both purred at the lovely meal. The village chippy never fails to provide delicious fresh cuisine.

I think about Eric Ward, and how the hell can an inmate be so badly murdered whilst locked in his cell. Very odd indeed. I would make a note to phone Brian Wagner in a few days. I wanted to be kept informed on this one.

My new cases were straight forward enough, so an hour later I decided to watch the film in my living room after all. Pud cuddled up on my knee, we were sharing some cheese nibbles. I was half-way through when my phone started ringing. I picked up the call from Tony hesitantly. "I thought you were in Milan?" I enquired.

"I am. I am just making sure you do not forget me. Actually, I have been ringing you a few times in fact, but you were obviously busy. Even too busy to ring me back?" I felt like replying sarcastically to his noticeable displeasure but didn't. "I am so sorry, but I have been occupied with work-so many new cases. I am literally sat here writing up reports. It is a never-ending vocation." I lied.

"I will let you off this time," he replied. Alarm bells were ringing.

"You're so kind." I said through gritted teeth. Why on earth did I give this man my time or phone number? To my surprise, we actually had a positive conversation, just asking questions of each other and talking about his visit to Milan. Telling me about the much-needed work he was doing on his parents' home. The call ended pleasantly, and he was to ring me later in the week. I was getting varying vibes from this gorgeous younger man. For God's sake, he was in Italy, the place of his birth, with his beloved parents, and he is ranting over me not answering his calls. For fuck sake, get a life man! One meeting with me was not worth this. I have changed my mind; I do not want him as a friend either.

Back to my TV. I pressed play and the phone rings out again. This time it was Phil. DVD back on pause as I answer. I giggled like a teenager, and felt similar. I liked him and my obvious answer to a date with him was yes! I had put on my pyjamas and made another brew whilst chatting with this sexy man. Finally, after we had finished our call, I got to watch my film: a war film with Tom as a pilot. You only saw his eyes all the way through the movie- until the very last moment of the film where he was captured on land by the Nazis. Those eyes could act. It was good: watchable. I love him in anything. Even better when I can 'phwoar' at his face. Oh no, apart from 'Waz'. A great horror film/thriller, but Tom was a drug-crazed monster in it. There are still a few of his films to add to my collection. I'm sure Brian whom works at HMV is sick to death of seeing me, and that's only after three long appearances at the shop. I put everything together needed for tomorrow's workday and I fell asleep before my head hit the pillow.

The working week went as usual, and fortunately passed quite quickly, appointments assessing felons was like water off a duck's back. Now I was pampering myself in preparation for tonight's date and felt a little nervous. Apart from our bedroom antics this was the first time we were to be on our own together.

I had nothing to be worried about. We started the date from where we had left it last weekend. Phil looked lovely; I liked his style, his choice of clothing. We were both dressed smart-casual, and he complimented me on my attire immediately. I echoed the same words. I was very happy with his choice of venue- a Chinese restaurant that served plenty of delicious choices. Our conversation through the meal was interesting, educational and funny. I was having a lovely evening. God, I had missed this. In fact, the last relationships including my marriage had not been half as interesting at the start of the affair, as this was.

We moved on to a quaint little pub out in the wilds and settled on a sofa in a cosy little room. I had three glasses of wine, and although I had eaten, I felt a little tipsy. In fact, the naughty side of me could not wait to get him back to mine. Hopefully he would accept my offer of coffee! I knew he had plans to be at a football game tomorrow afternoon, so he was not in a rush to get home. It was the first question out of his mouth when we were seated in his car. "Coffee at mine or yours?"

"Where is the nearest?" I ask, not having any sense of direction, not even knowing where we were. I was just desperate to feel him inside me as soon as possible. All mountains look the same! Turns out, we were not far from my house, which made me feel a little relieved.

I opened a bottle of wine on request and put out some nibbles whilst Phil chose some Katie Melua to play in the background. It seemed like we had so much to say to each other; there was never an awkward moment or a silence. "You're so beautiful. I cannot believe you have not been snatched up, but I am deliriously happy that you have not." Phil says, taking me into his arms. I would have said something similar to him, but his lips were on mine before

I had time to answer. There was a lengthy kissing session before hands started to wander, so I took his hand as I stood, and he followed me to my room. If I was happy the first time we were intimate, then tonight I was in ecstasy! The only way I could describe our sexual relations tonight would be immensely steamy. Wow!

I just heard Phil start to snore very quietly, then the world went black: I was out for the count. Contented.

We seemed to both have the same vigour in the morning, and that's before I had a chance to brush my teeth or have a brew. As wonderful as the night before, with the added feature of Pud jumping on the bed and interrupting. As soon as she had, I put her behind the closed door. (Definitely the wrong moment for 'Dreamies'!) Twenty minutes later I was in the kitchen apologising to my cat and added a few extra 'Dreamies' (not that she had any idea that I was feeling a little guilty). Phil made his way into the kitchen and came at me from behind, wrapped his arms a little too hard around me, so that I could feel his excitement against my body. Fuck, I thought, he is ready to go again. My lady garden (as Daisy calls it) was still suffering from last night's session. It was going to be a little rough on my sensitive parts- going another round. Over the kitchen table- why not? I did not have the heart to disappoint him! After the initial stages, the soreness left me and was replaced by more pleasure. I was not complaining; I just hoped he was not a nymphomaniac.

We had bacon bagels with two cups of coffee, before he asked if I would like to join him at the match in a few hours. I politely turned him down and told him I had work to catch up on (which was a lie). I needed to soak in a bloody salt bath and regain some energy and get rid of some soreness. "What about tonight?" he asked.

"What about it?" I joked.

"We could go to the cinema, or eat out again, go bowling, anything you would like to do." He nearly pleads.

"Cinema sounds great. I want to see 'A Star is Born' if that is okay with you?" I reply.

"That is sorted then. If you text me with the times then I will know when to pick you up." Phil says. Another coffee, and kisses goodbye, then I run upstairs for a bath. Ran back down for the salt with desperation. You cannot enjoy a bath as much without bubbles, and the pain from my poor lady parts was making me wonder if I should have declined another date with Phil 'til I had healed somewhat. I will just have to tell him, but in the mean time I slapped a handful of bepanthem cream on there. Well, it worked on babies' bums!

Pud was out in the garden by the time I was ready to take a walk into the village, so I just left her out. It was literally less than a ten- minute walk. I wanted some crusty bread, some bagels, maybe a couple of cream cakes, and see what they have in the way of pastries. We were now into October and the day was yet again beautiful. I strolled in a dream-like state, said hello to the very few people I met on the way. Everyone I had met here was so friendly. There was a great community spirit here. I think this is my forever home.

Once in the bakers, it was laughable at the number of sweet treats I had placed on the counter, but this had become the norm! I had already built up a rapport with Manny the owner because of the amount of times I had already been there, the short time I have been around. He was a comical character and we always had a bit of 'banter'. To be honest, 'taking the piss would be a more accurate statement! His wife Jan became a friend and she worked in the pharmacy as well as her days off in the bakery.

I decided to go into the chemist to buy some more cream,

as I would need it for my next tattoo as well as my sore bits 'n' pieces. The ladies in there were really friendly and incredibly helpful. When I first arrived in Penmaenmawr and enquired about doctors' details, they just went ahead and put everything in place for me. So jovial they all were. It makes a difference to see people happy in their workplace and every shop here had happy faces.

Walking back home, I decided to take the scenic route. This place was perfect; I was so happy to have discovered it. Just as I was about to enter my gate, I turned and saw a figure approaching from the corner of my eye. "Hello Joseph, how are you and the girls?" I say in greeting to my neighbour. "Hiya Laura, we're all fine thank you, how's it going for you? Settled in a bit more now?" he asks. I have a feeling his approach is not really to find out how I am, but to update me on these two similar murders. After some small talk he proves me right and I invite him into my home.

He compliments me on my ongoing décor of my downstairs rooms, after I had told him to have a wander whilst I put my shopping away. "Fucking charming! Ooooops! Pardon my French." I say to Joseph as he enters my kitchen in a rush. He sees me holding a rat up by its tail, then looking at Pud as she pops in through her cat flap. "Lovely." Joseph remarks.

"Yes, lovely present Pud, but I can quite honestly do without your gifts, if you do not mind. I apologise again for my outburst Joseph, but I must warn you French is my second language." I say looking at my mystified neighbour. "That's okay, not a problem." he replies. I make us both a coffee and tell him: "I am thinking this is not a social call?"

"No. I thought I would come and give you some update regarding our conversation last week." he says.

"As long as it is good news I do not mind. I do not like

talking work once I am off the clock, so to speak." I inform him- now and for a future reference.

"I had better speak to you when you're on the clock then, because it is not good news in the slightest." He responds with a little agitation in his voice.

"I am sorry yet again, I did not mean to sound rude, but I have this rule that work and home life do not cross paths. Obviously in our line of work, it has to be kept separate. In the past, it has caused a lot of upset with my husband and growing family. But you're still quite young. I learnt to cut off with time, being nagged and nearly losing the people I loved. Now it happens naturally." I say sincerely. "Let us start again. If you found me quite curt, I can be. I may sound quite abrupt at times, but those who know me just shrug it off. I think it is some form of Tourette's. Even though it is a neurological disorder that affects mainly males, that with age usually fades or ceases altogether, I unfortunately started with compulsive utterances in my fifties. Now you know me Joseph." I say as we laugh together.

"I think you are a bit of a character, but I have also learnt that you are first class at your profession, and your commitment has been described as exceptional. I would not describe you as having Tourette's, and I cannot fault you on your ethics. I am here to see if you have any insight into what we are now calling, just between ourselves, 'The vigilante murders." he says almost grieved.

"I had used the same words whilst discussing the homicides with a work colleague. In fact, I have just had a client that was looking at a life sentence regarding the Blake massacre in Manchester. He was slaughtered in his cell, and from what I have gathered reading the autopsy report, his injuries resemble the accounts you gave me about your investigation."

"Really? Maybe this is something I will have to look into. What is the name of one of the investigating officers?" He asks, whilst taking out his notebook and pen. I give him Brian Wagner's details. We discuss the demise of Eric Ward for a further ten minutes, giving him the only information I knew, which he noted.

Fortunately, with going to the cinema I did not have to spend time sprucing myself up. It doesn't matter when you're sitting in the dark! Joseph and I sat for two hours discussing his cases. I was even kind enough to share my pastries with him. I offered as much of my expertise as I was able, with the information he had given me. He asked if I would be available for a few hours in the following week, with the intention of meeting the detectives heading the investigation, and going through all the evidence, not that there was much from what I understood. He would meet me at the station on the agreed day. I must admit, I was more than a little curious with his case load now. Would it not be marvellous if I could make the transition from Manchester, to covering the North of Wales, in my role as a Criminal Psychologist? No use getting excited about something that was unlikely, but who knows?

I asked Phil if he wanted me to drive for a change and he declined my offer. I was not complaining. My ninety-minute drive to and from work and to various prisons, offices and homes everyday were more of a hindrance than I had initially thought it would be. I cannot complain, after all I live in one of the most beautiful places in Wales. I just wish I could spend more time enjoying my stunning surroundings.

I do not know who decided what, but when we reached the cinema we called into the public house adjacent first. Did we decide between ourselves or was I talked into eating and having a drink, rather than seeing a movie? I wanted to see

'A Star is Born', so I was a tad disappointed. The original film starring Barbra Streisand and Kris Kristofferson was one of my favourite movies. I think Phil changed his mind when there was not a film showing that he wanted to see. I was more interested in seeing Marvel's newest release 'Venom' but at this point in our relationship, I thought I would keep my passion for the main character to myself! We still had a great evening though. We ended up being joined by a young couple, the male being an employee of Phil's. I must say that the two of them had made up for my dismay at not getting my popcorn and movie. When we left the pub, it was nearing twelve-thirty. Time had flown in the company of Sean and Katie. We were in hysterics and my stomach hurt from laughing. They were very similar to my friends with their enormous charm and sense of humour. We were definitely going to meet up again.

How did I guess that it was to be my home that we headed for? I would rather be at mine, but I would also like to have a choice. This time Phil did not even ask. I will make sure that the next time we go out, it is Phil's house where we spend the night. I am quite impetuous at times and would have brought up the fact that I did not like him taking command, making decisions for me, but fortunately after the great evening we had shared this was not one of those times.

Once we enter and secure my property, my curiosity gets the better of me as I ask my new lover questions about his home. "After my divorce I bought myself a two-bed dormer bungalow. I was not looking for just ground floor accommodation, (with just one bedroom being upstairs) but I did not really have much time to be fussy. I have an acre of land with it and a couple of outhouses which gives it so much character. Like you, I wanted to be near the sea and the countryside. Being born and brought up in Anglesey, I was spoilt. Next weekend, if you have not got anything planned, maybe you would like to spend the weekend there with me?" I answer him with "Of course that would be lovely." I felt much happier now I had got that out of the way. "Good, I will plan something nice, as you have spoilt me and made me feel so welcome. I know we have not known each other long, but I enjoy your company immensely. You're beautiful, intelligent, and funny. My kind of girl." he says as he wraps his arms around me. I answer by raising my lips to his, just to confirm that I felt the same. We kissed and cuddled without our hands wandering for more than an hour, because at this moment that is all we needed. When he finally released me, I felt dizzy. I poured us both a glass of wine and before I could hand his to him, he took my other hand and led me upstairs. Tonight was so loving, a contrast from being a little mischievous at the start. He was also 'my kind of man'- absolutely no complaints there, except having to apply some soothing cream whilst in my bathroom!

CHAPTER TEN

J ust before I was about to leave to have a meeting with Brian Wagner at my office in Manchester, I got a call from Daisy. "Can I come and stay with you for a few days Laura? Or maybe for a year, ha ha ha! I won't get in the way I promise." she pleaded.

"For fucks sake Daisy, do you really need to ask? My home is your home. Are you okay?" I ask with concern.

"Apart from the hot flushes, the bouts of frustration, agitation and anger, I am fucking marvellous." We both laugh at her retort.

I was trying to ask her when she was thinking of coming, before she broke in with "I will be on my way in ten minutes. Sorry I did not ring earlier." I told her where the spare key will be and to go through the freezer and food cupboards so that she can prepare tea for when I get home. "So I am not going to be treated like a guest, more a husband or your lesbian lover?" Daisy is in true form.

"You're not my type! I will see you later then, my Sweetie Pie. Love you, bye." I tell her with a big smile on my face. I am pleased she has decided to come back. A good chill will do her the world of good, and on the plus side, she can cat-sit Pud while I stay at Phil's at the weekend. When he left yesterday (after a walk up to the Snowdonia National Park), he asked about seeing me during the week. As he knew my work hours were a little hectic, he was already sceptical about my answer. I assured him I would sort something out. I would like to have time to do that.

Brian was already waiting for me in the office. "Am I late?" I ask.

"No not at all. I don't have to travel as far as you to get here. I think Sian has gone into the kitchen to make us coffee; you have her well trained." he teases.

"Noooo, she is just a diamond. Have you been here long?" I enquire. "Long enough for Sian to educate me regarding the latest changes in your life, and to tell me how much she respects and loves her boss." His charm is working.

"I feel honoured to have her with me and the same applies to how I feel about her." I answer. Sian appeared with coffee and we settled straight into the subject that we were here for. It was not a long discussion, as there really was not much Brian could tell us. No evidence, no witnesses, no suspects. Was there some kind of cover up here? We learnt about Eric's abhorrent injuries in more detail. Whoever had perpetrated this crime may have thought he had committed an indecent attack towards the baby he beat so badly to death, suggesting a reason for removing his penis. Every nick and cranny was searched, and no weapon or evidence found. An instrument that tore through his larynx and windpipe was not any prison-made shank. The sense of pointless overkill came to mind- just sheer frenzied violence.

Our meeting came to an end, and as our previous encounter, I walked Brian out of the building. "Maybe we could meet up for a coffee, or an alcoholic drink sometime? Definitely. No talking shop." He asks a little nervously.

What could I say but "Yes that would be lovely." I was put on the spot and I did not want to say no and make the moment awkward. He walked me to my jeep, covering numerous subjects along the way. This was the first time he had observed me out of work-mode, and he made the comment. "I can see you're a bit of a funster out of your working environment. I have a humorous side and can be a bit of a prankster. I am rejoicing now at my decision to relocate here. There is much more comradeship in this region, and it makes for a more commodious work life." I totally agree with him, and he waits to wave me off.

Once out of sight, I can't help but say "Phwoar! What a fit bastard." God, it is like waiting an hour for a bus, then three turn up together! What was I thinking? I am expected to jump back into professional mode before this next appointment, and I am flustered by my, what's become a complicated social life. Brian is the third person in two weeks that I have promised to have a date with. Well, Tony is most definitely struck off my list of suitors now. What about my lovely Phil? I am not the type to have two lovers to alternate between. I will talk it over with Daisy tonight, (after she ceases with the derogatory statements) looking so forward to having her here again.

I parked my car near Manchester prison and did all the usual to get into the interview room. The young man, Sean Driver was seated, and if I had ever seen anyone that did not belong in that seat, it was him. His eyes were red and swollen with the crying that he still could not hide. Reading through his report, I found it quite questionable as to what had gone on. Sean was claiming it was an accidental death whilst 'Mucking about'- for reasons I have yet to gather. The investigation was calling Rikki Howard's demise 'murder'. I asked the officer if he could get this sobbing child a drink of water, and after it had arrived, I started with my interview; treading carefully, because this almost child, was at breaking point.

Sean and Rikki, both sixteen years old, were mucking about by the railway in the Guide Bridge area of Ashton-Under-Lyne. The bridge they were on has strong wire meshing that stands approximately twelve feet high. Both being very close friends since primary school, there was nothing to suggest there was any angst between the two. Several witnesses had signed statements confirming the lads were just being silly-which was apparently the norm with them both. Neither had ever been in trouble with the police, and they attended full-time college, with part-time jobs. Sounded like the perfect scenario to my ears. The two had been warned by passers-by to be careful, as they were climbing up the mesh guard. Sean states he was several feet away when Rikki fell from the bridge into an oncoming train. This I totally believe to be true.

Although a little immature for his age, Sean was fluent in his interpretation of the event. The only dilemma with his account was that there was only one witness at the time of the fall- an eighteen year old young man. His account states he saw Sean pushing Rikki from the bridge. Without being judgemental, I query this account, as this person was on the police radar and was of a questionable character. I will request an interview with this young man. If there is anything I am good at, it is getting to the truth using my charm towards the interviewee, or if need be, my subtle demands. Sean was mortified. He was not shedding tears for his incarceration; he had lost his best friend and witnessed the offensive sight of the aftermath. Good god, this child should not be here. He needed some counselling immediately.

I phoned Sian for her to start getting my plans into action. We had to get this young man out of there and I would acknowledge there was a chance of self-harm. I phoned Brian Wagner to see if he could get the ball rolling with regards to interviewing this so-called 'witness'. He was as charming as ever and said he would ring me with the details when he acquired them. Before the call ended, he also mentioned his earlier offer of a night out. I fancied the pants off him, so it was an easy answer. "Fuck yeah." Not exactly as I put it but the yes was there.

From the prison I go to the hospital to meet my next client.

Neil Saunders. Admitted into hospital for his third drug overdose in the last twelve months. Under twenty-four hour police custody, this thirty-one year old substance dependent had beaten to death a homeless man- David Bateman, aged forty-nine.

Neil found him sleeping, his body lying half-way in a shop doorway and proceeded to kick him to death. To say he committed this atrocity for money or goods to sell for drugs, he only came away with half a bottle of cider and a silver St Christopher on a neck chain. The mind boggles. If you intend to kill someone for money, or items of value, then why on earth do you choose a person whom has nothing? Easy target: assumes he cannot defend himself. (Which proved to be so in this case.) Nothing more than a murdering coward. My work here was to eliminate two of three reasons Neil Saunders would violently kill this poor man.

As is the norm in these situations, lies just spill so easily out of the bastard's mouth. Professionally, I cannot use these terms, but after interviewing him, I thought (as with the minority of cases) 'what a fucking oxygen thief'-not because he is a habitual heroin user, not because he had committed this murder. He was what I term a 'wrong one.' Case closed: throw away the key. Even better, let him die from the damage he has done to his body after his overdose. Save the National Health Service some money.

A quick call into the office to collect some files, I just catch Mark on his way out. He is just about to phone for a taxi, as his car would not start. (The AA had taken it into a garage.) I told him I would give him a lift to pick up the courtesy car he had been promised. He was grateful, plus it gave us a short time to catch up on some cases. After dropping Mark off, it took me a further two hours to get home; the traffic was diabolical.

Daisy came running out to meet me and we embraced. 'Moo Moo', as I call her affectionately is like a sister to me, along with Rae and Liv. I love them to death. I do actually have a sister and after years of her lies, greed, attention-seeking jealousy towards me, I have decided she means absolutely zot to me. She can keep her narcissism and shove it up her arse. Never met anyone living such a false life. The narcissistic side comes from her mother (that we both share). She also means nothing to me. Just as much as I ever did to her. "Why did God give you to me?" she would scream at me from an early age.

My sister and I are two total opposites. I like to be happy and never suffer others' negativity. She lives off misery, lies, attention seeking and gossip. You would not believe we came from the same twat!

"Aww, so lovely to have you back. I have missed you. Is tea ready?" I jokingly ask. Oddly, there was no retort. In fact, with her rushing me through to the dining room, I had guessed the table was already set to dine. I had given her notice half an hour ago, without admitting that I was famished.

"Surprise!" Rea and Forrest get up from their seats and come to greet me. "Oh my God, wow, how wonderful to see you. Have I forgotten something? Did you set this up between you?" I say with such glee. We are so incredibly happy to see each other. "I will just sit down and read the paper whilst you three gab on till breakfast shall I?" Says the usual selfish Forrest, but in a funny way of course. Daisy and Rea eventually make themselves busy in the kitchen and 'Pain in the arse' as I call him, and I have already got the banter flowing.

"That cat must be hard of hearing by now if you only have her to talk to out here- especially with your language, poor little thing. She never shuts up your mummy does she? How do you manage Laura? No glass eyes to talk to sleep in this neck of the woods. Eh, no, on a serious note, it is really gorgeous here. I have never been this way before." He says creeping to me after his initial insults.

"No, and you won't be coming back this way again if you do not behave yourself, ya friggin' retard. Lovely to see you anyway Forrest. I could not think of a more delightful way of being welcomed home, having you sat here. But on a serious note, it is great to see you as well, and it is a fantastic surprise." I respond. I go over and sit on his knee and give him another big kiss and cuddle. If anyone in this whole world was made for Rea, the strongest, most self-sufficient woman I know, it has to be this funny delightful man. We always rip each other to pieces, but only in fun. I think all of my closest friends and their partners are the same. We are a close family of rejects.

Daisy and Rae made a superlatively palatable array of food, including spinach and ricotta cannelloni (which was to die for). We caught up on each other's news, filled the dishwasher, then settled in the conservatory watching the stunning sunset we always get here. We're in October, so getting a little chilly in the evenings. I would not generally put the heating on for a slight chill, but Mr Wimpy Forrest was always cold. "I have a few things to get together for work tomorrow, then I can relax properly with you. So, while I am at it, you can pick a DVD or music- choose between yourselves." I announce.

"Soaps are starting on plus one." says Forrest.

"Fuck off: no chance I am watching any soaps. You can piss off into another room or go to your bedroom." I say vehemently.

"You three will be chatting anyway," he replies.

"Even more reason for you to put it on in another room, unless you're frightened of missing out on something, ya big girls blouse." I chastise him.

"God you are a ruffian. Roughneck, hoodlum." he squawks.

"They all mean the same thing." I say, before he interrupts.

"No wonder you do the job you do, you must feel right at home with all them hooligans, now go and get on with your sorting, you bloody fishwife."

"Fuck off, I am going now." I turn and tell him as I walk out of the room. "Your language is disgusting." Follows me up the stairs.

"Fuck off." I tell him again. I doubt if Daisy or Rea had even heard any of our sarcasm, because they were sitting together, deep in conversation. They had heard it all before with Forrest and I, it was all the same old, same old.

I was a little envious when I left for work this morning. Everyone was up and planning their day, which obviously could not include me. Then my phone rings, it was Phil. We had a lengthy conversation that saw my journey into the office seem to go quicker than usual. I invited him round for the evening so he could meet Rea and Forrest. He had met Daisy on her previous visit and I was desperate for my other sisters to meet my man.

I had been in the office for ten minutes when my personal mobile rang. It was Tony. I took the call and told him I was busy at my desk, promising to ring him later. He sounded quite offended to my trained ear. He reminded me that he was out of the country. He did not have to point out what I already knew. I had said I would speak to him later just to finish the call; I had no intention whatsoever to do so. I pressed block- what a dick head. I did not owe him anything, especially my valuable time. A chance meeting at a store helping me pack my bags, and now he wants me at his beck and call.

I commenced with typing my reports on the two clients I had last interviewed, when Sian approached with a look of pity on her face. "Good luck with this one. I will speak to you later; I am in the middle of interviewing for the secretarial job." I thank her and she rushes off. My extension line rings. "For fucks sake." Mark does not even look up; everyone in the office has become expectant of my foul mouth. This is why Sian is doing the hiring today. Maisie, our last executive secretary had taken ill, and was not going to be returning due to the nature of her condition. She was ideal and will be missed. I must remember to send some flowers. "Oh hi Brian, I am fine thank you, and yourself?" My change in tone made Mark look up He gave me a cheesy smile. Sergeant Brian Wagner was asking me out on a date, indicating that Friday would be good for him. How could I deny him my company, especially when he makes me go weak at the knees?! I felt a little giddy just hearing his voice. Oh dear, what a predicament I was in! I wanted to discuss my love life with Daisy last night, but that will have to wait 'til either my two friends and I are alone, or till Rae and Forrest leave on Thursday. I would hope Sian would let me follow her home on the night, so I could shower and get ready at hers.

"How many men have you got on the go at the moment?" asks Mark. "From zero to three in as many weeks or less! One of them I have not even met up with yet, since he helped me pack my bags at the till in Asda. He has clearly decided that we are already an item, by the way he has spoken to me since on phone conversations. I have blocked him now. The prick, ha ha ha, what am I like?" I answered to Mark's laughter, his mingling with my own.

"Watch yourself Laura." Mark says with sincerity.

"Actually Mark, are you busy for the next fifteen minutes? Can we have a chat if I make us both a latte?" I say, hoping he did not want a drink. "Knock yourself out girl. Do you know where the kitchen is?" he enquires. I just laugh. I am used to these remarks. Well I am always the busiest- at brew time especially. Nothing to do with being lazy. Truth is, they're all right- I used to be the one whom made sure everyone was contented with full bellies and thirsts quenched. Age has brought on this procrastination, charming myself out of doing menial tasks. I will put up with the lazy title as long as I get my own way!

Seated opposite him at his desk, we go on to discuss my love life. Who better to discuss it with than a brilliant psychologist? Fortunately for our office, Mark is one of the best. We have a serious discussion on my circumstances. We reach a conclusion. I met Phil on a night out and was drawn to him, when he and two friends introduced themselves to Daisy, Livvi and I. I had not had any relations with a man for several years, so Phil might just be an introduction back into the world of fun, lust, and the end of, the lack of companionship. He was a very caring, handsome man with an eagerness to please in the bedroom. In fact, he was constantly eager. With Brian it was more the effect he had on- making my legs go all rubbery because of his bloody gorgeousness. He had what I would call having the 'naughty boy' look. My decision was to spend some social time with Brian before throwing away something good with Phil. I would tell Brian about Phil, but not vice versa. Tony did not even make the short list. Arrogant prat.

I enjoyed our little chat. Mark was such a lovely young man. Nearly forty, but young to me. He was very happily married; his wife Becky was adorable, and they had been together since their teens. Two beautiful children, a boy and a girl. They were in a good place in life. I truly admired and respected this extremely qualified man who I considered a role model.

Back to my reports and some phone calls. I had managed to secure an interview with Paul Anderton, the witness who alleges Sean Driver pushed his life-long friend Rikki Howard off a bridge, directly into the path of an oncoming train, resulting in a very gruesome death. Sean was now safely in hospital, where he is being given the care that he so desperately needed and was entitled to. I finish my assessment of Neil Saunders, and hopefully will not have any more contact with this abhorrent criminal.

No wonder Sian had looked at me like she did, when she handed me this latest incident. She knows how passionate I get when a child's life is taken from them, especially when it is allegedly at the hands of her own mother and stepfather. Mother: Brogen Childs Alexander, not an appropriate name to have, if what I was reading was the truth.

Thomas Alexander: step-father. Lilly Rose, eleven months, deceased. At eleven thirty yesterday evening, there was a call from the home of the above, to the emergency services. Brogen states that she goes into her baby's bedroom to do the last check of the evening before she and her husband retire. She finds the baby non-respondent and did not seem to be breathing. Before the services could arrive, she claims Thomas and herself followed instructions from the gentleman on the line. Ten minutes later, the police and paramedics enter the property to find the baby deceased, and although time of death is not yet announced by the coroner, it would be believed that Lilly Rose was extremely cold, and rigor mortis was already beginning to set in. Brogen claims she had checked on her baby an hour earlier-which was obviously impossible if the body was already in the said state. I finish reading through the case, then start with the phone calls, putting interviews and appointments in place. This takes up time which could be spent on research. (I hope Sian has found a good applicant that can start immediately, to relieve me of this inconvenience.)

My so-called 'buddies' were sending me pictures of them having fun; some undoubtedly were taking the piss. I just sent them each a text saying, "I am not your friend." I had spoken to them earlier to inform them that we had a guest this evening, so to set an extra place. I was told that it was not a problem because I was buying Indian take-away tonight. Fine by me. They were just making their way to Anglesey for lunch. I hoped everywhere was shut. An electrical fault perhaps. How awful am I?

By the time I had finished my notes on the Alexander case, it was clocking off time. I left the office with a spring in my step. I was looking forward to tonight, and I did not have to be at court until tomorrow afternoon, affording me a good evening. I knew that Phil would fit in comfortably. I could imagine Forrest (whose name I have always bullied him for) would pull him aside and try to deter him from ever stepping foot in my home again. He thought I was the maddest woman he knew, with Rae coming a close second. I loved his name now for some reason, and I complimented him on it just last night, whilst in the middle of a phone conversation.

"Come to think of it, it is a beautiful name, Forrest. I love forests, every kind of forest." I told him.

"Funny that, numpty. It has nothing to do with Tom Hardy going to name his future son Forrest, is it?" he goaded me.

"Oh really? How wonderful. Errr…not sure whether I had heard about it actually."

"Bloody liar." he called me. He was up for a slanging match but he did not get one. He called me a 'numpty'. How dare he? 'Bloody liar' fair enough, but a 'numpty'?! I do not think Tom Hardy's child could possibly have any similarities to this plonker. I loved my best friend's husband, really.

The girls were in the garden sheltering from the light rain under the umbrella. Forest sat in front of the box with a newspaper. I got a glass of water and joined them (at least we could talk about my dilemma regarding my man problem). After an hour, we are all in agreement. I left them to it whilst I attended to my ablutions. I came down to some Leonard Cohen and a full glass of red wine. I announced that all this drinking every night was doing us no good, but what do I get for my care and concern? A mouthful of retaliation from each one. "Listen, what I do not know about alcohol would fit in a flea's jockstrap." I tell them.

"Are you having one or not?" asked the impatient Daisy.

"I will have to now you have poured me one, I would

not be so rude as to refuse your efforts." I said, taking my glass from Daisy's hand. The gate buzzer sounded, and we all looked towards Forrest. He complied and went to answer, opening the door to Phil. Well, at least I do not have to introduce them now, as I do not know how I would have introduced Forrest.

We all settled down to a great meal at the dining room table. There was not any space left with all the dishes we had ordered. Phil had offered to pay tonight, to celebrate an illustrious contract from a big company. We had a toast to his success, but I would not here of it. My guests: I pay. We're all quite relaxed with spending money, except for Jewish Forrest or Scottish Forrest. He was a tight bugger. I suppose thinking about it, his way was much more logical.

We stayed at the table for the entire evening, still dipping into food and changing CDs 'til bedtime came. I asked Phil if he was staying, and his answer of "If that is okay, I would love to?" put a smile on my face.

"Just look at the bloody smile on that face! Well it was nice meeting you Phil, and if you are still alive in the morning, I will see you at breakfast. I would not trust her looking after an inanimate object for me- good luck!" I do not find Forrest amusing.

"Shut up, I would not look after you anyway, Inanimate Forrest." I say, giving him the finger behind Phil's back. A few more words of discouragement to Phil were heard before we made it upstairs. I ran back down and hit him.

It was nine o'clock before we came downstairs, and we were the last to arrive in the kitchen. "Just dig in Phil," I told him, and was met by the first usual gob in the morning- the 'inanimate object'. "I bet that's what she said to you last night, hence you being late down this morning." No surprises that Forrest was the first the bring down the tone! "Forrest, shut up and pour some hot water in there please." We were all seated again now. I placed my hands in the praying position. "Oh God, let's get through this breakfast, so I can get in decent time for my court appearance, and please keep Forrest quiet. Amen. I just thought I would say grace this morning before I acted like a disgrace." I think we both try to out-do each other to be funny. No, I do not, thinking about it. I confess to be the funniest. I always have to have the last word. We are just a bunch of happy people with the souls of old hippies with my little bit of goth thrown in.

I was not planning on going into the office after my court appearance, but I had so much to catch up on with feedback and interview reports. A couple of hours would still be in general working hours. Rae and Forrest were leaving tomorrow, so I did not want to get into anything lengthy that would shorten my evening with them. The office was quiet. Sian had a day off. Everyone else was out working on cases. Without even stopping for a coffee, I sailed through three reports, putting me back on track. I was thinking how dishonourable I had been this morning when I had lied to Phil about not being free on Friday. Well, I was available, however it is the reason I gave him that sees the teeny guilt feelings nagging at me. I thought about it all the way to the car, then realised that in the end this would benefit the three of us, mostly me, but I had to know. To repent means I have got more than regular feelings for Phil. He does seem to have a controlling side, which doesn't go down well with me. He has made all the decisions, down to what time we go to bed. It won't be long before he finds out I don't like it.

I was in shock when I entered my house. Home-made soup with crusty cobs, salmon fillets with new potatoes, asparagus and a salad bowl. Jam roly-poly with custard followed. "I want this every day." I shrieked.

"Get yourself some hired help. Washing, cleaning, ironing, then they can prepare you a meal each day. Go for it Laura!" Rae suggests.

"I do not need someone to do my once-a-week washing, ironing, and cleaning. For God's sake, there's only me living here, and I am not untidy or unclean thank you very much; but I do like the idea of a cook-just during the week!" I say. I am even more shocked when Forrest shows me what we're watching tonight. "It is not you that only likes him you know. We all want to watch it. I need not ask you because it's a cert. Legend." says Forrest.

"I know he is" I say.

My phone rings. It is my beautiful son on face time. Everything was going great for him, I loved that. He was loving his time at university. Forrest mentions my infatuation regarding one certain actor. "She is his biggest fan or psycho stalker- take your pick. Either one is not good at her age." Ben never was any good at sounding sincere. The call came to an end, leaving laughter in the air. Silence followed and the film was critiqued by all at its end. We all then went our own ways after cleaning the kitchen and conservatory. I needed to do a bit of pampering, then I started a new Jonathan Kellerman novel.

It was sad saying goodbye to my two friends, but Daisy staying made it easier. I was in the office first thing, until I got my interview confirmation through. It was actually at the time I should be leaving if I was to make the appointment on time.

Fortunately, the traffic was light and parking access was simple. I went into the interview room, already having an unpardonable view of this character. (This from reading his record sheet.) I do tend to prejudge In a case like this, mostly right the majority of time.

Paul Anderton was the witness in the Rikki Howard case. I was fortunate again to have investigators that knew how I conducted myself with clients, dependent on their demeanour. I will not take any shit off anyone, nor sit and waste my time with liars. If it turns out he has given a false statement to the police about the incident (his allegations being for attention) meaning he is willing to put an innocent child in prison, then this consistent law breaker will get a wake-up call. Something tells me that this interview was going to infuriate me. Not a good idea when I needed to vent any anger that may be ready to surface. I hate liars, especially one playing God.

If there ever was a face that looked like it was asking to be slapped, this was it. The judgement I made of him through his notes turned out to be warranted. Two hours. Two bloody hours wasted. "Alright I made it up." the arsehole says eventually. He knew that I acknowledged from the beginning of the interview that he was fabricating the whole scenario, yet it took him all that time to admit to it.

"Can we lock him up?" I say in a pleading tone.

"Job done. Rikki Howard, you are under arrest for..." I left the room muttering expletives as he was having his Miranda rights read to him. I will arrange an appointment to see Sean Driver over the next few days. I wanted to make sure he got the help that he needed for the awful tragedy that he had witnessed and the time he had suffered interrogation at the hands of Anderton. He has experienced a detestable time this past week bless him. Another case closed.

I was now on my way back to Wales to call in at the police station. It was to be part of a feedback session on the 'Vigilante Murders.' There were to be investigators attending from the borough where the other homicide was committed. I have attended many of these over the years, but not any in which I was not a part of the investigation.

Joseph introduced me to everyone in the Incident room, from constables to the psychiatrist, and detectives. I just listened to every word, took notes and wrote down a couple of my own views. There was so much to listen to regarding the injuries of these human beings. The implement of torture was something bloody big, heavy and sharp. The crimes were connected; of that there was no doubt.

When the meeting was over, the room emptied slowly and I stayed behind.

For the first time since I have lived in Wales, I could not wait to get home. I did not like today. I think I just felt a little sad. I will start looking into my finances. I am definitely going to re-evaluate my earlier decision. I am working full-time adding to that, the time spent on admin at home, (not counting the two, sometimes three hours spent on travelling each day). My work was overtaking my life. How strange that I have made that ruling within five minutes. I have moved to Penmaenmawr, hoping to spend my quality time appreciating my enthralling views. Walking weather is good, and I am still in Manchester five days a week, weekends too in some cases. I have got to make this priority. No-one knows when their days are up.

It was a treat to have Daisy here when I got home. Pud greets me as usual and I spend ten minutes playing fetch with her in the garden, where Daisy was sat reading. It is amazing how much fun she gets with just a hair bobble; her toys left untouched. Daisy was apologetic because she was so enthralled by the book she was reading, she had not thought about the time. I made sure she knew that I did not expect her to have a meal on the table when I arrive home.

We were happy just having sandwiches with salad for tea. There was still quite a large amount of food and treats left from the extra shopping the girls did on Monday. My mood was somewhat solemn due to my five minute revelation regarding my decision to cut my hours. Another tell-tale sign of getting older. Something I do not like being reminded of! I was showing my age on the outside, which did not have any kind of resemblance to what I felt on the inside.

My appointment with Joseph and his comrades, listening to all the details of their case did not help my mind-set. Was I a bad person for not feeling any sympathy for the victims of these crimes? Daisy listened whilst I brought her in on the reason I went on my last appointment. I told her that I did not really have anything to add to what the investigation had already covered, just a few details regarding the suspects, my profiling and adding another motive to their pot. With the crimes that the two victims had marked up in their life, it could be so many people.

Daisy was rejoicing when I told her my decision to drop my hours. We got engaged into talking about why we were making these compromises. Daisy felt as I did. Although we accept that we are adults, I would not say that we are fully grown up yet. Surely you would acknowledge this when it happens? We grow every day in some way or another, even if it is just trivial knowledge. The chat did us good, because now Daisy was rethinking her hours at her veterinary practice. Rae and Forrest had recently let their diary decline a little. It was all good. Livvi was like me with her workload, and was also looking at going part-time. She would then move back home to Northumberland (where she had lived for many years previously). She had a house there that she rented out.

Livvi phoned and broke the ice on facetime. It was just like my dear friend was in the room with us. She was envious of my news and about Brian: she had already got her eye on him. "You bloody sly old cow." she shouts on Skype.

"Fucking Hell Livvi calm down love, ha ha! You might have seen him first, but he saw me first. Stop being a spoilt child and behave. He is definitely one you have not had yet - maybe never now!" I threw at her. "Slapper." she utters.

"Bit of pot calling kettle there." my retort. It went on like this 'til we all ran out of expletives. The conversation then turned to the crimes we were working on.

As soon as I ended the call, my phone rang. I disconnected it from my laptop - it was an unknown number. This was my private phone and only people I had given it to have my number. I declined the call. Before we knew it, midnight was here. I will get up half an hour earlier so I can get tomorrows work day organised. I Did not even want to think about it now.

How ironic that Sergeant Wagner was an investigator on the Alexander case. He was to accompany me to the interview room where I would speak first to the stepfather, Thomas.

On the walk there, Brian asked if I was still okay for the evening, then mentioned that he had seen Livvi earlier. 'Oh God' I thought. I needn't have worried though. Apparently, she had told Brain that I was one of her dearest friends. Thank fuck for that.

After everything was put in place, the interview was being recorded. The sergeant began, whilst I took notes. Another day: another liar.

The scenario the investigation had brought to light, was nothing like the version this bastard was giving. "Mr Alexander, you do not know how to lie well. That means, that every word that you just uttered, is a distortion of the truth. The evidence the investigating team have is conclusive, and there is no way of getting away with that. You're just wasting time: ours and your own. If you did not shake and smother your stepdaughter, then her mother did. I can see how ravaged you are. You have suffered a shocking tragedy. As from today, I will throw you in the cells that house the worst murderers in this country, and you do know what they do to baby-killers Mr Alexander?" I threatened. That is all it took. We got the full story.

I wish all cases were this easy. I knew from his body language and the pain he was in- with what he called 'his baby's passing with the help of her mother'.

"I am sorry that you had to witness my outburst, but it has been building up. I don't have any excuses. Anyway, I will always react like that if you're getting nowhere." I half gave an apology and sort of took it back again. I am a bugger. "You were absolutely right, and I would not usually go with the softly-softly approach, only I knew that you would be the bad cop. Everyone knows that you are tough, passionate and a bit bloody scary. If looks could kill!" he says, meaning it.

"Right on to the so-called mother." I nearly spew out.

"God help this one." he fires back.

This woman was hard-faced. Tough. She had a story, and she was sticking to it. A mother of a loved child would not cover up for her husband in this scenario. She did at one-point edge the blame in Thomas's direction, but we already knew the truth. She was so adamant. This epitome of scum sat there in denial. She had murdered her own baby. The investigation had now changed with the truth coming from Thomas. She did not show any remorse, or anything like the emotional state that her husband was in - Lilly not being his own biological daughter. Sometimes you get perpetrators that cannot show their sensitive state. Mrs Alexander was indeed one of these, if she did care at all that was. I would be interviewing this woman again for court purposes.

"What a team: result." Brian says.

"Aye, we did not do bad - coffee?" I ask.

"Yeah definitely, I might even treat you to a pastry." Brian puts in, smirk on his face.

"Bloody Nora, you have been doing your homework! Pastries at any time of day-especially when we have just solved another case. Good rewards, I will probably have two." We walked to the nearest café that we knew sold the pastries that we desired. We were to see each other later, (for socialising purposes, not business!)

By the time I got back to the office and did two hours work, it was nearly clocking off time. I just wanted to get this report written up before weekend and then I will head to Sian's. The unknown number called again.

This time I answered.

The fucking stalker - it was Tony. "Why did you block me?" he asked as soon as I answered.

"Christ Tony, who bloody cares? I do not even know you." I could not say anymore over his rant. I listened for a few minutes to gather what his problem was, so I could work on it. He was accusing me of being unkind. This one's got problems! Thank God I did not exchange addresses with him! "If you are just going to speak badly of me, then you have the wrong person. I have done nothing to upset you. I was finding it hard to concentrate on my work with my phone constantly ringing. Friends know not to ring during work hours. You gave me no option. I blocked your number. This is what ladies do when a man is coming on to her too strongly. I am going to put my phone away now as I am about to leave work for the evening. I may or may not speak to you again. Good evening." After saying that I immediately hung up. I really did not relish knowing the outcome from that.

CHAPTER ELEVEN

Whilst sitting talking to Sian in her spare room, she teases me for trying to make myself look different from what Brian had already seen of me. (I always like to look how I feel at the time.) I had chosen a dress that could be worn for any occasion (dependant on the accessories). I chose boots and a riding style jacket. "How can you feel nervous? You have been with him most of the day." Sian asks.

"That is just it. I was in work mode. I am never nervous in work mode. Sian, this is totally different. I feel dithery. Oh God I am too old for all this!" I sob light-heartedly.

"You are never too old. You are a woman with needs." she sang out. It broke the ice, we were laughing. I am a woman, and I do have needs, it turns out.

Brian turned up dead on eight o' clock. Well that does not happen often, being on time! I am talking about myself there as well. It would have been easier for us both if I had picked him up and driven us tonight, as I only had to come back here later and pick up my car anyway. Sian did offer me a bed for the night, but I just want to wake up on my weekend off, in the countryside, next to the beach. Ahh… That means my home in Wales then, I thought to myself. Yes, I am not holidaying there, I actually live there now! It was still a little weird getting used to the fact. Especially coming from Manchester in regards to beaches and mountains.

I mentioned my ideas for driving, and the Sergeant took command and would not here of a lady picking him up on a first date. "Yeah, but I am no lady." I told him.

He looked just as gorgeous in his civvies, as he did in the couple of times I had seen him in his uniform. He also wore well-tailored suits. We complemented each other on our attire. I was happy with my choice, and his.

In the restaurant, Brian was the perfect gentleman, taking my coat, holding out my seat for me. We had come somewhere we both knew and obviously liked. I love Indian and Chinese buffets. I can just fill myself up with salads and starters.

"I have decided to cut my hours, so I can have more leisure time. It has not been put into place yet as it was a recent decision. I have so much to investigate in my new surroundings. Still investigating, without the burden of a criminal act to start it all off you might say." I inform him.

"Big step really, it must have taken a lot to come to this?" he asks.

"No not really. I made the realisation within five minutes of driving home from a meeting with the homicide team dealing with the 'Vigilante Murders.' The case I was talking to you about previously. I have relocated for more reasons than a few. When my youngest left the nest, I was rattling around in our family home. I do not have any dealings with my eldest son, nor do I ever want to again, so he did not come into the equation. There was only my Daddy left in Manchester that I cared about, otherwise I would have made the break sooner. My close friends were moving far and wide, and all my attempts at trying to get Dad up to Wales failed, even though he loved it there. I would have stayed in Manchester forever if Dad was still alive. I lost him last year and what little I have left of him is with me. So he is in Wales now." I had said all this and a bit more while we were filling our plates. Once seated and delving into the food divine, I learnt a little more about Brian's family and his move to the Manchester area. We got on famously and did not have any awkward silences. You know it is going well without those moments.

We got (or he got) onto relationships. I did not want to lie to him. The reason I did not tell Phil about my date tonight was because I do not want to upset him - if there was going to be no reason to. Brian might not ask me out again and I might not want to be asked, who knows at this conjecture. "So, you will keep this guy hanging till you get to know me a little better? Will tonight determine Poor Phil's fate?" Brian asks in quite a hostile manner.

"Would you rather I'd have said no to your invite? Putting a couple of dates with Phil as priority?" I answer him quite abruptly.

"Not if you put it like that, but I have a right to be a teeny bit jealous." he admits.

"I do feel slightly guilty because I have lied to him, that is the worst part. I can explain everything else - lying you cannot. He will always keep that in the back of his mind." The conversation lasted 'til the end of desert. It is where we go from here now that counts.

"I would like to ask you back to mine for more chat and a coffee, but I think you may decline, in the predicament you're in" Brian offers.

"If you do decide to ask, I would love to." I assure him.

"Mine it is then." Oh God, what was I thinking? I should have declined as he thought I might. The rest of the journey saw us laughing about what other people think of our little foibles. My co-workers' gossip giving him the heads-up about my 'dippyness', passion, and compulsive utterances. He had already seen my no-nonsense approach and my aggression. Everything about him was so nice. No arrogance, great sense of humour, so dishy and sexy. Oh dear…it just might be a lust thing. It cannot be, surely? He is just so honest as well, even if he's telling me something, not exactly showing him in a great light, he still shared it with me. I am contented now that I told him the truth on the first date, it was still early days though. As the evening wore on, the worst I felt about letting Phil down.

He kissed me before we got out of his car. I swore to myself that I would not go further than that tonight. Oh my God! (How many times have I blasphemed today?) What can I do? My body was leading my head. We made it into the house, five minutes later and we were pulling at each other's' clothing. With only my knickers left on, he dragged me up to the bedroom. He had better not let any hesitation set in because I was ready to change my mind. I am in my fifties and I am carrying on like a teenager! The next few hours were wild and wonderful. We were both equally aroused, and when it seemed to happen quite abruptly for us, it was not too long before we got back into rhythm.

I will not stay over, like I have been requested to. I will leave that for our next evening together. I offered to get a taxi to my car so I did not have to disturb him, but he would not here of it. We kissed and cuddled in the car and we were soon ready to ravage each other again. I quickly got out, said my goodbyes and left for the ninety-minute drive home.

I felt somewhat sick driving back to Wales. I will get Daisy up and make her listen to my dilemma, even though she will not want to listen. I am supposed to be staying at Phil's tonight, yet here I am at one-thirty in the morning just approaching home.

"You dirty stop out! Ooh… do not come near me, I can smell him all over you! Stop it you filthy tart, get off- gross." Daisy just would not have me near her, I was chasing her round the downstairs.

"I need to talk to you seriously Daisy, if you're putting the kettle on after my long drive, it would be much appreciated, and show me how much you love me." I utter in my child like voice.

"Fuck off." I knew she would say that, but also knew she would make me a brew. I sat there with my make-up wipes, whilst telling her the outcome of the evening. "For fucks sake Moo Moo, stop saying 'oh dear'. Do you not think I feel bad enough, do not say 'oh dear' to me again. You will have to phone Phil later and tell him I am unwell." I say holding my hands in the prayer position.

"No, you got yourself into this mess, how the fuck do you expect me to get you out of it? It is not me that has been shagging a copper all night behind your lovely new boyfriend's back." she digs at me.

"Thank you for my delicious cup of tea and if you feel like you would want to help me out of this situation at all, then please feel free to do so. Goodnight Moo Moo, I love you." I said sincerely.

"Goodnight Dippy, I love you too." she replied. I showered quickly then hit the sack. I felt I had behaved appallingly. Daisy had every right to speak so harshly, even in jest.

CHAPTER TWELVE

The last few days had been dull, and the chill was indeed settling in from dinner time onwards, but the days still stayed warm. I woke late, to the sun streaming in through the bedroom window. I had zonked as soon as my head hit the pillow ten hours earlier. Apart from the circumstances I find myself in, I feel great. My head still full of lust for my new lover, but I did not care about Brian in the way I cared about Phil. I could not keep lying here going over scenarios, I needed a long soak in the bath. Bloody chaffing again-my age! I giggled to myself.

"I made you a latte, my wounded child. Haha! I am taking mine into the conservatory, so come on and tell Auntie Daisy all about it. When you have got yourself together we can go for a walk up to the Fairy Glen if you fancy it?" She's such a suck-up sometimes.

"Sounds good to me. I do not really have anything I need an Aunt Daisy for this morning. I am enjoying myself more than I have done in years. Life has just begun again for me, is that not why I am here?" I say fully meaning it, but just for that moment, who was I kidding?

"You are absolutely right, and I just hope I come out of this fucking menopause the same as you. I find it quite cute really. You're happy Laura, and that is all anyone wants for you. Come here, give us a big cuddle." Daisy grabs me as she was saying the words I needed to hear. I did not want anyone to have any angst against me. I would never intentionally upset anyone. I would apologise after, if I did so unintentionally.

We set out for our walk, when my phone rang. It was my neighbour Joseph, asking if I was around to talk to on the clock. When I said we were just at his garden, Daisy's face could have killed me right there - if looks could kill. He came out to greet us and acted like he was in a rush to catch a plane. "I am just on my way to a crime scene in Leeds." Joseph tells us.

"Don't tell me you want to take Laura with you?" Daisy asks.

"Go on." I encourage him.

"It is up to you whether you want to attend with me. It seems certain that we have another victim." He announces.

"Same M-O?" I enquire. (Modus operandi is a police term meaning a characteristic way of committing a crime.)

"Yes, but this was committed maybe ten or so days ago. Nobody had looked in on the victim. It was only the stench that got the neighbours' attention." Joseph says without precaution in front of Daisy. He had listened to me previously when I told him I could trust my friends with my life. I did not feel the need to go to Leeds in any way shape or form. I let Joseph know that I would speak to him on Monday morning if he was available. I agreed to call in at the station first thing that day. My morning off, after the court case I was appearing at, had been adjourned. I wished him good luck and we said our goodbyes. If no one had checked on the victim Joseph was talking about in all that time, it would suggest this person did not have anyone that had missed him - just like the other two victims.

"I do not get that with all the crime you're involved in you can just switch yourself off." Daisy states as we take off our cardigans and tie them round our middles.

"I just learnt to detach. Look how I used to be compared to now. Maybe age has brought me this gift, because if I did get involved emotionally now, I think it would be time to give up all together. Also, I think with what Saul has taken from me, I find that I have grown in strength, and the part of my heart that went with him years ago has been replaced with stone. I am not suppressing feelings; I am using all of them daily." I say without sadness at the loss of my child from my life. Daisy pats me on the back after my statement and gives me a smile. Always on my side.

Daisy walked in front when we found ourselves on a narrow footpath. I was a bit hesitant and slow, as I did not like heights, and we were pretty bloody far up. Once off the path we took picture after picture of the breath-taking views. I wish I had a pound for every time Daisy called me lucky!

This was wonderful. We were in awe, sat there with our bottles of water as though time had stopped. We did not even speak for what seemed like an age, and then Daisy surprises me by saying. "I want to move up here too. This is what I should be doing, not stuck in a fucking supermarket every Saturday and cleaning up after the boys on a Sunday, making a bloody roast dinner, getting all the bills in order..." I feel bad for her, but she has yet to come out of the menopause - the new Daisy. I tell her there would be nothing I would love more, but to make those decisions when your hormones reach the places they're going to stay. I do not want to encourage her for my own selfish reasons.

Daisy knows perfectly well I would be over the moon if she moved here too.

Phil ringing me broke into the silence. I knew I was not going to have to lie to him again. I looked at Daisy and held her hand. "I am so sorry, I was about to ring you, but the signal keeps going in and out. We're in Snowdonia sat having a drink. Unfortunately I will not be able to make tonight; I am staying with Daisy and that is all I can say at the moment." Clink. The phone went off, I wasn't sure whether he put the call off on me. I still had full signal, so it would seem so. "Do not think I used you as an excuse, because I did not. I was going to stay at his tonight, and it would have meant going home now to get ready. I don't want to. I want to relish this some more, and not have the worries of being ready or rushing for a certain time. I want to spend more quality time like this with you. You have always been there for me, through some bad shit as well Daisy. I do not know what I would have done without you when I was menopausal, and with Saul. My two most hated things in life. Come on before we starve to death, the Glen will be out of food."

We had to, well, we did not have to, we chose to share a table with a couple (I would put in their early forties). Their smiles welcomed us, and we did not have to wait thirty minutes for a table. I do not know who made the first daft comment, but it took the theme of the rest of the early evening. I think I always came the worst off, with the barmy things that I have done, and you cannot dare me, because I am more likely to do it. I do not think I have ever turned down a dare, and I still am pretty much the same. We were having such a good laugh, no-one really wanted to leave yet, so we took a seat outside. The twilight was mesmeric, you could just dive into the stunning colours, they were so blatant. Another hour's chat and a pint of lemonade with pineapple juice later, we came to an accord and started the 1.8 mile walk back home. This, after refusing a lift from Nea and Dave! We wanted to walk a few of the calories off. Boy, did we eat in there! Approximately fifteen minutes from home the bloody heavens opened. We blamed each other for refusing the lift. The evening coolness we could take, it was the fucking pound size raindrops that were pummelling our heads that were the problem! We certainly did not need any more damage to our heads! We still laughed, with some songs in-between 'til we got home.

I had promised Daisy that when I had dried off and had changed into my pyjamas, I would ring Phil. She had thanked me, and believed me when I told her that I truly had meant what I had said to her earlier on the mountain. I was not really sure what I was going to say, but I was not going to lie to him anymore. Once is enough for them never to believe you again.

"Hiya Phil, are you okay?" I ask when he answers after several rings.

"Yes, I am fine thank you. You?" he asks quite jovially-phew!

"All good thank you. I am so sorry I let you down, and I did really mean to be with you tonight, I was stuck in the moment. Daisy needed to put some things straight with me, and I her. We both had to get rid of some cobwebs, that is what my friends and I are there for, each other. I do want to talk to you about a couple of things though, but not on the phone, and not now. We were walking without coats back from the mountains, when that bloody storm hit, were-drenched and squelching! Can I ring you or even pick you up tomorrow and take you out to lunch? Can you decide though, I don't know anywhere near you." My waffle near enough comes out all in one big breath!

"Good grief. You're still blowing the cobwebs away. Sounds like a good idea to me. I will email you with details of how to get here in the morning and with a time. Enjoy what's left of the evening, take care, goodbye."

"Phew! That turned out to be easy." I announce as I jumped over the sofa to join Daisy. "I take it you have spoken to Phil?" she enquires, asking the obvious question. "Tomorrow will be harder, but it is what it is Daisy. I told him from the get-go that I did not want a full blast-in-your-face relationship. It seems that is just what it is becoming. I have felt guilty all week, yet I did not say I was exclusive to anyone. I was being too hard on myself. Have I become selfish again Daisy?" I implore her to answer me with the truth.

"No Laura, you have done the right thing; I did not realise you had felt that bad, and all I was doing was taking the piss out of you. Forgive me my dear friend." she says, ever so sarcastically.

"Fuck off. Cow by name, cow by nature." I throw at her.

"Well, Tom Hardy film night?" she says.

"I love you Daisy." I say as I go to kiss her on her cheek. If I get her into 'Taboo' (which, if I am honest I would like to watch again, now I know the plot) I'd be getting at least eight hours of Tom and would be able to pick up on some of the things I missed first time round! I have only ever felt like this about one other celebrity and that has always been the one-and-only Mr Bowie.

There was definitely something bad going on with Daisy's hormones; she did not make any utterances about Mr Hardy's favourable appearance throughout the two hours we sat there. "Yeah he is good looking." She said

WHAT WOULD TOM DO?

when I suggested that she go to Specsavers. She suggested I see a therapist!

I got ready slowly in the morning, and sauntered in and out of the house. Daisy had decided to do some gardening and had already been to the retail park to pick out some items that she thought I needed. "That is why I have a fucking gardener Daisy, and I forgot to tell you that Handyman Dave is coming for two days next week to put up and take down blinds and curtain rails and put my pictures up properly. I have bought wooden blinds which I have had made to measure. Dave will bring them with him. Now, he is a married man so behave yourself! Mind you, if Tom could not do it for you, Handyman Dave has no chance." She was laughing whilst I was chastising her. "Are you on your way now? (I nod my head towards her.) Good luck honey pie." she says.

"Thank you, laters." I reply with an air- kiss.

CHAPTER THIRTEEN

DAISY

I sit out in Laura's garden with all these lovely ideas. I have to tell myself this is not my haven. This is Laura's home and I am just digging myself in further and further. I do not want to go home. I am only there for the kids and my dogs. I just hope that when all this mid-life crisis shit ends, I have it in my power to make a shot at a better life. I know my amazing friends have kept me sane these past couple of years. How long does it fucking take? I just hope I can come out of this in the way the girls have. It does not stop me worrying about Laura. As if I do not have enough worries of my own. The poor girl has had some very much undeserved crap thrown at her and at the wrong time of life as well. This 'man domination' she has at the moment will settle when the right one fits (pardon the pun). I am pleased she is not putting herself in any danger- by being up front with the guys to start with.

Fucking hell, I have just managed to squeeze into the perfect place to plant some flowers and the bloody gate buzzer has gone. Instead of walking up the side of the house and randomly just opening the gate, I take off my walking boots and enter the house to someone who seems to have their finger stuck on the button. It was constant and overbearing. "For God's sake. I'm coming. Hello!" I shout.

"I want to speak to Laura please." an agitated male voice on the other side says.

"Who is it? I cannot see you on the camera. Right, I can see you now. Who are you?" I ask very curiously.

"My name is Anthony I work with Laura. I found myself in the area and thought why not call. She is not answering her phone." He lies.

"Do you want to wait there just for a minute Anthony while I try and ring her because she is not at home right now?" I say as I am already trying to connect to her. "Sorry to bother you honey, but there's a guy that is a little bit suspicious-looking at the gate. He is asking for you. He says his name is Anthony, he works with you. He says he is in the area so thought he might call on you. I have not seen him before…Okay, will do. Hello…hello. Anthony are, you there? There's no answer now Laura, looks like he has done one… okay sweetie, laters." Pretty strange, I am not liking him. Very suspicious indeed. I think she might need to speak to her neighbour about that one. My only hope is that Laura settles with one of these guys. Phil seems ideal for her; in fact, I think they are a very good match. I have not met Brian - Livvi says he is gorgeous, and that he catches all the ladies' eyes-even the young ones! It is not about looks and wealth though. Laura did not just work from her office in Manchester, she supported her wider circle of friends and families, taking on much homework and court appointments in the process. In fact, in some instances, Laura did the whole court thing. It is this she needs to relieve herself of. But will she say no to a friend? It would be extremely hard for her to do.

I am going to have to go back to the practice for two days next week, as the other veterinarian on duty, Maggie, is taking the week off. We only do two days of surgery a week, and as the client list is rising, I have taken on a full-time vet as well as myself and Maggie-all in place ready for cutting my own hours (if I ever do get the courage to do so). If I am to keep coming here throwing myself into Laura's kindness, then she is going to have to accept some money (if nothing else) at least towards bills. I will go into work for those two days, but I will come back here when I have covered them. I am not ready to go home yet. I might just stay over at Livvi's the one night I am back in Manchester. I carried on with the garden and all my worries disappeared.

CHAPTER FOURTEEN

LAURA

I was a little hesitant as I approached Phil's. Another beautiful area. (He lived in Beaumaris.) I have been here many times throughout my life, but never paid any attention to the residential areas. I parked at the foot of his garden, maybe I should have gone up the drive? Phil was stood by the car as I looked up. I'd still not made the decision whether to go into the drive or not when he said he would just grab a jacket. Decision made: we were going straight off. We embrace before I told him he was to give me fair warning when I have to turn a corner, because I am the worst of the worst with my sense of direction (or lack of). He was his normal self (thank God), and I was very happy to be with him. We made our way to the Treaddur Bay area to a seafood restaurant.

I had actually been here a couple of years ago with a friend, with the view to maybe having a relationship. That was Steve, and no, never did he get the chance to be fully that (nor anything sexual for that matter). I always felt a little sorry for his deceased wife. Married for thirty plus years. She must have died a virgin or without knowing what an orgasm was. God, I was so vulgar! When you get to my age, why settle for someone who makes me more unhappy than I already was? I think it was he who actually put me off men for a while. I had forgotten what it was like to have a man at your side for the best reasons. The things that run through my mind! Well, the things that run through all our minds (but some people are unwilling to admit it). He became a great friend of my fathers and did so much for him. My Daddy thought a lot of him. I respected him for that.

Phil had actually booked, so our table was ready for us and we ordered an array of food to share. "Now, what do you want to talk to me about?" Phil asks, as we settled.

"Not anything in particular, really. Well, just one little nagging voice. That nagging voice is my head and it is speaking to my heart. I just thought that maybe we have jumped a little too much, too quickly. I cannot fulfil a full-time partnership role. That is down to me, because of work commitments in and outside the work place that I have taken on. I am going to lessen my hours, still probably be a four-day week, but that is including admin work I get involved in personally, and driving. I want my hours to coincide with a general working week. Forty hours would be ideal including commuting, I want to be home by five o' clock each evening, without any thoughts of work until the next working day. Sorry- I am rabbiting on now!" I say (not sincerely), before he stops me. "I am listening, carry on. You have come to a big decision, I am happy to be sharing it with you. Carry on." he insists.

"Do you know, you are such a sweet and caring man, and I am very happy with what we have. If it becomes more, my work is going to get in the way of us having time together. It always has; from my children, husband, friends, everyone. Whilst I am getting all of the above in place, I suggest we try and get one night a week, and weekend together. Plus, Daisy is not herself at all. Never has she really left home before. You know what I am trying to say. I don't want to upset you in any way." I sincerely mean it. He was security- I had realised that today. I think Brian is the bit of fun, the naughty boy I have been missing out on. I have no intention of becoming the local ride and I don't want to lose Phil. Our conversation ended, then Daisy rang.

She told me about Anthony (a colleague from work) stood outside my front gate. The name Anthony bothered me a little. I told Phil the story of Tony the weirdo. At first, he seemed uncaring of the issue, as if I had nothing to worry about, but when he read my expression, his demeanour changed. Maybe he thought whilst he was on my arm that no one could touch me. He then feigned anger, which had me at a loss really.

We went to the cinema- wow! I would have stayed to watch Venom again! Marvel was another one of the common loves of Ben and me. We always watched a new Marvel film together a few times when it is first released on DVD and many times after. He was worse than me!

"Wow, I cannot believe you are a mad Marvel fan- that is just the best." (I was acting like a child with him, letting him into that silly, charming side I have, that gets me my own way)

"I know what your favourite is, having just seen that." I say smiling from ear to ear.

"So who said that was my favourite? You forget I know about your Tom Hardy infatuation- Forrest told me all about it. That was one of the best though, and yes-Tom Hardy was brilliant. Only I do not see him in the way that you do. I can see we will be getting the Marvel movies out soon." he says.

"It is not an infatuation!" I protest. Forrest talks through his mouth- that's his only problem! "He is someone new to me, not having seen any of his work until a couple of years ago. It was love at first sight, but only one-sided unfortunately! I became aware of just how amazing his acting talent is. It is true, he is an amazing actor as well as..." We both laughed at my outburst. Phil was adamant he was following me home after Mr Weirdo's appearance at my house, so now he was bothered. With my knowledge of reading body language, I must admit I was having a little difficulty with Phil. I had phoned Daisy when we came out of the cinema. This Anthony had not shown up again. Daisy had not been beyond the gate, so she did not know if he was waiting somewhere, and she encouraged Phil when he said he would be with me. I was happy he stuck to his guns. This business with Tony was getting silly.

Everywhere around the lane looked quiet. You could not see much, it was dark now and the lighting was very minimal. Phil had picked up what he needed from his beautiful home. (I did go in for a coffee at last!) His home was beautiful and modern, whereas mine was one room in one-style and one room in another. All different, with what I am told is 'crazy old furniture'. Who cares? It's quirky and I love it! His décor was manly with minimal furnishings; it was so tidy. This man had a lot going for him relationship-wise. He is a keeper. I was happy he was staying over. I had had such a lovely day. (Apart from the idiot interlude.) The more I saw, the more I liked. Daisy kept Phil company whilst I got engaged in some note-typing ready for tomorrow's lectures at Manchester University. I made us all a latte, gathered some snacks from the fridge, and we sat down to chat together. What a lovely end to a perfect day.

CHAPTER FIFTEEN

O n Monday, I made my way to the local police station where I got the update from the so called 'Vigilante Murders'. The connection was obvious, and so was the lack of evidence. I finished early after my stint at University, then made my way home. By the time I get home it is five-thirty, and I think that is early.

Tuesday: I caught up on a case I was working on for a friend in Manchester regarding her son- drug related. It went well. The afternoon saw me in the office typing up my report on a new case that came in on the previous day. A gay couple, Lewis and Luke Manford-Jones. One alive, the other deceased. Allegedly, at the hands of the husband Lewis.

Wednesday: interview with baby-killer, Mrs Brogan Alexander in the morning, alongside the mighty handsome Brian Wagner. He had asked me when I left his privately-rented pad early Saturday morning, if I fancied doing something Wednesday night. I declined, blaming work. I went into the office and wrote up my report for the lawyers working on Brogen's case (defence and prosecution). Brogen was still denying causing the death of her daughter, and as of yet, I have not witnessed her shedding a tear. Absolute bloody cow. She admits to smoking crack. Not an excuse nor would it inhibit her memory. Did social services or child protection have Brogen on their radar?

Thursday was here, and I had just declined a case I would normally take, but found another on my desk when I came in. Hooray, I was learning how to say no! I booked a holiday in my diary for two whole weeks off. I would decide what to do when the time came. I could get my Christmas shopping done before I nearly break my neck doing it on Christmas Eve (as has been usual the past several years). I will phone Rae and Livvi tonight, and make sure Daisy is still around by then. We should get a few days together. We have to visit each other at least once monthly or we get disengagement manifestation. It is not that bad is it? My two weeks off are at the start of December, then I have the whole Christmas and New Year period. I might change that time together now, and we all have Christmas over at mine. A decision we will make together.

I decided to go home. It was three o'clock and I only had to write up my pre-interview report from the case I had received. I will do that sat in my conservatory later. Just as I was about to leave, Brian came into the office, and my personal phone began to ring. I had forgotten to block the number that Tony had rung me on the last time we spoke. Oh well, maybe it is a good job I had not. I put it on speaker and made a sign to silence Brian. "When are you going to speak to me like you did the first times I phoned you?" he asks.

"You were ringing me constantly, demanding my attention, and because I was unable to give it to you for good reason, being very busy at work, you were very rude to me. We never arranged a date or professed to be anything that meant anything to each other. So this is me saying I do not owe you the explanation you want. I do not need to be told I have to speak to someone at a time I am unable." Speaking slowly, I articulate my tirade clearly. I want him to hear every word.

"You were not in work for a few days, you lying bitch." he spews out. I am glad I thought of pressing the record button. Brian had motioned me to do so after he picked up on the threat in Tony's tone. I nodded my head towards him- it was already pressed.

"You told me you were in Milan working on your parents' homestead. You specifically told me that the last time we spoke - which was on my day off. Tony, or Anthony, as you called yourself when you spoke to my house guest last Sunday, clearly not in Milan. You lied to her about ringing me and who you were." I said, being ashamed of what this sounded like to Brian.

"I came back because Mum and Dad did not need me anymore and I wanted to see you again. I loved your company. We kissed." When Tony said this, I could see wonderment on the sergeant's face.

"You helped me pack my bags in the supermarket; you helped me transfer the bags to my car. We stood talking because it was a beautiful night and we were having a pleasant conversation. I wanted to meet new people whom I can become friends with in my new location. Just as I told you. Someone I could share walking with or just to natter to on the beach, any kind of new hobbies I could try. I saw a caring young man in you, whose company for an hour was engaging. I gave you my number. I thought that you could be one of those friends, but..." I was stopped there by his next comment.

"We fucking kissed, you knew I wanted you." he yelled.

"Let me stop you right there Tony - if that is your real name. Firstly, I do not believe that you are forty-nine years old. That means, straight away you lied to me, you looked too young for me to harbour any kind of romantic ideas, or thoughts of anything other than friendship, and if I remember rightly, I went to kiss you on your cheek because you were a big help to me. You turned your face towards my lips. How dare you think that one kiss gave you the right to curse at me over the phone - on several occasions, I might add. I think you had better come into the office or an interview room at the police station. I do not want this conversation to end. You know too much about me: you know where I live, and I want to know what you have been doing to get this information. So you either come in, or I will report you to the police." The rage I felt was not hidden by my voice. God is this guy for real.

"I do not need to go anywhere. We need to meet face-to-face, so you can look me in the eye and tell me you don't want me. You will feel that chemistry - that bond we had. You will change your mind." He sounded intimidating.

"Do not put the phone down Tony, we need to keep talking about this, otherwise you're scaring me a little, and I am sure you do not want me to spend my days worried that you might turn up and be cruel to me." (Brian gave me a sign that he had made contact with someone in the office.) This is the truth after all.

"Why would you feel scared? I like you a lot. I would not hurt you; I'm not a fucking madman." He so obviously is. The click: the phone went dead.

I looked up at Brian and said, "I am a total weirdo-magnet - my friends call me that!" I was trying to make light of what just happened, but the truth was I was scared.

"That was threatening. I heard danger there without

doubt. I guess I heard what you wanted me to here, so now I know the whole story."

"You got the entire relationship known in that several minute conversation." I was a just a little embarrassed.

"Well now you have to go to the station. Let me do a statement with you so we can start an investigation into this idiot.

"Sorry, I have not even asked you your reason for coming in?" I realised. "Oh, it was not actually to see you. I had to go into probation so I was just walking past your office, so I thought I would pop in before I ended my day and see if anyone was putting the kettle on?" Brian says.

"Well I was just leaving; I suppose we could go to the deli and have a coffee-up to you." I say.

"Come on then; I am buying. Actually I am starving." he utters, rubbing his belly.

"I am behind you." And I am.

When we had ordered, I started the conversation off about Tony, just to get it out of the way. (I do not want to talk shop while I am dining out; I have clocked off.) It seems Brian had the opposite in mind. I was only just enduring the long-winded ninety minutes we spent in the deli. He bored me shitless, and every time I tried to bring the conversation back to civilization, he would carry on about all his acts of bravery. What a hero he was! I was quite shocked when he came round to my side of the table and planted a big kiss on my lips, then said, he had wanted to do that since he saw me in the office. "Okay…thank you, erm…right, sorry, I'm stuck for words. I did not see that coming." I just about managed to say. We had been to each other's personal places and spaces, so I suppose it was a natural romantic gesture on his behalf.

"You look gorgeous, I could not help myself, here let me

help you… Should we…?" he said as he helped me with my cardigan, then took my arm to lead me out of the restaurant." Oh dear. I want to go home. How can I, when I need to put Brian in the picture regarding Phil? I am surprised he left it this long to find out where he stood. "My place?"

"I am so sorry if I gave you that impression, but I have a plethora of paper- work to do. I have to get my essentials together for my work day tomorrow, sort bills for the house… God, I won't get to bed as it is." I said in response.

I had been wondering through the course of the meal how tonight was going to end. What I told him was true; I had so much to do. We had a couple of kisses in between me trying to tell him that I wanted to chat to him first, about where this relationship was going, or not after a few reality checks tonight. I promised him I would call into the station first thing in the morning, and I take my leave.

I drive home in two minds. The first being I am thrilled that I saw Brian in a different, more governing light. Although one I am not particularly fond of. A week of worrying what decision to make, and I felt a slight lightening of my shoulders. Now I knew that I could tell him the truth. It is not a good idea anyway, to get involved with a colleague, especially in our line of business. To be honest, I could never see a copper and myself as a couple. I want away with crime in my personal space - not a cop who thinks it is okay to talk shop, when not on the clock. A certain arrogance comes with the job, for the majority, in my opinion.

My second thought is a bit more daunting. I feel a little unsafe with the reality that someone whom maybe dangerous has a grudge against me. Brian was coming up with scenarios regarding the idiot, and what he thought he may be capable of. Does not help me much, that. Pillock. I asked him several times not to talk shop, but he just had to go and bore the fuck out of me. The next crime on his agenda for this evening was 'The Vigilante Murders'. This was the subject that brought us to the end of the evening and my revelation about him. Fancy talking about slicing through a victim's thorax while were eating. What a plonker. I even showed him my 'I'm so fucking nerveless face', and he still carried on. I think if Brian had not talked about the horrific vigilante killings, I would not feel this little irritability going on inside my head. I was constantly looking in my mirrors to make sure no one was following me. Thank God for mobile phones! I rang Daisy and asked her to buzz open the gates when I pressed my horn. The jerk had obviously put the fucking fright up me. No signs of Tony as I drove onto my drive. Gates shut and secure. Daisy had changed the alarm system so that we could have it working in the rooms we were not in while we were in the house. Through the night it went on a different setting, and another setting for when the house was empty.

"I have to be honest with you Laura and say that I am worried about you and this Tony, especially after what you have told me of your evening. Food, wine and crime! Fuck me, some slashing went on there, I don't know how you could eat while he was talking like that. Holy cow." Daisy went on.

"Well at least you are here, that eases the pain somewhat." I reply and cuddle her. I was just about to tell her about my decision, when Phil rang. After our hellos I told him about the idiot's phone call, and the presence of the plod as a witness, was how I put it. Then Phil gets onto the 'I'm worried about you,' speech. Fucking hell, I feel like locking myself in a cupboard, until the bastard has had a speaking to from 'The Law'. He asked if he could come over just to settle down and watch a film with Daisy and myself, to which I answered "Yeah, why not." I quickly collected my items needed for tomorrow, and got my 'before interview report' done before Phil showed up. He looked so handsome. He had had his hair cut, and it made him look younger in a very pleasant way. I was so happy with the choice I had made or had had made for me. Daisy asked for a bowl when I complimented my boyfriend on his hair, cheeky cow she is! We gave Phil the choice of DVD, he chose Pulp Fiction. Great for me. Daisy will be going to bed early with a book; Quentin Tarantino loses her at his name. My favourite film ever: pure genius.

I was quite shocked, but pleased, that Daisy decided to read her book in front of the TV; it was nice to have her company. (Unlike her to be so thoughtful.) As ever, despite the twenty plus times I have seen this film, it has never failed in entertaining me. The end of the film took us to bedtime (with the obligatory brew, of course). I felt really safe, restful even, lying listening to the first murmurs of sleep from Phil's chest, upon which my head lay. Tonight, for the first time we really 'made love'. I was feeling very much 'in like' with him. I fell asleep thinking about tomorrow's events, this is something I do not usually do, worry. I think having to go into the police station to report a potential crime for my own personal safety, is so much worse than having to go to report anything that comes up during the course of my work.

I got to the Manchester 'Cop Shop' at eight thirty. After a five - minute wait, I was called into an office. As well as Brian, there was another Sergeant, Colin Burrows. After the introductions, I did try to say that I did not feel that this issue was to be made a big thing of. I am in denial. "I am sure he is just a wimpy guy whom has not had his own way." I say, but I'm not sure I even believe myself. Fuck me, would you believe it, the bastard was only ringing me - right on cue! Brian and Colin picked up on my reaction straight away, and the record button was pressed on my phone and connected to a cable that had been passed to me.

"Hiya Tony are you okay?" I say simply.

"Not really, you are pissing me about. First, you're all over me, then you start ignoring and blocking my calls. You're probably leading that copper you're always with up the garden path as well. You cannot behave like this Laura Timmings. What do you have to say for yourself? It had better be good." he threatens. I just want to tell him that if I ever saw him, I would poke his eyes out. How fucking dare this freaky individual (who seemed a good, caring man) be following me? God, he could have jumped out on me at any time. I hated this cretin for putting hurdles in the way of my personal happiness. Well, if I was not worried before, I am now. "What are you expecting me to say, that I did not say yesterday?" was all I could think of, all work ethics out of the window. I have great negotiation skills, where are they?

"Do not treat me like a fucking idiot. We started seeing each other before you started seeing them, so I have every right to be angry with you Laura." he says in a very controlling and intimidating manner.

"Do not patronize me, Tony. Every time I answer a call from you, I get nothing but anger. Why would I think of having a male friend that is going to scare me every time he talks to me? Someone whom, so very kindly helped me with my shopping, hence our swapping numbers. Where in the conversations we have had, have we talked about seeing each other on a boy/girlfriend basis? Never, Tony! Which leads to the fact that I owe you absolutely nothing at all. There will be no apology yet again." I managed to get out before his rant got worse. He was just threatening me with harm now, and to be honest, I just switched off, I did not listen past the first punishment he was going to treat me to.

I was sat in the canteen with both officers now. Tony was not really Tony. He was called Alex Dunne. He lived in a small village near Llandudno. (My favourite shopping centre in North Wales.) Great, I will have to find somewhere else to go if I am on my own. He will obviously not approach me when I am with company. Sian cancelled my afternoon appointment and Brian was going to come with me to my local nick. How fortunate that the Sergeant on duty was my neighbour, Joseph Keil! I let the two Sergeants discuss my case (as it was now). I had made my statement. I did not have anything really to add: everything was recorded. The man was deluded. He needs help.

They were both here talking; they decided they might as well talk on the car journey to Alex's home. Hopefully by the time I get home, my new remote control gates will be near finished. I will not go back to Manchester, so I will get home earlier than if I had gone to my appointment. I will perhaps catch up on the new case I had found on my desk when I went into the office. I was under threat at the moment, so Daisy was aware I was nearly home.

There were two men working on my gates, so I parked on the end of the drive. Both were looking around with concern - Daisy must have given them the heads up. I am pretty handy myself but having these two here whilst Brian has gone to see the idiot (along with Joseph), makes the place a lot safer. He must have known he was being recorded! I am going to have to do an assessment of him as I do with my clients; I do not think he is very well. I am on pins waiting for Joseph to arrive home so I can see where I stand. His shift does not finish 'til seven this evening and it is only one o clock.

"Daisy, why is the jet spray here? Or should I ask with that look on your face." I laughed 'til I cried. Daisy had combat gear on and was using the jet spray as a gun. She started acting the part. At least she has lightened my mood! The gate guy's were laughing along. Looks like Daisy has been entertaining them. Nice to see her like this again.

"Go and see what's sitting on the kitchen table. I apologise now for changing the mood. I was not going to let you see them; I didn't want to add more shit to what you have already had today." my best friend tells me.

"Wow! That's a bloody big bouquet - no need to ask who they are off." I see in Daisy's face that they are. "Shit, shit."

"But on the plus side, come into the dining room. These flowers are not off the imbecile." she says.

"Wow! Not as many, but more beautiful. Aww, they're from Phil - how adorable. I had better ring him to let him know what's going on. He will probably come and stay here, that is if you do not mind Daisy?" I have to ask. I don't want to make her feel uncomfortable. "Why the hell should I mind? It is your home after all. Safety in numbers is it not? I like Phil, seems like he has been around us for a long time. He is good for you Laura.

Please don't keep the two, do not be greedy. You're a damned right fucking tart." I was wondering when she would get that in! She smiles.

I sat in the conservatory whilst I rang Phil. He started to go mad before I got even half of my news about Tony in - I mean Alex. "Tell the gate guys to stick around until I get there if they're thinking of leaving beforehand. I mean it Laura. If that twat can climb, he will get in somewhere. I am on my way." he says, then disconnects. The workmen outside would be here for several hours yet.

"Bloody fucking Nora. This is putting a lot of people out." I shout out loud enough for Daisy to come in.

"Who are you putting out? Police? It is their job. Me? Am I not here anyway? Phil? He wants to be here. I think he has got his eyes on you as a keeper. Let's get through the weekend with some fun, and let the cops do their job. Who the hell is that now?" She hollers the last sentence over the sound of my phone. I walk into the conservatory to get away from my lunatic of a guest.

"Hiya Brian…okay, that is fine. Phil is on his way. He will stay depending what you have to tell me. Bye."

"Daisy, oh God, you're there. What are you doing lurking behind me, listening to my personal calls, ya nosey cow?" That started our bombardment of insults upon each other. As is typical, we end up falling about laughing. "It is not funny Daisy. Brian is coming here with Joseph." I say in a more serious tone.

"And?" she replies.

"What do you mean 'and'? Phil is on his way too, ya plonker." I said, meaning it.

"And?" she repeats.

"Eat more brain food Daisy. Yours is dying from a lack of something! Take it out of your arse and put it back in your brainpan." I tease.

"Oh bloody hell, fuck, I forgot for a second. Anyway, you seriously do not need me to be panicky about your conundrum of men when 'The Vigilante Murderer' might be preparing to take his next victim." she says, acting as though she is in terror and coming at me like a monster.

"Just to make me feel better, you bloody moo. Do you want a latte my 'special' friend?" I say, acting out the word special, as we do. Not nice, but there it is.

CHAPTER SIXTEEN

D aisy and I have been the best of friends for over thirty years. We have always been able to be honest with each other. I had made her like that, because I give my opinion, whether it is wanted or not, and I welcome everyone else's with respect. My close friends are like that too, especially with me. What you see is what you get.

Daisy has never lived further than a few miles away from me, so we saw much more of each other than we did our other friends. As we got older, the ones I keep very close and share my heart with have become a force to be dealt with when we are together.

I have known Livvi nearly all my life. Even though she moved to Northumberland for twenty years, we still stayed great friends.

Rea, I have known for twenty plus years. I met her when she was producing a crime documentary, and they had chosen a client I was working with to be part of the production. We hit it off instantly, and became the greatest of friends.

Phil arrived first, an hour later. Number one item on the

agenda: food. It was still a little early, but we put our order in place with the Indian restaurant near the Fairy Glen for eight o' clock. Twenty minutes later, the boys in blue arrived. (Out of uniform, but in blue suits.) As soon as I clocked Brian, I got 'that' feeling. 'Stop it!' I was saying in my head. He is bloody gorgeous. Daisy gave him a "Ooh, hello!" Introductions over, we all made our way to the conservatory with various drinks and a plate of biscuits.

"There was no sign of him at the property." Brian says. "As far as your safety is concerned, we have put out an 'all-points bulletin'. I am going to leave you my landline number. I will revisit his property until I find him in, if he is not picked up in the meantime. There will be police surveillance vehicles passing through the night. Let us see what tomorrow brings. I am going to pay him another visit before I clock off. He does work, so evening is probably the best time to catch him in, mind you he has not been working while he has been following you." Joseph is just telling me, what I already know. Brian asked to be shown around my home, and the wonderful Daisy linked his arm, pretending to flirt with him, so he had no chance of denying her request. Brian threw me some 'bad eye vibes' when he came back into the room. I could tell he was impressed with my abode, but Brian was the least of my problems at the moment.

I was elated when they finally left, with the idiot's flowers in tow. Let's get this weekend started: I really needed it. Sian had phoned earlier to say she had sorted a more favourable working schedule out for me for the next few weeks, and to tell me that we had a new secretary (which will help with some of my workload). It also leaves Sian more available to me again. Hooray, it has only taken three weeks to find the right person!

The Indian meal was delectable, along with the

company. Daisy wanted to play Scrabble and Phil and I complied. God did we laugh! If we did not have Google, I would have lost because they would not accept some of the words that I put on the board. "I cannot help it if I have a much wider vocabulary than the two of you!" I told them. I did warn them that I would win! Sometimes I might cheat a little to make sure! I am doubtless I would make a very poor loser, only at Scrabble. I was the scrabble master.

Ben face-timed me, and I introduced him to Phil. I had not told him about my new boyfriend because I was unsure that it was actually the case when I last spoke to my son. I had to tell him a little of what was going on, as he had just informed me that he had booked his train ticket for his surprise visit next week. I was delighted. I was dying to see him. Circumstances could be different. If he had pre-warned me, I would have made sure I had some space in my work schedule: a few days leave to spend some much-needed quality time with him. Ben had a bit of a warning for me. He always tells me that I am too friendly, and that it will get me in trouble one day. Well, that day was here. All I did was be friendly, accepting the help of a stranger to pack my shopping. Although I think I have seen and heard the worst, I have to say that the position I am in with Tony was concerning.

I have worked on cases where a disgruntled person has killed for what they think is their right, for being rejected by another for the sake of love. It would not stop from popping up in my head. I just have to hope that his bark is worse than his bite. We spoke about his social activities, had a bit of banter between us all, then he left the call to head for his night out with a girl he told us he was interested in, but not the same one he took out last week! I looked at Daisy, knowing she would be itching to give a retort. With Phil being present I knew she would not do such a thing. 'Like mother like son' was on the edge of her tongue. She bit her lip to prove to me I was right.

We sat and watched a horror film that was on TV. It was so good I cannot even remember what it was called! (They never fail to put crap on the box.) I filled the litter tray for Pud whom had been snuggled up on Phil's knee through the film. I was not taking any chances by letting her out. How dare this bastard do this to us! As soon as I put the litter in her little toilet, she decided to go and dirty it. That sent us all upstairs to bed. I had forgotten to put the humidifier in there, and her scent spread like wildfire around the bottom floor of my house. Pud is definitely a stunner on the outside, but her insides were rotten.

Our lovemaking reached greater heights, the more we were now 'in like' with each other. I fell asleep wrapped in strong, calming arms. It was not long before we were awoken by what sounded like an explosion in our silent surroundings. As we came together with Daisy on the stairs, the phone began to ring. "That is either Joseph or the idiot." I predict.

Fortunately, it was Joseph, saying he had called a squad car but he was heading outside to have a look around. I tried to stop Phil from doing the same, but who can stop a man on a mission? I know he carried something with him, not sure what. I put some milk in the microwave so I could make us all a hot latte. I was just pouring it into mugs when the boys came in together. As earlier, we reconciled in the conservatory. Joseph took a small evidence bag out of his pocket. It held two bangers that he had picked up from my patio. What was left of them had evidence of what looked like, some kind of pin holding them together. Evidently calculated, that is unless they have started selling them like that (which I doubted).

They had been directed straight towards the French doors. We took it for granted that this had something to do with Tony, though we should not judge like that. He must have had something to hurl it with, to have come this far into my garden. Whoever did this must have entered the neighbour's garden (that joined mine at the back of my house). However, this may mean nothing personal. Just a coincidence, hopefully.

There was nothing else we could do, so we just finished our drinks and headed back to our rooms after Joseph had left. I did not want to speak about it once we had got back into bed. I will call it a coincidence rather than a threat that the idiot wanted to blow my house up. Really, if it was Tony, he could be just letting me know he could get to me.

I do not know how I slept, but I did, 'til twelve-thirty that afternoon. The day felt chilly. I was on my own in my room. I surfaced after I had showered and made myself look decent. Daisy was on the phone in the living room. The radio was on in the kitchen, and it was like a sunny day with all the daylight bulbs turned on- Handyman Dave's idea! What a bloody good idea that was.

Bowl of cereal and two brews later, Daisy gives me the heads up on what has transpired whilst I was unconscious. No evidence regarding the fireworks had materialised. Phil had work this morning, which he had informed me of yesterday. Poor soul must be knackered. Joseph had phoned and sounded positive but would not leave me a message. He told Daisy that he would call in after his shift. Oh, and the gates worked perfectly.

"So Daisy, Daisy, give me your answer do." I sing to her, as I most often did while she was holding her hands over her ears.

"Christ Dumbo shut up! You cannot sing, but that is why you do it, isn't it?" she says.

"You're just jealous ya miserable old sod! What are we doing today? I am putting you in charge. I have got to keep busy, mind you, having you with me is like being at work. The clientele is similar. Argh: that hurt!" I shout out after receiving a Chinese burn.

"You deserved that, come on let us go for a drive, see where it gets us." says the heavy-handed bugger.

CHAPTER SEVENTEEN

W ell, the heavens opened again! So, the drive out was
literally just a drive out. This rain was not going
to give up. I ordered some flowers for Maisie, my
poorly former secretary. She will not get them 'til Monday,
but I had done it now, got it out of the way. I phoned Brian
to say a big thank you. He already knew, what I did not, but
he was not going to say anything in regard to my fucking
scary stalker, knowing Joseph was coming to see me later. I
need to know something about his background. At least then
I would know what to expect. Mind you, it is always easier
for the victim not to know, that is if the culprit has a record.

We found a nice café in Conwy. Rather than have a meal,
we opted to eat unhealthily this evening, just for a change.
So, after our drinks and sandwich, we took advantage of the
pies, cakes and pastries that were on offer (it would be rude
not to). The rain was much lighter now, but persistent. When
we get free time (like we have now) we always decide to get in
front of the TV to watch a film. We should take up knitting!
We could not do this until our children left home. Video and
DVD technology was invented in our children's life- time.

We were too busy bringing them up to watch anything we wanted to. Now it is the epitome of relaxation. Daisy still had Mark living with her, so it was nice for her to enjoy chilling on the sofa, with the goodies stacked up on the table.

This is where we found ourselves watching 'A Star is Born'. I was still planning on taking a trip to the cinema to watch the newest account, starring Lady Gaga and Bradley Cooper. Hmm, should be good. I was a fan of the said Lady. I started singing. I was soon shut up!

Like magic, I pressed the stop button for the DVD at exactly the same time as the gate buzzer went. I thought it a little too early for Joseph, so we were both a bit jumpy and we got into cautious mode. It was Joseph. We took him straight into the kitchen and I put the kettle on.

"Daisy, you can finish them off." I say with a chuckle.

"I wondered what had got into you when you put the kettle on!" she answers. We waited whilst we were seated before we spoke of 'The Idiot.' I knew his real name and the area he lived, but that is as much as I know. I opted not to speak until Joseph had finished telling us all he knew.

"He has a record for domestic violence, but I think you knew that was on the cards. So, he has had several protection orders against him. They never learn, do they? (Meaning Alex and his behaviour, not the victims.) Obviously he has threatened you. You know I cannot arrest him for that. I left a note for him when I returned to his premises yesterday. He has rung into the station and has offered to come in and see me on Monday. I am sorry I cannot tell you any more than that Laura. Until I speak to him we are going to keep the barriers up. Regarding the bangers, there's nothing we can go on. I have visited the family that live in the property behind you. They heard nothing, and there is nothing left at the scene. We cannot call the Crime scene investigators in just for being the target of two bangers, particularly as we are not even sure that he is responsible. We have got your back Laura, don't worry."

I was not going to dwell on this issue again, until Joseph has spoken to the 'freak of nature'. We went over what had occurred since we last spoke on the murders he was investigating. The body of the man in Leeds: Michael Gorley got to the age of forty-eight before he was so severely slaughtered, same M-O. The investigation team had come to the conclusion (with such a lack of evidence) that it was a one-person crime. The homicides were exact in their injuries. Mr Gorley had molested, then caused the death of an eleven-year-old girl. He had recently been released from prison after doing a life term. "Fucking hell. His life was just beginning at the age of forty-eight. They call that life- my God. I am sure the family of the victim are over the moon that someone has done a good job in getting rid of him." I rant with anger.

"Exactly, I agree whole heartedly with you. It still does not give the committer the right to play God." My neighbour replies.

"Would you think like that Joseph if it was one of your girls that were the victim of his depraved crime?" Daisy asks.

"No." was all he could say.

Daisy and I were just settling down again to carry on munching and watch the film. I think we had had enough of talking and were happy to have our evening taken up with being entertained by the TV. Phil arrived just before the film trailers had finished on our second DVD. Daisy made brews and sandwiches with various fillings, and we had our lovely pies. The table reminded me of a children's party buffet. I think Daisy just wanted to be kept busy so she would not have to listen while I echoed Joseph's words to

Phil. Ben, Rae, Livvi, Sian, Brian and Tracey (a friend from Manchester) rang. "For fucks sake. I apologise for leaving your company and will going into the dining room because I am sure you don't want to hear about the idiot any longer." I know everyone was concerned, but I was absolutely sick to death of repeating myself. I turned off my mobile phones (work and personal), and unplugged the house phone. Enough was enough. Film?" We watched 'Everest'. Daisy and Phil had not seen it. Daisy and I ended up with tears in our eyes. Phil was a man, say no more.

The three of us retired together-not in the same bed! Truth be known, I could not wait to get into bed, and that means I wanted to ravish the man with whom I was falling very much 'in like' with now. I sneaked out some sexy underwear, changed and entered the bedroom from my en-suite bathroom. Let's just say, it had the perfect effect. An hour later, we succumbed to sleep whilst our erratic breathing became normal.

The morning came with sunshine. On awaking, I thought it would be nice for the three of us to get out -away from it all- somewhere together. As soon as Phil opened his eyes, he pulled me towards him. Round two. He certainly knows how to make me happy! I hope the same applies from his perspective.

I made brews and took them to the bedroom. Daisy had nipped into the village, to buy supplies. God knows what supplies we need. The fridge, cupboards, and freezer were full. Daisy is a fan of bakeries though, like me. We showered together before we descended to face the world.

Daisy was in the kitchen. She must have ants in her pants. She offered to make us all a big breakfast. Just what the doctor ordered. She even did bacon, sausages, and some black pudding for Phil. I declined the latter. Even though

Daisy is a vegetarian, she did not mind cooking meat for others as long as she did not have to touch it.

It was nearing eleven o'clock. The buzzer for the gate sounded. Looking at the camera, we could see a man with a parcel. Daisy and Phil looked at me, I shook my head, I was not waiting the arrival of a package. Phil went out to greet the courier and came back yielding the item. "I do not think we should open it." said Phil, anxiously.

"Since when do they have courier service on a Sunday?" I asked.

"I questioned the delivery guy with the same. And yes that particular company do." My handsome man answered." The three of us just stared at the package, the size of a large shoe box. Daisy put the item in the old coal shed and we decided to wait until Joseph had finished his shift to speak to him and go from there. My mood declined.

I sat in the back, whilst Daisy took the front passenger seat. Phil had volunteered to drive. I was not thinking straight. I felt a little bit numb. I hope this situation with the idiot does not drag on. I feel like my freedom has been taken away from me. I am a sucker for my own space. God forgive anyone that encroaches on it.

As we approached the junction we were to leave, Phil gave out a loud screech. He did not use the language that I would have. "The breaks have gone." he said, trying to stay calm. No one spoke. Best for the driver to just take control. Apart from a couple of quick glances at Daisy, we also stayed still, with what I know now as shock. Fortunately, the traffic was minimal, and the length of road we had yet to travel before we had to stop, was enough for Phil to get control of the car and pull over as soon as we got off the motorway.

Phil rang Joseph, who was just taking a coffee break. He told us to wait with the car. We had driven twenty miles and were not far from Anglesey which was to be our destination. We would be picked up and Phil's car will be towed back to the police mechanic's yard. His car was not even twelve months old and had minimal mileage; thank goodness it was still in one piece. Obviously, once again we believed it to be the work of the idiot.

It took two hours for the whole procedure, and now we were travelling in a taxi back from Llandudno. It was five o' clock by the time we got home. I phoned my insurance company straight away to have Phil's name put down as a driver on my Jeep. I could not see him without a car and did not want him to pay the expense a hire car would incur. I felt that it was my duty: Phil had become a target now. He could have been killed; we could have all perished. Thank God there were no children involved. I seriously think I am going to have to hire a bodyguard, especially through the week while trotting about from place to place, doing interviews and having meetings. I am sure Daisy would lend me her car 'til I got something in place. Shit! I had forgotten with all the horrors of the day- my son's arrival.

Ben was arriving tomorrow, and I wanted to purchase some gifts for him to take back to university- typical Welsh items like fridge magnets, tea towels, rock, flags- anything that advertises how beautiful this country is. I had to buy him some new clothes as well. It was funny, because he never bought anything that I didn't like. He knew I had a good taste in clothes, I think that's why! I loved the way he dressed; he was a six foot three very good-looking young man.

Ben had not asked for the train fare up front- which was new! He has loved all the videos and pictures I have sent him of my time here, especially when we face-time each other when I am out and about. He was going to love it here. Mountains, views and the sea; he was in his element.

His walking boots will be thrown over his shoulder, one hanging in front, the other resting against his back. I won't do it every time, but his first visit to his Mummies new home has to be remembered. Now it was all put in jeopardy. God, I would give the bastard a fucking lights out before I referred him for assessing, so we can gather the information from professionals as to whether or not he is mentally unstable, then obviously this being so, he could not contain this madness. If it is not, I would be extremely unhappy and very, very angry.

Joseph was to be sending someone to pick up the package and check the security cameras. We do not know who it will be until it has been discussed between the investigators at the station. As we left, my situation was the topic of the meeting they were to start. This was extremely serious for me now, and obviously for anyone who was with me. How awful to be on the other side. A victim. I pray that if someone is to get hurt, just let it be me- I am the target. How dare another human being put the life of another person in their hands and destroy it. I do not want to think like that. I see it every day, what happens in scenarios like this.

There was a message from Rae on my answerphone. She was on her way, and she was coming here by train. It was too late to try and stop her. I did have to turn my phone on silent when she rang the first time because we were busy at the station. I had rung Livvi, Rae, and Sian whilst we were waiting for assistance. I now rang Ben to tell him what had occurred today.

As can be imagined, he was very angry. Having studied in martial arts for many years (full-contact), you would not want to get on the wrong side of my boy. He is an adult, but your last child always stays your baby. I asked if he would prefer to leave coming up for a few days until we knew more, because as it stands, his stay would mean being house bound. To say he was insulted would be an understatement. He got upset, knowing what could have happened without the brakes on the car. "What is he going to try next, Mum? I don't even want to think about it. I will rip his fucking head off if I get hold of him. Me and Phil will go looking for him." He spits out.

"Ben, calm down. I want to enjoy the time you are here even if we cannot go out. I have plenty of board games, and Daisy is here for you to bully." I say, trying to appease him.

He was arriving at two-twenty tomorrow. The station was only five minutes up the country road, but we would go together, Daisy, Rae and me. I had to threaten Livvi with violence if she took leave and came over as well. She was going to spend her four days off here and would arrive the day after Ben left. Nobody needs the sofa, unless I kick Phil out of bed, and I cannot see that happening! I did not need the office bedroom any longer, I did not use it. I will have to get a bed in there as soon as possible; I needed the room for Ben. Rae will have the room I allocated for Ben. There is plenty of room on the big sofas as well, if need be. I would rather a guest have a room, with all their own belongings in it. I am bordering OCD. Obsessive compulsive disorder. Worse since my children flew the nest.

Phil went 'out and about', this was all he was willing to say. I made Daisy and myself (with enough for Rae and Phil when they arrived) a Quorn pasta bake with salad, and Daisy's obligatory buttered bread. This one was walnut- how could I refuse? We were in and out of several different conversations, just trying to keep off the topic of the day. I am lying if I said I was not scared now!

After food, we went up to make what we could out of the fourth bedroom. By the time Ben arrives, our morning shopping would yield a modern boy's bedroom. All the rooms were quite big, but only two had an en-suite- Daisy's room and mine. When friends asked why I was buying such a big house when I was retiring on my own, I would tell them I will need it for my guests. They all hold double beds except for my extra-large big wooden four-poster. I saw it in an antique shop, wanted it, bought it. It cost me a fortune, but I got pleasure from having it, as well as having so much pleasure in it! Phil thinks the same- might as well get my money's worth! Us woman get a bad rep about our sex lives after we have hit our fifties. Not me or Livvi: both of us make the most of the occasions!

In the end, Phil picked Rae up from the station. He had fixed himself up with another vehicle, so I could use my own car for work. He was going to use a work's van. He also had the beginnings of a black eye and the reason he gave for acquiring it was, he did it when he was looking under the car. His body language suggested he was lying.

Now, there was a little tension while we were talking regarding my work. Who was going to accompany me? The list goes as follows: Rae on Monday, Daisy for Tuesday and Ben is pencilled in for Wednesday. I do not have to go into the office in the morning now, so I can work at home. I cannot cancel the interview that I have in the afternoon, not for a second time. I had a new case left on my desk apparently, so Sian was going to drop it off at Manchester police station for me to pick up while I am there. I was anxious, in fact we all were, waiting for the someone to arrive and pick up the package, so we could finally look at the cameras. There was no doubt that the person who cut the brake line would have been captured. There was also no doubt that the individual knew there were cameras, so likely they will be disguised or covered in black from head to toe.

It was eight-thirty, I felt like I had been awake for twenty-four hours. I did not feel tired; in reality I felt the total opposite. Being anxious does that to you. The buzzer went, and we all stood. There were two people that could be seen on camera. We established who they were before Phil let them enter the gate. We had an Inspector Craig Phillips, Sargent Joseph Keil and Constable David Evans, as our guests. The package was placed on the table in front of the three men that were sat on the same sofa. I knew I needed big furniture. (I knew it would come in handy!) There was not a sender's or company address on the item; that in itself was suspicious. I was thankful when the decision was made with regard to the bloody shoe box item. It would go back with them. The constable was here for a reason; he was an expert in CCTV, so knew how to retrieve what they needed, to hopefully get a conviction against the obvious offender.

To say I felt sick is an understatement. A figure in black, even footwear and face, came over my ten foot high fence at the rear of the house clutching a small handbag sized item. The next sighting is of him drawing something on the French windows with his gloved finger. He walked up the side of the house, straight to Phil's car. He did not even look at Daisy's or my own. A tiny ray of light came from under the car where he was committing his wickedness. I have only met him the once, so I could not tell by movement or body language whether it was him or not. The footage was now in the constable's hand. Eight of us got closer to the window, to see a smiley face that the culprit had left. We then went to the drive, to show the guys the area where the brake fluid was camouflaged by the black slate tiles. Alex had made sure that not the slightest of evidence was left. Why bother covering himself when he had almost admitted to the offence when he had phoned me?

It was ten o' clock on a Sunday night, it had been a long day, but I needed to eat again and have some time to relax. I did this by picking items I wanted out of the fridge. Everyone followed suit, from pizzas to beans on toast. Each to their own. I then stuck 'Phantom of the Opera' in the DVD player. I was surprised that they all joined me. I had seen this film with Rae and other friends when it was first released at the cinema. It always blew me away. Got to have a bit of Gerard Butler looking gorgeous (even with his badly burnt face) as the Phantom! My favourite musical. I did not speak a word all the way through, and no one asked or expected me to acknowledge them when they were having some banter between themselves. Not one of us lasted, and we each went up to bed at different times. I joined Phil after I had shut everything down and played with Pud for ten minutes (fetch the ball, made from tin foil). Pud had a thing for the shiny item.

Morning did not see me in the usual jolly mood. My whole life had changed in the matter of a week. I woke with my circumstances bursting at the seams in my 'brain pan'. I had to start work, with the conservatory being my office for today. I hoped this was not going to be the case for long. Phil left for work after a cereal breakfast together. Rea and Daisy appeared within ten minutes of each other, showered and dressed. I got a peck on the head from both of them. Phil was meeting Ben at the station, bless him. I cannot believe how lucky I am, to have friends drop their own lives to come, and probably help save mine. They are a God-send. We talked a little about his appearing at the police station today. I had a feeling he would not turn up. I needed news. I focused so hard on my laptop working, that two hours later saw me finished. I got ready for my appointment, gathered the items I would need, then had a coffee and a sandwich with the girls.

Rea and I left Penmaenmawr at one-thirty. The interview was written in for three-thirty. The employees at the station were aware of my circumstances, and we were greeted at the front desk by Livvi, Brian and the desk sergeant. Rae had not seen Livvi for a couple of months, so whilst I went in to do my job, the two went to a café. Brian, again, was assisting me. "If we crack this one as quick as the last, I think you and I should become partners." Brian sounded quite serious with his words.

"If only it was that easy," I replied.

"Oh, I can see you're going to love this fella, talk about dramatics." Brian sweeps his hand over his hair as he spoke.

"Is he still claiming self-defence?" I ask.

"Oh yes, and I will not reveal anymore; you can enjoy yourself for a change, Laura."

Everything in place, his interview started. I picked up so much about him just by his demeanour, he had yet to speak. I introduced myself, told him what my role was and why I was here. It was so hard not to giggle when I had first set eyes on him, and I still had the urge to give a compulsive giggle. Brian would not know what part of this person I found funny. I had to focus on his face or blow my professionalism, which would make me incompetent. He did not know about my relationship with Tom, not that Tom has one with me! Lewis Manford-Jones (alleged to have killed his partner Luke) was wearing an 'I LOVE YOU THOMAS HARDY' T-shirt. I wanted it! In the two hours it took me to educate myself on this very bad actor, I could have lurched into laughter at many moments. This man would send his own grandmother to jail, rather than admit to what the evidence has made quite clear. No defensive wounds on Lewis; Luke had many. The only injuries that Lewis sustained were the ones he inflicted upon himself. (Nothing that needed hospital attention.) He could not cope with my suggestive questioning. He was contradicting himself, repeating some of the argument at variance and his defence system was barricading his sadness, at what he had lost. This obviously means he was not feeling or showing any remorse. The son of a bitch was a lying, creepy, over-dramatic cry baby. Boy was he going to get it in the nick. Why had he carried on stabbing his husband of six years, whom was fifteen years his senior, after he was dead? That does not cry of 'self-defence'.

The argument had started early in the morning, on the day in question. Lewis was deceitful throughout the whole session. There were no signs of any mental health issues. Just an actor, performing a false and utter piss-take on his imaginary stage. My meeting with him put him directly on the spot. He had no choice but to come clean. I had come pretty near to unfolding the scenario of their day, from the information I had gathered through the two hours I was with him. His face was a picture; he looked like he had been caught on camera.

"Well, another case closed Mr Wagner. Are you available to join us for a coffee?" I had just said when we walked straight into Livvi and Rae. The latter was holding the file that Sian had so kindly delivered. She never fails, that girl. The first thing I told them about was my entrance into the interview room and being confronted by a life-sized face of Tom Hardy with the words 'I love you' and his name written above. They burst out laughing, and now Livvi was telling this handsome man about my obsession. "It's not anything like that, it's admiration; from his looks to his acting and general concern for people. He was a very, very nice man." 'Fit as fuck', I thought in my head.

Rae asked. "Did she wear it well?"

"No he did not", I replied.

We walked to my office; after all I had Rae, Livvi and Brian with me. I was safe. I made lattes to everyone's amusement, and we all sat round the kitchen table. Fucking Jaffa cakes or Jammie Dodgers- selfish sods! We were now joined by Mark, who had only heard bits and pieces of what was going on. He was livid to say the least. Sian was out on a visit, and I was introduced to Eva Mistry, our new secretary. First impressions were good. I gave her details of how to manage the report I had printed out at home this morning. She was actually working off the clock. She should have finished an hour ago. Good, I love a person who has to get the job done before they leave, either work or in the home. I told her to always put her overtime down on her time sheets and thanked her for staying to finish some work from the growing back log.

Brian took a phone call and moved into the corridor. Ten minutes later he walked over to my desk and placed the chair he had picked up next to mine. Oh dear, what now? "That was Joseph Keil I was talking to. He knew you were in my company. The package you received, held a soft toy. It was a replica of your cat and had red paint around what looks like knife marks. He had been stabbing at the toy." Brian expresses with sadness. The wanker had never seen my baby Puddles. How would he know her identity, never mind that she was a full ginger cat with white paws? Who was giving him information? I did not want to hear anymore I did not want to talk about it. Thank God I had decided to keep Pud indoors since these horrors had begun. This man had a fucking death wish most definitely. Rae and Brian moved out of the office, most likely to discuss what I did not want to hear.

An hour later saw us going our own ways, but not before Livvi and Brian had walked us to my car. Brian wanted to be kept informed, and I was dying to get home to find out the result if any, of the idiot's visit to the police station in Llandudno. I was so eager to see my son. I would forget what I had just been told about the package for my own sanity and Ben would be mortified if I told him how serious this situation was. Even though what he did know what was going on, he did not know the extent of my feelings about it. Alex was wanted for questioning, so if he did not turn up, the cops would be doing whatever they could to find him. I do not want to talk to him or see the bastard; I wanted his balls in a mincer. Not literally, obviously. I would not trust myself not to react in a somewhat aggressive manner though- if I was face-to-face with him.

I enjoyed our drive home. A good ninety minutes of Joshua Tree and Bowie's 'Changes'. Singing away like a pair of mentalists! It was so good to have spent some quality time alone with this amazing lady. The circumstances are not great for her, and she felt the hurt that I was going through. Rae had taught me so much, and I loved this woman with all my heart. Some years back, I had taken two years leave from my profession to learn about Rae's. I was intrigued. I became her assistant in a documentary production. I apparently did so well, that there was a job offer towards the end of my twenty-four-month stint. I enjoyed my work with her that much, that I did actually think about a career change. My passion lay in psychology though, and I was sat back in my office chair a week later. Rae was admired for her hands-on work, resulting in gaining quite a name for herself. Rae was my sister and a fantastic auntie to my children who adored her as much as I did.

Joseph followed my car as we entered the drive. We

spent ten minutes talking about my new gates before we walked into my home. In only two months of living here, I had a crime scene across the road, and a real mentalist on my back. Let us hope disaster does not come in threes. Mmm, dinner smelt delicious-good old Daisy! Where was my son?

The conservatory was the room of choice and we gathered here with our brews. Phil arrived before we got down to the nitty gritty, with Ben in tow. How strange that I should burst into tears. I was overwhelmed. This action proved to all, how much my circumstances had broken me. I was surprised myself. I had not cried since disowning my eldest son. Poor Joseph, who should have been on his day off today, had arranged to go into the station to be present at the questioning of the idiot, and was now sat watching me have a meltdown. This situation was inconveniencing too many people and taking away my freedom.

Eventually, we got down to the reason why we were gathered. First of all, the bastard did not keep to his word: he was a no show. Well, that did not shock anyone. Someone was hiding him. I was not happy having Ben in the room, I did not want him under stress. So be it. I was happy to know there was now a warrant out for Alex Dunne, after his car registration was taken by a nosey neighbour of the people in the house of which Alex had trespassed two nights ago, when he turned Phil's car into a death trap. There were only four cottages on the lane behind my house, and Alex had parked in front of the wrong one. A very suspicious home watch volunteer. Thank God for nosey neighbours! I am the total opposite. What goes on on the other side of my gate, does not interest me in the least. A cast was made from the shoe prints that were in my garden, and the neighbours. Alex had a sister living in Shropshire. The police there had interviewed her. She had not seen her wayward brother for six years. Alex, nor his sister's parents lived in Milan. In fact, their family home had been in Shropshire. He was more British than I was.

Alex had not turned up, at what is now known as his rented property. The young lady that lived adjacent to him had not seen his car or lights on in the house for two days and nights. His work- place could not help with any inquiries, as the idiot had phoned in to say he was ill. He was telling the truth there; he was bloody ill. Joseph suggested I keep up with taking someone to work with me every day, until this lunacy was over. I thanked my wonderful neighbour for the extra work he had put in over the last week, and for all of his care. I will buy his favourite alcoholic drink (if he had one) to show my thanks. I felt quite humble with the love and help I was surrounded with through this time.

After the news, I did not know whether I felt better or worse. We spoke a further thirty minutes on the subject, then gathered round the table to eat the amazing food Daisy had prepared. A Monday roast. Being a vegetarian, Daisy had made herself stuffed peppers to go with the roasties and vegetables, whilst we had beef. Chat was pleasant and funny throughout the meal.

Phil took his leave at nine o'clock. He was satisfied that I had enough people around me to feel safe. Ben kept us entertained, not with tales of his life at university, but was more a stand-up comedy routine. We all had our input, and we were in hysterics.

I brought up the time he had shown me up so terribly in our local Asda. Ben was not one for tagging along to do a food shop (or any kind of shopping), if the items to be purchased were not for him. I had met him in town after I had finished work on this particular day, perhaps six years ago. After treating him to some new clothes from his favourite expensive store, he needed some bits from Asda. I needed groceries. Once inside, Ben wandered off with a basket of his own, whilst I pushed my trolley around the food isles. Fifteen minutes into the shop, my youngest child appeared and emptied his goods into the trolley; this I was used to. I was also knowledgeable of the fact, that once Ben had acquired his own items, he did not want to carry on doing a general shop, because he was so impatient. As ever, he kept pulling at my coat sleeve like a child, something he had done since he was one! "Come on Mum!" he called, over and over again. He wanted to get back and play with the PlayStation game, or watch the DVDs he had just chosen for his mummy to buy. He annoyed me so much that I gave up. I made my way to the till, and he twitched until we finally got to pay for our goods.

As we entered the foyer, there was a tombola, raising funds for breast cancer. There were many people around, and I made my way to the queue. "You have got to be kidding me, you're not doing this to me Mum, I need to get home." Ben urges.

"Oi you, ya selfish sod. This is for cancer and I am giving my donation. Stop tugging on my arm, it is bloody aggravating me." I request of him. Then as loud as he could he shouted.

"Who cares what people think, we love each other. We want to be together, fuck anyone else." I wanted the ground to swallow me up. I stood open-mouthed, along with all the folk surrounding us. Ben started laughing as well as walking with his very long fast legs. I looked around at the faces staring at me. "He is my son he thinks he is being funny." I said, and made my way out of the store. "I will fucking kill you for that, you absolute fucking arse hole." I shouted after him. Thankfully, there was not anyone in the vicinity to hear my outburst.

Once in the car, I looked at him and we both burst out laughing. I did give him a slap, and he did acknowledge that he had gone a little too far. I cannot believe he played this prank without thinking it through. That is what I found so funny. Usually he would get me out of a store by acting as if he had Tourette's, insulting shoppers so much that I had to apologise, as well as tell them that he suffered with Tourette's syndrome. What he just did then left me speechless. That put an end to our shopping expeditions together for a long time. It saved me some money!

The girls remembered my telling them after Ben had done this, but found this rendition so funny, we were all convulsed with laughter. I jumped on Ben and we proceeded to play fight then I wrapped my arms around his shoulders, kissing and cuddling him, until he picked me up and placed me next to Rae, still laughing at our antics on the sofa. I cuddled each one of my friends and my son then made my way to bed. I left them all in the living room. I loved having my son with me and never got fed up of his company. Saying that, I did keep out of his way when he was in a blue mood. The nearest person to them always gets the brunt of it.

I was sat up comfortable in bed with my laptop on my knees, making notes on the new case I had received today. Carl Lever was an old client of mine, so I was not shocked when I read the report in front of me. Only this time, I would not be working with Carl; I will be meeting with his alleged killer. I remembered quite distinctively saying at the time of Mr Lever's last incarceration, that he was going to be taken out one day. Well now that day had happened. The accused, Paul Davis was claiming self-defence whilst drunk and 'out of it on drugs'.

Carl Lever was found bludgeoned to death. My job was to gather whether it was self-defence and also determine if Mr Davis would have committed the crime if he was not under the influence of substances. After an hour, I put everything away, ready for my morning trip into the office with Daisy tomorrow. I would be conducting the interview with Paul after lunch. Ben had wanted to come with me every day- this was not fair. He was supposed to be holidaying here. Instead, he was babysitting his mum.

Rae was taking Ben for a walk; one we had done together on a previous visit. Lucky buggers were going to have a ramble up to Snowdonia National Park. The walk started at the bottom of our lane. After breakfasting together, Daisy and I headed towards Manchester. 'Bat out of Hell' had me singing again at the top of my voice. Daisy had her ear phones on listening to her seventies faves. (Certainly not mine!) She gave up in the end, saying I was too loud, and gave her own little input with myself and Meatloaf. The CD was in her glove box, not belonging to her, but one of her sons. It stopped us talking about Alex at least. Every conversation we had always led back to him.

After having a brew together with the few that were in the offices, Daisy took herself off to the Trafford Centre. I got on with reading yet another case I had waiting on my desk. I did not want to take any work home with me tonight, and between Eva and myself, we pretty much covered all that was needed to be done. I think our new secretary was fitting in nicely. Sian was looking after her poorly little boy, something she would not have been able to do if Eva was not as efficient as she turned out to be.

Brian turned up thirty minutes early to pick me up so we could have a little catch up over a coffee that Eva so kindly made us. It was a part of her job to make sure my thirst was always quenched, but we all took turns here. Maybe I, not as often as I should. Why would I if someone else was willing to do the honours? I had to put up with all the lazy comments for payback. Sticks and stones.

Brian and I made our way to the station, which was only a five-minute walk. He wanted to discuss our relationship. I told him, at the moment I had too much going on, that it was the last thing on my mind. He tended to agree. I am not so sure he did. As we got into the station, my personal phone rang. It was Alex. Did he know I was here, like the last call he made to me? I answered and put the call on record, whilst rushing with my bodyguard of the moment to his office. "I am sorry about that Tony; I am in a rush as I am running late." I say, because I had asked him to hold on for a minute, whilst I got to where we were heading to. He asked me to put Brian on the phone, he did not want to speak to me yet. I told him Brian had already left me, and could we not talk like mature adults, until the Sergeant returned. In actual fact, he was stood in front of me with two other officers. They were tracing the call. I needed to keep Alex on the line for as long as I could. I was not going to lose my rag; I would stay in professional mode. Why would he want an audience, especially in a police station when he was threatening me? Putting himself on a plate.

"You are a bitch Laura; how many dicks are you sucking? You're filth." he says quite calmly. I reply in the same manner. "Tony, I am really sorry that you think like that. I also apologise for any wrong-doing to make you feel like this." I wanted to carry on, but stayed quiet whilst he interrupted me with. "Shut the fuck up. I know what you are doing. I am too clever to fall for that. Women like you need to be taught a lesson." he said before I stopped him from saying anything further. "So you think your behaviour is acceptable?" I ask.

"I have not done anything wrong yet, you're still alive aren't you?" he so creepily replies. I butted in again, telling him Brian had just walked into the room and I was handing over my mobile. Brian had given me the nod, and it seems they had him. The two officers made a prompt exit. "Mr Dunne. How can I help you?" he asks.

"You know what she is, don't you?" says Alex.

"I am afraid I do not know to what you are referring, why don't you tell me?" No answer. The phone went dead. And I fell apart.

Alex had left the scene before he could be caught. That is probably why he cut the call. We all know how the cops can monitor calls if you keep the culprit on the line for a decent length of time. It was now time to track him by GPS. He had gone way too far now. Two different localities of the police force had his card marked. Manchester along with North Wales. Brian understood why I was so upset. It was not the actual threat of me still being alive, as he put it. This proved my death was his aim. It was the waiting, the watching every move. Putting people out. Upsetting my son and my friends.

CHAPTER EIGHTEEN

To say the interview with Paul Davis took my mind off my situation with Alex was an understatement. The guy was diagnosed as having PTSD. Post-Traumatic Stress Disorder, diagnosed six years ago, after a stint in a mental health facility. Thirty-eight-year-old Paul claims self-defence, due to Carl's retaliation when he found his stash tin empty. (A user's 'stash' is any object used to hold their gear.) Mr Davis stole some crack from the deceased. Whilst under the influence of this drug, Carl returned to find his stolen property had already been used by his so-called friend. Paul's declaration states he was attacked by the victim after a verbal exchange. He did have wounds to prove this. There were several places where stitches were still obvious: two severe lacerations, caused by a frying pan of all things. An array of bruising and lumps were also evident. These were wounds of self-defence.

When you are a sufferer of PTSD, and you face a situation like Paul had, you see red. His brain went into alert mode and he would fight for his life, whether warranted or not. There is no real cure. It is a mental health disability that can be worked on in time. Counselling and therapy is always encouraged. Paul had been struggling with his diagnosis since serving six years on the front line in Afghanistan. He answered all my questions without any upset and I understood his actions, due to his drug addiction. I say I understood. That does not mean I agree with what he did. How many times had I come across this type of scenario over the years? He was respectful and articulate. He gave a truthful view of the day in question.

Brian wanted some other answers from Paul. I cringed, knowing the interviewee was not going to like the manner in which he was being spoken to. All hell broke loose. I pressed the alarm button that was in my reach. When a person sees red, their anger becomes more intense. I stayed silent and in my seat. To me, this was a normal reaction under the circumstances. I had seen it many times. Sufferers of PTSD are as vulnerable as any other person who endures any kind of mental health obstacle. I watched as the accused man threw both Brian and police officer Mike Chapman from wall to wall. Paul had the backbone of a horse. I could not tell who had the injuries that caused splatters of blood on the wall. It seemed like an age before help for the officers arrived. I took my leave when the interview room door opened. I was of no use.

I was sat with my laptop making notes in the station's kitchen when Brian walked in. I regarded this incident as an incitement by this 'law man'. He certainly did not have a good bedside manner. I will most definitely put this in my review. Brian had quite a bad cut under his eye and his nose was gashed- so obviously broken. I felt no sympathy for him. If he had followed my lead with his questioning of Paul, this would not have happened. I just thought of him as a prick now. It is a shame that the criminal justice system does not make sure that all officers are given training in regards to working with vulnerable people.

I demanded to see Mr Anderton again after he had calmed down. Without doubt I knew he would want to speak to me. This man was also a victim. The worst part being, that someone had lost their life. The victim in this case died as a result from hitting his head on a cabinet after Paul had pushed him away. I believe the incident to have been committed in self-defence. Purely an accident. Carl Levers' injuries did not suggest that Paul Anderton had intended to cause his friend's death. He showed remorse. Not only was Paul incarcerated, he was racked with stomach cramps from withdrawals from his crack and alcohol addiction, adding to the violence he showed in that room. Fortunately, I had some time before Daisy picked me up to make sure Paul was provided with care and medication.

Brian did not agree with my assessment of the occurrence. I didn't think he would. After he made sure I was okay, he left for the hospital along with Mike Chapman. He would not be as pleasant with me after he read my report.

Once again, I was seated in the interview room with Mr Anderton, now in handcuffs and leg restraints. He apologised to me instantly. I had to speak to him now regarding the earlier incident. He acknowledged that I was there to make sure the right treatment was handed out to him. He was very respectful towards me. Usually, in cases like this, the prisoner was happy to have someone to talk to that did not judge him. I disclosed my intentions. He accepted the terms, then spoke to me of his relationship with Carl. This man was once a soldier that witnessed the most horrific episodes imaginable-such a shame that there was no help for these brave human beings, once they have come home from their term in the armed forces. Paul was such an interesting and educated man, who knew his actions were wrong. His substance misuse issue was an escape from reality. I understood. Many ex-service men suffered in this way.

I was all done by the time Daisy came to pick me up. Her car was loaded with items from her shopping spree and she was in great spirits. I could not wait to get back home and see what she had bought for me! It took the whole journey home to tell her about the events of the day. She was horrified and came out with more expletives than I care to remember! God help the idiot if she got hold of him. Brian got a few unpleasant names also. Daisy did not take to him at all. She had his card marked and I tended to agree with her.

As we approached my lane, a car came at us at speed. My good friend did not have any warning of what was next to happen. Even if she had applied the brakes the inevitable would still happen. "Fucking hell" we screamed together. I lost consciousness.

The next thing I knew, a group of people (some I recognised) were standing around the car. Daisy (thank God) was one of them, although creased up in agony. Ben was devastated and I wanted to put him at ease, even though I was feeling severe pain coming from my chest. I tried to speak to him, which made the agony worse. Fire fighters were in attendance using machinery to take off the door of the car, this one most likely a write off due to the same culprit that had caused the damage to Phil's. He was here, and bless him, he put his arm around my son and led him away from my eye line. A paramedic was trying to alleviate some of my pain with an injection of what was most likely to be morphine. They had managed to get Daisy out of the car, and I could just about see her being led away. Her cries of pain will stay forever embedded in my heart. All I could think was that this was my doing.

The crash had caused the seat belt to injure some of my ribs; I had broken some years ago in my boxing days. I did have sparring partners and wanted to be totally part of the sport, but I did not compete in fights outside of our gym. I also had swelling and severe bruising to my legs. The paramedic was sure I had not broken any bones in them. Daisy was suffering with a dislocated shoulder and was in terrific pain. Within fifteen minutes, we were both travelling to hospital in the same ambulance. She had insisted on waiting and taking the seat whilst I lay on the bed. The car that had hit us intently was still in situ. Many police in uniform were at the scene I noticed as I was being strapped, ever so carefully onto the bed. I heard a male voice I knew to be Joseph asking for a path to be cleared as the Crime Scene Investigators were here. After the second shot of morphine, my lights went out again.

We were both now patients on the same ward but in separate rooms. Daisy's shoulder was broken as well as being dislocated; now being put back in place. I had three broken ribs as well as some internal bleeding and bruising. My legs were swollen and bruised also. We were both a little dopey on morphine, so neither of us could leave our beds to visit the other- not that we could have anyway with what we had suffered. I needed therapy after this. Fucking scream therapy.

When a nurse came in after I had awoken, she informed me that Daisy had gone into theatre to have her shoulder operated on. The tears so easily spilled from my face without an utterance of a cry. I could not move or speak; it just made the pain more unbearable. I did not want to take advantage of the little button I had been given to release the pain killer, as I wanted to remain focused. I was shocked when I was told that it was one o'clock in the morning. Daisy's break must have been severe if she was being operated on at this time.

Was Alex hurt in his murder attempt of two people? I would fucking hope so- and badly. In fact, I could not care less if he had killed himself. If his attempts of taking a life was just against me, I would not feel the absolute loathing I did. He was trying to kill the people close to me as well. This broke my heart. He knew we would be returning home around this time and must have sat there with his engine on waiting for us to turn into the lane. Was he in this hospital? Was this the end? After I drank a cup of tea, I went out like a light again. I had intended to wait for Daisy to return from theatre, but with the events of the day, the crash, my injuries and the morphine, my body had no other option but to shut down.

I had woken several times during the night. Pain being one of the main reasons, nightmares was another. When I pressed the buzzer for the nurse under the pretence of needing some water, a male nurse appeared. I really wanted to know how Daisy was doing. I was relieved to hear that she was back from theatre, and the operation went well. He left me to sleep after I had questioned him, as to whether he knew anything of today's incident. I needed to know if Alex was in custody or the hospital- which was a frightening thought. Unless some mistake had occurred then the latter would not be a possible option.

I woke to see daylight but could not even move to alter my body's position so I could see the time. Silly as it seems, I was mortified at the fact that I could not and would not for some time be able to return to work. I was in the foulest mood. The thoughts running through my mind were giving me a headache. I needed to see Daisy to comfort her and apologise to her. Saying sorry to one of the friends I loved was not enough. I was getting panicky with all the scenarios eating at my brain. I pressed the buzzer for the nurse and the one for the morphine. I felt like I was going mad.

The nurse from last evening came with a cup of tea and sat with me whilst I asked her all the questions that were eating at me. Daisy was fine and recovering well. Two officers had arrived not long after we were admitted, and Becky (a lovely, helpful nurse) recalled an officer on his walkie talkie, saying that the culprit had left the scene on foot. Every swear word that was so ridiculously invented, went through my mind. I told Becky she was fortunate to not know what I was thinking. If that fucker does not get me first, I will kill the bastard myself.

She informed me of the many phone calls from friends and relatives enquiring about Daisy and me. God, I had not even thought about Daisy's boys. I knew Rae would make sure that everyone was looked after and sleeping space was made available. She was a nurturer and carer like me. We all had a similar ethos. I needed to see my boy and I am sure he would feel the same.

I let the tears flow, remembering the man I loved, admired and respected more than I could say. I missed my Daddy so much; he was all I had in my life that loved me for me. Out of the three children he had, he always said I was the only one that loved him. We were the best of friends and I could talk to him about anything. We could not have been closer. He was a big softy, with the strength of ten men and a caring side that was so seldom seen in a man. He had a list of friends that would run the length of a football field. Time does not heal, and there is never a day that my heart does not ache when I realise, he is not with us anymore. He was more a father to my children that I raised as a single mother. I do not know how I would have managed without him.

My eldest brother had died from alcohol misuse five years ago. Having his problem from such a young age, he was rotten through and through. From violence, to having a filthy mouth and being a thief. Yet, he was loved by the mother we shared, but only for some years before his death. I would say that half his problems stemmed from the neglect he received from her as a child. The woman being narcissistic, only gave her heart to the one child, probably the least one to deserve it. Money-obsessed, with an evil eye and lack of empathy for others-again attributed to her upbringing. She was extremely protected, not giving her the value of any family love or loyalty. I wouldn't mind but when away from her mother, she hated her. It was all to do with her mother's will. My brother did not deserve the life he had or hadn't had. He did not know any other.

Christ, how were Daisy and I to stay sane 'til our stay here was to come to an end? I had noticed a police presence and I wondered if it was in aid of our safety. This I would expect under the current circumstances. From the angle I was positioned, I could see anyone who passed my room. I was exhausted from thoughts and anticipation. I wanted questions answered, I needed my lifeline and hoped that my first visitor would bring it-my phone.

As it was still early morning and breakfast had yet to be served, I did not expect two police officers to arrive to take my statement. Daisy's room was their first port of call. My dear friend was still comatose after her night surgery. The thought broke my heart. I sobbed before I could manage to speak. As long as I kept my breathing balanced, the pain was not as bad.

Introductions over, I preferred that we acknowledge

each other on a first name basis. I started the questioning off, as my life still maybe at stake and the same with everyone around me. He should be tried for attempted mass murder. "Please tell me you have caught him?" I asked. "Unfortunately, and I am extremely sorry to say, we haven't love." Oh God, I hated being called love. Why at a time like this would something so fucking trivial even present itself in my thoughts? A twat of a man is on the loose and I am affected by how I was addressed by this policeman, who was here for my welfare. I am cracking up. "Do you know if he was injured in the planned collision? I am sure you realise that it was planned?" I could only say slowly and quietly. I needed to press my meds button, but I did not want to fall asleep at this significant time. "Yeah, there was blood found in several places of the vehicle. Not seriously injured obviously, otherwise he wouldn't have 'done one'. Let's get what you can remember in ink down first, then I will do my utmost to try and answer your queries." Adrian suggested. I just wanted to get this over with. I needed something to eat, a brew, to find out from the nurse how Daisy was, then sleep. I was overcome with fatigue.

I could not give any details, other than turning into the lane and instantly hearing then noticing the oncoming car. I could not even say what type of vehicle it was, or colour other than, it was 'dark'. Daisy was now awake and having a cup of coffee. My new nurse, my namesake, Laura said there would be no reason why my friend could not come and sit with me later on this afternoon, depending on how she felt.

I woke to find a doctor and two nurses having arrived at my bed side. I told them how I was feeling and Doctor Munroe went through my x-rays. I was to go for a scan to see the extent of the internal bleeding that was probably caused by one of my broken ribs perforating something or other. I could not concentrate, not able to keep focused on what was being said. My mind was in turmoil. All I needed to know was when I could go home, and depending on how I was faring, and how long it would be before I could return to work. I think he said a few days regarding going home, the rest of the conversation evaporated into thin air. I told the doctor of my difficulties. A script was sent to the pharmacy for benzodiazepines. An hour later, I was given ten milligrams of diazepam, along with another shot of morphine. I did not have my little drug button now. If the pain got too bad, then I was able to receive the morphine through my cannula. When the evening meds were handed out, I was to have a higher dosage of diazepam.

When I got back to my room after my scan, I had a welcoming party. Obviously Daisy was the first I was ecstatic to see. Rae, Phil, Livvi and Ben stood to attention as I approached them on my stretcher. No one could cuddle me, and I would have preferred not to have them in the room whilst I was so painfully put back into my bed. I was overcome again. It must have been catching, as Daisy, Rae and Ben cried also. I think it was partly relief and partly worry about what was going to happen next. I got kisses and well wishes from all, after I was made comfortable by the nurses. As flowers were not allowed in the hospital, many items of edible objects were placed on the bottom of my bed. This did bring the first smile of the day. I loved fruit, along with plenty of chocolates and sweets. All my favourites. No one spoke of the bastard or the incident-something that must have been discussed before they arrived. Livvi was pacing, agitated. Being a police sergeant, she would be in that mode. She was going to stay for a few days and make sure everything was being done, to catch Alex Dunne. She did not have to say anything; I knew this would be her aim.

Thirty minutes later Daisy and I were left in my room. We held hands and talked between us, about our horrendous ordeal. I was the first to see Daisy's two sons and daughter-in-law coming through the door. I welcomed them, then told Daisy to return to her room, so they could have some quality time together. I noticed that her husband John was not with them- but that's another story. I was glad of the reprieve. I was shaking with anxiety, my mind-set all over the place. I rang the buzzer for the nurse. I was offered food as I had missed the lunch time break, whilst waiting for my scan at the other end of the hospital. The thought of food made me feel nauseous. I declined and asked for as much medication as I knew I was allowed. As part of my work, I have prescribed such meds many times. I was not fond of taking sedatives, being the hyperactive freak magnet that I was.

CHAPTER NINETEEN

For the first time in my life I knew what it was like to need to have something I could depend on, to help me escape my world. I needed to sleep through the time I was here. I would not come out of this the same person. I did not care whether Alex had some form of mental health dilemma; I wanted his fucking head on a plate (just like the request of Salome for the head of John the Baptist). The bible states she got her wish; I hoped I got mine. My mind was failing now with the workings of my medication. 'Private investigator' were the last words I remembered before the blackness overcame me.

I woke and it was already dark. I was somewhat confused. I did not know what time or even which day it was. I focused and saw Tom Hardy was sat at the foot of my bed. I felt like it was the most natural moment to have my favourite celebrity right there in front of me. The most beautiful man I had ever seen. "Hello Laura." he says like I am familiar to him. "Hello Tom." I say weakly.

"I am not too worried about you Laura as long as you keep composed. You are one of the strongest women I know, physically and mentally. Do not let this man break you. When the time comes, you will take this bastard out, and I can assure you the time will come. You have to stay strong Laura. To overcome this you must fight. Do not wither in fear. Remember these words. I will be there with you. Laura, you will push on; go fourth and conquer. Think: 'WHAT WOULD TOM HARDY DO?' Now it is time to eat something to keep up your strength." Sleep took over again.

This time when I woke, it was twilight. Sadly, there was no sign of Tom, but his words were embedded in my brain. Fucking hell- I was hallucinating, audibly and visually. If any good came out of all this shit, it would be sincere empathy for those suffering escapisms. I was experiencing many consequences of my torturer's actions. I could hear a television in the distance. I probably would not have noticed if I had not heard the bothersome vagina's annoying tones. I would give my spleen to get her to shut the fuck up. I do not know how much longer I could stay here. If I was not discharged in the next couple of days, then I will sign myself out. I had enough friends at home to help me if needed. I was turning into a monster. I need food and drugs.

I had alerted the nurse to my requirements using my buzzer. It made me feel like I was an annoyance and would only press that button with necessity. I could imagine the raised eyebrows every time that buzzing sound was heard. I had missed dinner but I had a sandwich saved for me. (You can never go wrong with cheese.) Half-way through the last of my butty, Daisy's voice hit my ears before she turned into my room. She had asked the nurse if it was okay to visit me. I heard the reply and she entered with much amusement on her face.

"Hello you, what's so funny?" I asked.

"You. I came in earlier with Phil and Ben whilst you were sleeping. The bedclothes were lifting because you were farting like a trooper and talking in your sleep. It's a good job Phil knows about your compulsion, otherwise he might have thought you were seeing another man called Tom!" she takes pleasure in telling me. "Ooops, really?" I say with no real embarrassment. Farting and talking in my sleep was the least of my worries. I was pleased that I had amused my great friend. I was not going to repeat my hallucination to Daisy- I would never live it down! She enlightened me in that she was to be taking her leave tomorrow. "Bitch. I will see what the doctor says tomorrow and if I do not need anything but general care, I am coming with you. I cannot really move much, so I cannot really move much at home. For fucks sake Daisy, do not say a word against it. I want to spend some time with my son, also Rae and Livvi- if she is still here." I say adamantly. I am a stubborn cow and my language was uncalled for, but I had made my mind up.

Daisy turned on the TV to my annoyance. She flicked through the channels 'til she stopped at Crime Watch. Well this got my attention. They were doing a piece on the 'Vigilante Murders'. The major crime unit were now involved and a spokesperson for them was pleading with the public for information. Daisy and I watched in silence. This individual may have or had a background in something pertaining to law, purely due to the lack of evidence. (We took a quick glance at each other) Was there anybody who recognised a person they knew, who was behaving in a different manner to the norm? He finished his piece with 'The criminal's motive remains a matter of conjecture'.

The viewers were not given the identities or the history of the victims. It would have been more appropriate to say. This person was ridding the world of some of the scum that walked it. Surely a serial killer would leave some existence of his being, especially after four executions. Who could say, there may be more? To commit these atrocities as they were, may suggest he has been involved in the acts of murder before the vigilante slaughters started. A serial killer usually escalates with regards to injuries, until he is fulfilled with his final acts. It is not usual to start his spree with such severe mutilations. All the publicity surrounding these cases were not intending to build up a hero figure of the killer, but that is exactly what was happening. This was usually the case in vigilante killings.

We both talked a further ten minutes on the subject before I said "I hope to God Alex is not the culprit. If he was finally going to get his way, I do not want to suffer those types of injuries. A gunshot to the head would be more preferable." Daisy recoiled in horror at my statement.

"Do not ever say anything like that in my presence again. You are a fucking idiot Laura! You're here, you're alive and that is how you're going to stay. I am disappointed in you for even thinking that." she says without slapping me as she usually would for such a stupid utterance.

"Well they certainly have not caught him, not with the presence of the police officer still sat in the corridor." I reply, seeing the anger imprinted on her face. "Are you an imposter posing as my best friend? Laura, since when did you give up so easily. You're the strongest person I know and once you are on the mend, the fight in you will return." Daisy saying this made me think of the words I had heard so recently from Tom- my beautiful hallucination. I just knew the residue of what has occurred in the last several weeks will never go away.

Daisy started going through the channels again and stopped at 'E.R'. The worst of it was, it had just started.

"For God's sake Daisy, please no. We have got our own ER here- is that not enough for you?" I am cringing as I speak to her. "Sorry, I am watching it. Do you want to try and stop me?" She looks straight into my eyes at a very close stance as she said it. "You're a fucking coward, hitting me when I am down." I could not even lift my arm to hit her or move my head enough to head butt her! She had always had a thing for George Clooney. He (nor the series) did anything for me. I would let her off this time, only because it was my fault she was in here. I was so sorry that my great friend had to go through what she had because of Alex, but selfishness made me happy that she was here to take away the pain of it in my head. My thought process at the moment was no longer rational. We ate chocolates and Pringles as we watched.

Thursday came and went. Daisy had gone with it. I was in less pain and now on a lesser strength medication. I ate well and my demeanour was improving. I had many visitors who cheered me up no end. Joseph had called in and told me that the assumption at the station was that Alex's injuries from the crash were keeping him in hiding.

Friday (like for many people) was my favourite day of the week-even when I worked weekends. This Friday was especially good as Doctor Munroe had told me I could go home. After speaking to everyone at home, it was decided that Phil and Ben would come to pick me up. Rae was playing nurse to Daisy and getting ready for her next patient to return. Honestly, what would I do without these amazing people in my life? Ben was supposed to be returning to university today but he had now changed that to Sunday.

Hooray! I was home. My bloody ribs were killing me. The journey home did not help, and I felt every little bump on the road. I had my first beautiful latte that I had missed. The brews in the hospital were bleeding awful although the food was okay. I sat among my loved ones to open my get well cards. The first was from Sian which made me laugh. I had the nick name Gordon Ramsey for some years in the office, due to my naughty language and flaming nature. She had designed the card herself-wishing me a 'speedy fucking recovery'! In the pile of fifteen cards, there was a card from Alex. He did not sign his name but it did not take Sherlock Holmes to work out it was from the bastard. He was obviously well enough to go out and purchase a card. Rae rang the cops and within the hour I had two police officers at the gate, one of them being the lovely Sarah Parish.

The officers took the card with them after they had sat and had a brew with us. Written in it 'if I have better luck next time, I will be sending a sympathy card'. Fucking Wanker.

It is amazing how when you are not able to do something that you end up more eager to do it. I still had notes and a report to write up. That was simple, I could do this at home, but I had appointments booked in that either Mark would take on or I would have to have them sent out for someone else to do. This really pissed me off.

Ben stayed top-to-toe on the sofa with me throughout the rest of the day. My so-called friends were in comedy mode without being able to help themselves. I did not want to retire to my room until Phil came back from his visit to his brothers. He could help me with my attire. It was so painful trying not to laugh at some of the scenarios my visitors were telling us about what their children got up to as kids.

I remembered an incident Ben had forgotten, and we both now realised how horrible on that particular night he was to poor Saul. We were having a visit from a lady named Margaret Wilson who was to be Ben's first teacher in the reception class he was going to be attending after the summer holidays. Saul had been enrolled in this school now for four years and was extremely happy there, so it was an obvious choice for his little brother to follow. It was an introduction that saw all new young ones visited by their teacher to be.

She arrived and brought some pictures to show what this year's children had done to let Ben know how good it was in reception class. As it was a hot sunny day, it was hard to keep Ben in the house when she arrived. She wanted to get to know him a little. We gave in and were having a little chat when Ben came in crying- not an unusual event. (He was a little mardy arse at times!) Apparently Saul had thrown some crab apples at him and one had hit him on the head. Obviously, I did not admonish Saul as Ben would have liked, only because the small item would not have caused the damage that Ben was professing. He then went back out to play with his brother and the local children.

Ben returned minutes later and told Miss Wilson that he had a present for her. Margaret held out her hand to receive this gift and he placed a big orange slug and a scrunched-up mess of woodlice on it. She screamed and dropped the offending items on my living room floor. I picked up the mess with a wad of kitchen towel without pewking. Slugs were my most-hated thing on the planet (along with worms). I am sure Miss Wilson would remember her introduction to my son forever!

The day carried on as normal and eventually I made my way to bed to find that Ben was fast asleep in it. He often did this, and I hoped that when he went to school, tiredness would put an end to him making his way into my own private pit. We were woken at one-thirty in the morning by a screaming Saul running into my room. It took some seconds to realise what he was saying and what had happened, then

I noticed in the moonlight, a lump of orange surrounded by shiny lines, up his arms and around his face. I screeched in horror and pushed Saul towards the bathroom. I was unable to help, I was retching. I was horrified that my son had a big slug and trail marks all over him. Ben was giggling behind his hands. The slug went down the loo and Saul took a shower. I felt so awful for my child and was as sickened as he was. When I eventually went back into my room, my youngest son admitted to me that he had put the slug under Saul's pillow in revenge for the crab apple attack. I think Saul and I would rather be hit with a cricket bat than come anywhere near a slug! Ben was grounded that day and spent it in tears.

Ben was slated by my two friends that thought the incident horrendous- but it did not stop them from laughing. I could not laugh with them. The memory still made me feel nauseous. My youngest son also had a thing about tying sleeves and legs of clothing into knots, making it a hopeless attempt when trying to dress in these garments. Not only were they tied so tight that the item took a while to untie, they were unwearable with the deep creases that were in them. It did not matter how I punished my child; his fetish went on for months. After he had finished with tying up the clothes, his next annoying naughtiness was putting greasy substances on all the door handles, from hair gel to toothpaste. I thought of him as a nutcase whom did not take threats of punishment from Saul or me seriously. Again this went on for some time until Saul reaped his revenge by breaking the arms off several of Ben's beloved Marvel figures. Saul was grounded for a lovely day over the weekend and I had to buy new figures, even though I thought Ben got his just deserts. I was not too pleased that it was me who suffered by having to spend hard-earned money replacing the toys I'd initially bought anyway. Sometime later in the year, whilst tidying Ben's room, I found that he himself had taken arms and legs off his figures and was taping them onto the wrong bodies. It was not until he was older that I bought him anymore. Now at the age of twenty-four, he still loved his Marvel figures. Each to their own!

Phil arrived at eight o'clock in the evening and was talked into watching 'Taboo' by Ben, who had heard good reviews, although my review didn't seem to matter. I could see his point. The two of them (along with me) got comfortable in my room and watched three episodes. The image of Tom sat at the end of my hospital bed was still vivid in my mind. I would never tell anyone of his visitation, everyone thought I was potty already.

Daisy and Rae went to an Indian restaurant for their late dinner and brought a take-out back for us. We ate on trays whilst still watching the DVD. Ben did not disappoint, there were curry stains and rice everywhere!

I spent an extremely painful night, even with the strong pain killers and the ten milligrams of diazepam (a supposedly tranquillizing muscle relaxant drug, chiefly used to relieve anxiety). It was the anxiety that was not helping with my torture. I was so tense. Ben was going back to his apartment early tomorrow as he had some work to catch up on before he went back to university on Monday. To say I felt bad regarding this was an understatement. I told him I would send an email to the university's head office with an explanation for not being able to do his homework, but he assured me he would be able to get it done when he got back. As Ben wanted to finish watching 'Taboo', he and Phil took over the living room and spent the whole of Saturday watching the last five hours.

Rae, Daisy and I spent a lovely day doing nothing but

chilling and gabbing. The two of them kept us all fed and I thanked God for their love and kindness. The evening saw all of us playing scrabble. It was two hours of pure laughter. If it had been filmed, I am sure it would make high ratings in comedy TV. I was in agony, but the tension and anxiousness had been replaced with pleasure and laughter.

I cried when Ben left for the station in Phil's car. He held his tears back, but his voice was shaky and he told me he was scared for me. We all tried our hardest to alleviate his fears and once he had left my tears flowed. Phil was staying at home tonight, knowing I was safe in the ward of Rae, Livvi and Daisy. Livvi arrived for her week's stay in the early evening. The four of us were a force to be dealt with when we were together. The four musketeers. Sisters in arms. We had planning to do for the coming months regarding my safety amongst some other business. We knew Alex was still at large. The three of them made a lovely Sunday roast whilst I had a sleep.

Daisy helped me get ready this morning for the appointment Rae was taking me to, for more x-rays and a check-up. We were having a police officer in a squad car to accompany us. The pain I suffered when breathing had now eased, but movement was still torture. I was not looking forward to the journey in the car after my last experience.

I do not know if Rae was a better driver than Phil, or if my jeep (that she was now insured on) was a much more comfortable drive. Fifteen minutes later, we arrived at our destination. The copper had gone on a little further to park and due to the bad swelling and bruising on my legs; Rae went into the hospital foyer to get a wheelchair for me.

Within seconds, Alex jumped into the car. Rae had left the keys in the ignition, as she had to move into the parking space once I was in the chair. My heart stopped and the pain seared through me. He took off at speed and after a short distance away from the hospital when he realised the cop car was not behind us, he slowed to the normal speed limit, not wanting to cause any attention from other road users. Not much was said until ten minutes later he stopped the car on a side road, came around to my side and pulled me out roughly. For the third time in a week, my lights went out and my world went black.

When I came to, I was lying in the back seat of a car, my hands and legs trapped, with layers of gaffer tape around them. I could taste blood, so was obviously injured in the transfer of vehicles. We were stationary, and Alex was sat in the driver's seat. I did not want to alert him to my consciousness and needed some time to think. I could not go into 'professional mode', as I knew this would anger him. The harder I tried to concentrate on how I was going to handle this, thoughts of Ben kept entering my mind. Fucking hell! In what way would this psychotic person kill me? I could not fight; he had already broken my ribs on his last attempt of taking me out. For fucks sake, all these years of working with some of the most dangerous people on this earth and I get myself in a position like this, just because I let this twat help pack my shopping bags.

I still did not have a clue as to how I was going to verbally try and defend myself. I was positive Alex would not show any sympathy. I felt a dig in my ribs and could not help crying out. It certainly was not a voluntary cry. "Fucking bitch, wake up. "he says. I could only move my head.

"I cannot move Alex, the pain I am in will not let me." I can only just say.

"I did not tell you to move, you fucking bitch. I have got a lot to say to you and when I have finished, I will listen to you beg for your life, you stupid fucking slag." He spits at me, then starts up the car. From the position I was in, all I could see were trees. In fact, during the whole time he was driving, that was all I could see. I heard two or three vehicles on my voyage to death and noticed we did not stop at any lights. We were almost definitely in a rural area.

This guy was not stupid, he had to know, by doing this he was going to end his own life as well. In an un-identical way of course. I felt something in my mouth and tried to get rid of it with my tongue when I realised, I had a gap in my teeth. The unwanted object was a tooth. I thought I had passed out with pain and maybe took a knock to my mouth, hence the blood. The bastard must have punched me, as now I was more aware of swelling and soreness to my cheek and jaw. I could not say how many times the words, 'for fucks sake, make this quick' went through my mind. He poked me with a hard object. "Are you still awake, bitch?" he shouted at me.

"I am." Was all I could answer. I had no fight in me. How did a man who was so angry and aggressive get to this age without killing someone before? Did something happen to him recently to turn him into this monster? I was not given any details of his past, or whether he had a police record other than what Joseph had told me. Breaking confidentiality is not the 'done thing', but I knew he did have a domestic violence record.

My phone was in the glove compartment of my Jeep, it would be picked up by GPS. At least the police would get that far. For all I knew we could be in another country. How long had I been unconscious? It was raining now and the window screen wipers were making an awful screeching sound. Not that this would bother me being in this predicament. Alex was screaming with such aggression at the wipers, that in itself was very scary.

Well here we were. We had come to a standstill and the bastard was rummaging around in the front of the car. He was looking for some keys. I was obviously going to be taken into a house. He eventually located the keys and left the car with the words. "I will be back for you bitch." I had given him the name 'BASTARD'. It was unquestionable that he had named me 'BITCH'. There was nothing in the back of the car that I could take and use to help me in this situation. Then I remembered that I was filing my nails on the journey to the hospital and I put the metal file in the back of my jeans pocket. Please do not let him search me or notice it! Surely he would release my hands before he killed me. Oh God, I do not want to be raped.

He was back and again pulled me roughly from the car. The areas where I had pain seemed to have given up the fight and they became bearable. I assumed the damage had worsened and had affected my nervous system. My fear was now turning to anger and loathing. If I got a chance to defend myself with the pain now staying at bay, my God I will either go out causing him some severe bodily damage, or I would kill him myself and recover. Hopefully without needing psychiatric help. The physical scars will always heal.

I was literally dragged into a quaint little cottage. Was this place to be my coffin? Not if I could fucking help it! There were not any other residences as far as I could see, just open fields with some fences and trees. I lost my footing twice and fell to the floor. Although I had tape around my legs, there was still a foot of space between them. It was apparent the bastard had thought about this when he had applied the restraint. I was five foot ten inches and weighed eleven stone, not so easy for him to carry. In actuality, I was possibly a stone heavier than he was and it was doubtless I was carrying more weight, as in size. I received a punch to the back of the head which sent me forward and into the wooden chair arm where I was to be stationed.

I had not realised how filthy I was from my falls and being dragged along the ground. It had rained quite heavily, turning the soil to mud. If the police had got to my jeep instantly before the cloudburst, they should surely have enough evidence by tracing the tyre treads, left due to the light rain we had witnessed over the last two days. All these thoughts were going on whilst Alex had left the room. Within ten minutes he returned with two mugs and a sandwich for himself. My drink was left where it sat. I do not know what he expected I could do with it. "I'm not giving you anything to eat, coz when you die, your body empties and I don't want to clean up any of your shit. You made me fucking hate you Laura. Why did you do it? I would have treated you like a princess. I helped you, didn't I? Why did you do it? Why did you fucking do it?" He was screaming now. A punch to the face. How did he expect me to answer when he had punched me in the face yet again? This time there was a crunch. He had broken my jaw. Another punch. I would not be able to answer him at all now.

He took so much pleasure in hurting me. The metallic taste from the old and new blood made me vomit all over myself. The bastard's reaction was another punch to the head. The blood was running freely, I was watching it seep through my clothes. Thank God that last hit was not to my face as I do not think it could handle any more hits. He knew I could not move or talk, so he left me for what I think was a nap. If I could speak, I would have told him exactly what I thought of him and describe what I would do to him if I was capable. The severity of my injuries and the pain the punching caused must be akin to being murdered so I had nothing to lose.

I woke to a darkened room. A small lamp (allowing enough light to see) had been turned on. He was about. Bloody hell, that means he had allowed me to sleep and not hurt me any further. Tears ran down my face at the thought of not seeing my beautiful son again. It hit me, that I did not feel the same about my eldest son. God forgive me, I did not. Why he did what he had done to make me feel so ashamedly nothing for him anymore, I do not know. My face, especially the lower part of it, was so badly swollen, there was no movement in it at all. I could only see through one eye which meant the other was swollen shut. I felt no pain there, so again I had severe nerve damage.

Alex appeared. He helped me up this time without being rough. I put my weight on him. I wanted him to think my body was in worse shape than it was, just in case I did get a chance to defend myself, even if it was just to hurt him. He took me through a doorway that led into a kitchen diner. The table that stood in the middle of the room was set for two people. Candles burning, and napkins in place. My last supper I suppose and would have said if I could. He did not react to my shrieking in torture. I cried out as he sat me down. "It's okay my darling, you will feel better when you have had something to eat." Alex said so lovingly. He was off his fucking rocker. Eat, how the fuck was I supposed to eat? I would not even be able to drink through a straw. My face was dead. Some framed photographs on the wall stood out. They were of me. He had been taking pictures whilst he had been following me in the past weeks. Could this get any more deplorable? This was all vey scary, what you expect to see in a horror film. He wasn't really this insane, was he?

Alex started to cut through the tape that bound my hands. "See Laura, I am a gentleman. I told you I would treat you like a queen. I want to show you what you have missed because of your actions. We will not argue tonight; it is going to be special. We have soup first, your favourite. I do hope you like my cooking." I thought of the nail file in my back pocket. I did not know whether it was still there. He was too near and would notice if I tried to make any movement. He knew not to put temptation in my way, as there was no cutlery on the table. Imbecile.

He put the soup in front of me. Oh God, nausea overtook me again, even though it was my favourite, pea and ham. Where was his information coming from? How I managed to keep from retching was a miracle "I am so sorry my love, I have forgotten to put some music on, bear with me." He said as he stroked my face.

I did not even feel his touch. It was my chance to feel for my nail file. I managed to take it out quickly and place it in my bra. I just hoped his night of acting like a gentleman meant he was not going to touch me sexually. Was it coincidence that he put an album of Katie Mueller on, the one I had listened to with Phil some weeks ago? He answered my question when he reappeared. "I thought you would want to listen to this for the last time, but if you would rather something else you just have to say." I shook my head to his ridiculous statement, and as far as saying anything, I don't think the damage he has done to my face and jaw would ever allow me to speak again. I knew I was in a bad way.

We were now sat together at the table, with our bowls of soup and a spoon each in front of us. Once again, I hoodwinked him into thinking that I could not lift my arms and slumped further in my seat. "My poor love, I will have to feed us both." I thought about the weapon in my bra, but I would have to catch him unawares. I knew where I was going to stab him with it, but would it give me enough time to render him helpless so I could use his phone that was sat on the end of the table? He had a few spoonful's of soup, making sounds which would suggest it was delicious, and told me how much I was going to enjoy it. When was he going to realise that because of his beatings, I could not move? I was trying to access him, but my son's face kept coming into view. Please God, he still needs me. Alex looked up and his face registered my predicament.

He pulled his chair to touch mine and placed his bowl next to me. He filled my spoon with soup then made for what was left of my mouth. I felt some warm liquid on my tongue, but the majority dribbled down my chin. He ever so gently used the napkin to wipe it away. As he replaced the piece of cloth on the table, I saw all the dried blood on it, along with the soup. "It's okay Laura, don't be embarrassed. I have hurt you too badly for you to eat. I think you have a lot of broken bones. I am going to have to help you on our last night together. Do you want me to pour some soup into your mouth? Can you swallow?" I nodded my head. I had to have something inside me so I could gain a little strength. My nausea stayed at bay, which meant his cooking must not be offensive. He was pleased and said so as I tipped my head back a little, he took the weight of it with his hand at the back.

With his other hand he spooned the thick liquid into my mouth. "You have a loose tooth Laura. Here let me sort that for you, it must be uncomfortable." I couldn't scream, my body went into spasm with the pain. He had just wrenched the second molar of the day out of my mouth. One from each side. I should be dead by now surely. How much pain can a body take and most of it was aimed at my face which wasn't that far off from my brain.

I was pleased when the bowl was empty, and he then finished his own. "Would you like some more soup Laura?

WHAT WOULD TOM DO?

You will not be able to manage my seafood paella and it's divine." I nodded my head. Again, he was pleased. There were tears just running from my one eye, I couldn't stop them. Did it not do anything to show him what he was doing was so, so wrong. "See you would have loved being my wife, I am a very good cook. I am just sorry you cannot speak. We could have had some lovely conversations. I will get your soup and my dinner then we can sit and listen to the music when we have finished." I nodded my head. Before he put his own meal on the table, he brought me my next bowl. I finished that off too. My stomach felt good, the only bit of me that did, but unbeknown to the bastard, I felt stronger. Physically and psychologically even with the accustomed pain. I faked another slump and an utterance of pain. "My poor darling, I could put you out of your misery now, but I want to make love to you tonight. I need you to know before you die what you missed. How gently I will love you." I would rather he put me out of my misery now. If I was going to die anyway, rather than be raped. He had already told me some of this once, but it was the 'making love' remark that brought the words I was told to think, into my mind. 'WHAT WOULD TOM HARDY DO?' He certainly would not let someone rape him. Tom had said he was with me. Whether my own mind had gone or not, I believed these words. It was hope.

He ate his paella and made small talk whilst I watched. I was itching to make a move on him, but not with his knife and fork in his hand and me already being half dead. If only I could undo the tape wrapped around my legs, it would give me more confidence. I noticed the clock on the kitchen wall. It said four-fifteen. It would be light in three to four hours. Would I see the daylight? I stopped myself from thinking like that. Someone was looking after me. I felt strength returning to my body. My face had suffered too much and I doubt I will ever look the same again. Phil will find me grotesque and my son will be reminded of this for the rest of his life. At least now I was giving myself a chance of getting out of this alive.

The meal was over. Alex had some tiramisu for his dessert. I had decided against it even though I loved it and could have swallowed it, with it being smooth. I was not a big eater and the soup was sufficient. He took all my weight again and attempted to take me upstairs. It took him approximately twenty minutes before he realised it was fruitless. Why would he want to make love to me whilst I looked like this? He got angry with agitation and brought his leg up to my backside and booted me as hard as he could, so I landed right near the chair I had been thrown into on my arrival into this room earlier. The kick will have caused some damage, I felt and heard a crack, the pain made me want to die very soon. I just hoped my Daddy was waiting for me. "I will bring everything from upstairs and make a bed for us down here, then I can help you get undressed. I will have to tie your hands up again." I nodded. He liked me agreeing with him. He had the look of glee on his fucking bad bastard face. He went into the kitchen to get the tape with a spring in his step. I took the nail file from my bra with urgency and lodged it in my watch strap. There was nothing else I could do; I did not have time to think before he was back. It was on the underside of my arm and as he thought I could not move them he would not see it. Then realisation hit me. He was taping my fucking hands. If he did not find it, it would assuredly be stuck to the tape.

He stood me up to move me to the other side of the room, then let me drop to the floor to get me ready to put into the manmade bed. I screeched in pain and pretended to faint with it. It worked, although I got a kick to my broken ribs to check I was out. What happened to him showing me he was a gentleman? This repugnant bastard was a real monster, he was torturing me. I lay lifeless and he took off up the stairs. I thought again of Tom Hardy in his role of James in 'Taboo'. He had to take the pain to live. Give into it and I die.

I was still lying in the same position when he returned. I heard him setting up our bed right next to me. He rolled me onto a duvet, and I heard him fidgeting with something. He left the room and I placed the file under my side of the quilt. He returned within minutes with two glasses of champagne. I had opened my eye to let him know I had come round. "You're awake, my little Princess Laura. I will put some music on, and then we will make love. You will like this. It is my gift to you." he said as he put the CD in the player. One last insult. It was the album 'Ten New Songs' by Leonard Cohen. What a time to think about all the occasions I had had sexual intercourse to the wondrous sounds of Leonard. I could feel a slight vibration in the air and automatically knew it to be a helicopter. Please. Please. Please. Let it be in search for me. Alex did not seem to notice, and as the music kicked in, the whirring sound was covered with the sultry tones of my idol.

Alex removed his clothing before he started undoing my shirt. I noticed his already growing erection. Once my top was removed, my arms went back down to my sides. My nail file was there, under my hand. If I was going to be rescued, then I had to hurt this bastard before the coppers came in. I doubt they would let me stab him with my weapon in their presence. He was now removing my jeans and I had the nail file in the position I wanted it. He was talking to me, but I was not listening. The helicopter would have landed by now a little distance from the cottage. My rescuers were about to burst through the door; I knew it! As Alex came up to kiss my cheek and remove my bra, I brought up my arm, brought it back and stabbed hard right into this bastard's eye. I cannot remember anything after that. Pain seared through me and my brain cut out again. I came to on a stretcher that was heading towards the whirring sound. They were flying me home.

The tears flowed. My body was racked with pain. Was I still going to die? I did not hear a word of what anybody said to me. I did not even know who was with me. I was awake, but unaware. I needed to sleep. It was daylight and I was free of a man who had haunted and hunted me for weeks. I could not smile on the outside, but I was smiling within. If I lived, I will see my baby, my friends and Phil again. Sleep came on that note.

I was in and out of consciousness for what felt like days. I saw faces of loved ones but did not know if I was dreaming. Someone was holding my hand. I opened my eye, but that was also now so swollen I couldn't see clearly, the other still shut from my beatings. I still could not move, so Ben's face appeared above mine, his tears spilling onto my face. He gently wiped them away and sobbed. I tried, but I could not speak. My face felt like the largest pumpkin. I wanted to know what I could and could not move. I knew I had a broken arm because there was a cast on it, I could feel it. I could not move my legs because of the pain to my ribs as well as my back. With my tongue, I could feel metal in my mouth. I could not feel my lips, but I was free! I was with my baby and that was all that mattered. Ben told me to sleep. I thought I had slept enough. He told me I had not long since returned from surgery. He stroked my hair like I had done to him so many times as a child. It felt wonderful and it helped send me into a full night's sleep without nightmares.

Breakfast was in my drip, the same place every other meal would go for a few days. A few days, who was I kidding? I could only use my left hand and I certainly could not write with it, so my questions would have to be asked when my laptop could be brought in. The television was high up so I guess that is all I could rely on to keep me entertained. I could see through a tiny slit in my best eye. At least I was not agitated on this stay. I felt calm, but knew it would not be long before I was bored.

At least Daisy was not here, and I did not have to suffer ER! I did not have my glasses, so I could not find the menu button on the remote. I would just have to flick through the channels, God I hated when people do that, but I had no choice. My closed eye nearly opened, and the good eye nearly popped out when I saw a picture of Alex Dunne on the news channel. My hearing must have been damaged because I had to turn up the TV quite loud to hear what was being said, which brought the nurse in. I pointed at the screen and then at myself to let her know that he was the monster who had done this to me. She acknowledged that she knew what I was trying to tell her. She told me he was now out of hospital and in prison. Phew! Through my one-handed sign language, I asked her how long I had been here. This was my sixth day. I was not shocked to hear it.

The doctor arrived at lunch time. He was happy with how he found me. I was back on the morphine button and pain killers, so my pain had eased (as long as I did not move). I would have thought he would tell me the extent of my body's damage, but it was not forth coming. What could I do? Nothing.

I felt someone take my hand again and thought it was Ben before I opened my eye and saw my beautiful boyfriend, who had been through hell since our first two weeks of meeting. He had stayed by my side. It was a good job I had a private room because within minutes, it was full of the people that meant the world to me. Rae, Livvi, Daisy, Ben and Sian were here. I knew I must have looked bad because they all shed tears. My face was wet with my own. Sian spent the first ten minutes talking to me because it was imperative, she get back into the office in Manchester. Her work load without me there must be horrendous. She just talked about what her son and husband had been up to, what else could she say? I knew everyone must be on edge and it is hard to have a one-way conversation. She left after kissing my head and saying she would come to see me again. Rae, Livvi and Daisy were making small talk, not bringing up anything about the day I was kidnapped. Ben and Phil went off to get everyone a hot drink. Apparently it was very cold outside.

We were here together, the four of us. We have had such a strong friendship for over half our lives. We were an alliance. A relationship based on shared interests and values of care, trust and love. We had so much in common. The primary thing was: we had each committed murder.

END OF PART ONE

PART TWO

CHAPTER ONE

LAURA

It was the second day of my holiday, (the one I had booked off from work in October) and I was only just being brought home from my hospital confinement, making my stay there, over five weeks. We were now in December. When I eventually learnt the full extent of my injuries inflicted by Alex Dunne, I knew that my stay would be lengthy but never, would I have thought it would take so long, yet I would still be suffering the events of those days.

I was wheelchair bound and fortunately for my guests whom I was now sitting in my conservatory with, my jaw was still wired shut. For fucks sake I had not smiled in six weeks. My, now nearly healed ribs were allowing me to have belly chuckles without pain. It was wonderful to have Ben, on holiday from university, and the ever- present Daisy with me. Phil had followed behind the ambulance that was returning me to my much-missed house but veered off when we passed the supermarket. I had typed him a list of soups and fruits that could be blended for my meals whilst I still wore the wires that kept my teeth shut tight together. All I could think was, thank God for my laptop.

My broken three fingers on my right hand were healing nicely along with the broken arm, wrist and dislocated elbow, so it would not be long before I could put these to use again. The swelling and bruising from my fractured eye socket and several breaks in my cheekbones had become just slightly noticeable now. I had the stitches from several bad wounds out some weeks ago, leaving a few ugly scars. I was not going to worry about them at this moment. The two teeth I lost should not be too visible once I lose the wires. I thought of Phil having to look at me every day and be reminded of his own torment. God, what must I have looked like after having been rescued? I chose not to look into a mirror whilst I was in my private little room ten miles away, and still hadn't.

My spine was a different matter, hence the wheelchair and the ambulance that was needed to bring me home. There was a hospital bed set up in the conservatory that was to be my sanctuary for the next few months. I had had two surgeries to the damage caused by the kicks I had received to my back and at the same time the surgeons had put my kneecap back into place. When I had passed out for the last time, having been on target with the nail file to the Bastards eye, it was because Alex had removed the implement and stabbed me three times with it before the door was knocked off its hinges by my search team of great detectives. Not only did he manage to puncture my lung, he left the fucker inside me. None of the latter do I remember and was pleased I was unconscious at the time. It is hard to believe that my body could have withstood all this damage, and it was easier now to understand the reason I thought I was dying. I thought about Tom Hardy and his character, James in Taboo. The torture his body accepted and the pain that he managed to detach from. My love of Tom had nothing to do with the moment, but the words from my hallucination I firmly believe worked in helping me cope.

Alex had spent three days in hospital whilst he had the damage to his eye treated. He came off lightly considering the extent of injuries I wanted to inflict upon him. He was obviously receiving psychiatric care but was still housed in a correctional facility and not a place for the mentally insane. I had typed a full report of the events of my time in that cosy little cottage where I had spent, not one but two days. I have yet to work out how that happened. There is time unaccounted for, I can only assume I slept through quite some time of it. The whole experience was nothing less than abominable, but I can quite honestly say that not being raped by my captor makes the events of those days easier to cope with. I have no fear of seeing him again at all and hope one day I will be able to sit and face him. I want to know more about Alex Dunne. But that's just me. Witnessing what I have through the course of my working life also adds to my acceptance of the harm that humans can inflict upon others.

I will still be in my converted wheelchair when this case goes to court. I will attend willingly and gain the jurors sympathy much more, than I would if I could walk into the room unaided. I have argued with work colleagues and friends, as much as I can, using my laptop about doing some work from my bed. I was finally given the heads up, so I will be receiving new case reports and will still be able to give my pre interview accounts which have become very successful over the years. I will then work side by side with whichever criminologist is on the case after the interview has taken place. I could not just lie here and rot. It was however going to be some months before I could return to work and although the idea infuriated me, I had now accepted it. But it was early days.

CHAPTER TWO

O h God, I needed a big stick to slap Daisy with, and I had only been settled in my bed for ten minutes. My dear friend had gone on a shopping spree purchasing items that would keep me occupied during my bedridden time. It's probably a good job my gob was wired shut. We were totally different with what keeps us engaged in periods like this. Soppy love stories, true child abuse reading books, word searches, crossword and gossip magazines with tales of woe. Some games for a Nintendo three D DS, I had bought myself some years ago but only used once then got bored of it. Fucking colouring books of flowers with a choice of either felt tip pens or pencil crayons. God, she was out of her mind. Ben was sat holding and stroking my hand whilst giggling. My tension was reverberating through his arm as she went through the presents individually. Eventually I typed "Daisy, enough already" on my lifeline. She just dropped everything where she stood and looked crestfallen. I felt bad. "I'm sorry Daisy, I love it all, I'm just playing. I just want to have a latte and sit with you and revel in the fact that I am here with you both and Pud, who had been by my side since she set her eyes on me." I started crying. I just let go for the first time since I woke up in the hospital that day. This was a real let out, my mouth being cemented together didn't help and the sobs wouldn't stop. Phil walked in on this scene and the sympathy that was showing in their faces made me worse. We all ended up with tears and snot running down our faces. I brought it to an end after fifteen minutes by writing "I need a LATTE in my bottle." It worked. Daisy left with Phil to put the items he had bought away and make my much-needed favourite home-made drink. I looked at my son and wrote, "All I could see and think about whilst I lay there dying was my baby. Your still my Babyboy and I love you more than you could possibly know Ben." We held each other tight and I knew that if I never told him again, he would always know. I lost the other most important man in my life last year and was still suffering the effects from his sudden passing. The greatest role model there could ever be. I trusted no one more than him and my admiration and respect for my Daddy was immense.

I had got used to having my food, once blended to a smooth fluid through a special bottle. If it wasn't soup, it was fruit. I sure as hell was not going to eat any other meals in this way, especially not vegetables or my much-loved salads and seafoods. I could smell the meal Phil and Ben were preparing whilst guy chat was going on in the kitchen and I felt ravenous. Beef stew, what I wouldn't give to delve into a great big bowl of the dish. Fucking Hell, to add insult to injury, Phil had made dumplings and roasties. I was glad they were eating in the dining room. Daisy shouted to Ben to "Bring the crusty bread" pure bastards. With my various medication, I had some anti-vomiting tablets that were crushed and added to my other meds. I felt that hungry after smelling my carers meal that it also made me feel nauseous.

I sucked on my oxtail soup like a calf on its mother's udder. I can't believe my so-called loved ones were tormenting me like that. I started writing a little tale when I had finished my bottle, and at the end there was a moral to the story, which in effect was telling my friends that they had no morals.

I had literally fallen in love with Phil over the ten weeks I had been with him, even though my time spent in the hospital was longer than the time we had been an item beforehand. As well as being hungry for food, I felt like I was starved of sex. I was looking at him knowing that all we could do was snog with our mouths shut, when in reality I wanted to jump on his naked body and be as mischievous as you could possibly be and still regard it as making love. We had problems with wandering hands in the hospital, but my poor back made me screech in pain rather than pleasure and we certainly did not want a nurse to run in and catch Phil or I, with something we shouldn't have in our hands or in my case, hand. I have already put in words on my laptop regarding sex and what I have in mind once I am back in the land of the living, per say. Phil had become hardened to the fact (pardon the pun) that it was not a hands-on relationship at that moment. As soon as I get back on form, we had decided to take a holiday somewhere quiet.

Daisy, Phil, Ben and Pud gathered round me and made themselves as comfortable as could be with the space afforded them in the conservatory. We were just about to start watching the film Legend starring my saviour and midlife crisis crush, when the gate buzzer went. Ben returned with Joseph and Rosie in tow. More flowers accompanied with a new vase and various gorgeous looking chocolate drinks. My addiction is obviously becoming an item on many a friend's shopping list. I was not complaining, in fact I motioned for Ben to add one of the treats to my bottle. Bless both my lovely neighbours for their kind thoughts and our growing friendship and for not showing their displeasure at being squeezed into a small space. Phil almost forced a brew on the two, and Ben with Daisy left the room so my visitors could have a seat with their drink and 'Oh my God' pastries. Life back at home was becoming a torment. I just listened to the conversation that they tried so hard to include me in, and only used my laptop a couple of times.

Now we were left alone again, we settled to watch the film. Having my mouth wired still didn't stop me from making a few noisy sighs at the sight of Mr Tom Hardy.

Daisy had taken on the task of getting me ready for bed, even though I was already in the bastard. I was still to wash and dress the same as I usually would. "It all helps with physio" said the doctor. My eyes were already heavy and when my evening meds, that included a sleeping pill and diazepam were put into my last brew, I only just made it onto my bedpan before I crashed.

CHAPTER THREE

Daisy appeared early and first on this dull rainy Wednesday morning, she must have heard my bladder calling her. We had already spoken in detail about my toilet needs and I was embarrassed beyond belief, because whilst Daisy was taking care of me, she would be the one to empty my potty. The thought of Daisy wiping my arse was demoralising. It was true I would do the same if she were in my place, but it still doesn't make it feel right. I was given the option of keeping the catheter in place that I had during my stay in hospital, I wish I had taken that option. Daisy was going to have to be on hand every time I wanted a pee. Fortunately, I had a bladder like a bucket. I told her to go back to bed with her brew when she had seen to my needs and she surprised me by doing so. Livvi was coming over at weekend to give Daisy a break. All this fucking trouble I was still causing. I had decided to write a diary of every day's events since I was rescued from the Bastard. I believe he is now blind in the eye that I stabbed him in with the nail file, and I felt pleasure at the thought that he also had a reminder of his evilness towards me for the rest of his life.

As if things couldn't get any worse. I woke to the smell of bacon coming from the kitchen. At least at the hospital, the smell of food was not as enticing. I was getting very runny porridge. Ben stuck his head into the room to ask if I was ready for my breakfast. I nodded and gave him the two fingers. "What" he said. I sniffed and he got it. I thought maybe I should have stayed in hospital after all and meant it. I did not want Daisy, Ben and Phil to feel obliged to look after me. I was not happy, in fact thinking about it only made me feel low, maybe a little depressed. When Daisy came downstairs after reading a book in bed, I had to type that I really needed to open-up to her, on the subject of my care.

When Daisy realised how badly I felt, she had no option but to agree with what I thought was going to make life easier for all of us. I was going to hire a carer to come to my home twice a day. These people were used to dealing with all types of casualties so my embarrassment would be lessened. I could not thank my best friend enough for what she was willing to put herself through and I held her tight and motioned to her how much I appreciated and loved her.

Daisy had got on the phone instantly as per my wishes. I would be having a carer twice a day starting this evening at eight o clock and again at nine o clock in the morning. It was to be a female and she had to be at least in her thirties. My preference.

After Ben and Phil had eaten their breakfast, they joined Daisy and I in the conservatory. They both accepted that my choice of care was now in the hands of the professionals and agreed it was a good decision.

Ben picked up the word search magazine that Daisy had so kindly purchased for my entertainment. We sat quiet with our brews, then Ben said something that had us in hysterics. He threw the mag back on the coffee table and said, "Fuck that, the words could be anywhere in there" Either he had not realised what he had said, or he was just bloody dumb. All we got from him was "What, What." 'Plonker,' I wrote. This started him off on a comedy routine. I had just raised my bottle to my mouth when Ben said, "What's hard, red and bad for your teeth?" I thought it to be a serious question so thought about it logically. I said, "A can of Tango," as I associated his question with me drinking from my bottle. "Your wrong Mummy, it's a brick." I just wrote "FFS." Daisy and Phil found it laughable, or they were just humouring him. I loved watching and listening to him, he was extremely funny. Not all his jokes were that bad. We laughed till we cried, and I kept writing derogatory men jokes, for example. "What do you call the useless piece of skin at the end of a penis?" Each one had a guess but got the answer wrong. It was "A bloke." I then typed that "God must have been a man because if it was a woman, she would have made sure sperm tasted like chocolate." I was on a role and my earlier predicament forgotten. The whole morning carried on in the same vain. I had finished with, "What do you call a man with ninety-nine per cent of his brain missing?" The answer was "Divorced." They did come up with some funny answers though.

The afternoon saw me typing up the events of the morning regarding my feelings and choice of care. After my medication, I had a nap. I wanted my guests to get on with something they wanted to do rather than think they all had to stay by my side. There was no threat now, I could spend some time alone. I think they took it as a hint and the three of them set off in Phil's car to Llandudno. Shopping spree, so I gave Ben my cash card and allowed him to spend two hundred pounds on some clothes or whatever he wanted. I made sure Daisy knew his limit but typed her a message saying that when he got to his limit, she could tell him he could have another hundred pounds, then that would be his Christmas present. It was highly unlikely that I would be able to go and do any present shopping. However, I will buy some gifts online.

I wanted to sleep. I think all the laughter had really tired me out. I had been woken from my sleep earlier by the noisy Ben. Bloody foghorn. I only hoped they ate out so I would not have to suffer any delicious food aromas. It had just gone dark and that along with the miserable weather saw me falling into a deep sleep.

I woke again at the sound of voices and I was feeling the pain in my back. Medication time. It made me think of 'One flew over the cuckoo's nest' I'm not just meaning the phrase 'Medication time' I meant with this house and its occupants. I suppose I would be Jack Nicholson's character, R P McMurphy. No one was coming into the room yet and I could feel the stirrings of a stomach-ache. Christ, I knew what that meant. I looked at the clock and it was only seven o clock. Could I hang on for Steph? A great introduction to my new helper. Gosh, I had slept all that time. I wish I could sleep away the time I was disabled. I was so anxious to be back on my feet. I could hear the three stooges moving about and chatting. They had obviously been Christmas shopping and I heard Daisy say, "You may as well leave them in here, Laura won't know their here."

I turned my laptop on just as Phil and Ben walked in. I got kisses and cuddles and a big box of Cadbury's flakes. I could just break them up and put pieces in the side of my mouth and they would melt, and I was in heaven. The only orgasm's I could have at that moment. I will probably have to have more teeth out as well as the wires when my jaw was healed. The sweet must be rotting the enamel on them. Ben had bought some DVD's, but none of which impressed me. I suppose I can't always have my own way and Phil seemed quite interested in them. Sci Fi does nothing for me. I was overly thanked for Bens Christmas money and you could tell he was in his element with the new items he had purchased and was now showing me. Several items of clothing, a skull ring and some trainers. I would buy him some surprise items as well. Ben, Phil and Daisy were getting on like a house on fire. This pleased me to no end.

Daisy appeared with a latte and my meds, she asked me what I wanted for dinner? I wrote, "Just One of my protein shakes, after the carer has been." I was clenching my cheeks. She disappeared and returned with a couple of books. These were more apt for me. Crime novels. I checked my emails and I had been sent my first report from Sian. Bless her. I would get straight onto that in the morning. Apart from needing a poo, I was feeling quite happy.

The lovely Steph arrived fifteen minutes early due to her not knowing the area and just in case she got lost she would have that extra time. God must have sent her because I was just holding on. Touching cloth as Ben would say. She introduced herself and I wrote "Steph, I am very pleased to meet you. I apologise beforehand for what I am about to say. I am dying for a number two. I have been holding on for an hour and I have probably a minute left before I ruin this bedding." Steph was going to fit in great, she laughed and saw to my needs immediately. I was then treated to a bed bath and put in my jimmie's. She went on to tell me that twice a week it would be another lady called Sarah and she was a lovely lady. Just someone else to see the places I like to keep hidden and do the jobs that are so personal in one's life.

To end the evening, Daisy and I were reading, Ben and Phil (who was on a week's holiday) watched one of the newly acquired DVD's.

One of the books Daisy had bought, saw me reading it

from front to back in one go. It was a crime thriller and kept me enthralled all the way through. It was four am when I had finished it. I made a note to purchase further novels by this author. I was a bit pissed off when I had realised the time and in quite a bit of pain. I had been looking forward to an early rise so I could get back to work and start on the report I had received yesterday evening. Oh well, I had enjoyed my reading for a change.

It was nine o clock and Steph had arrived to sort me out. I was groggy and miserable when I first woke each morning, partly through the medication, my body needed more to bring me back to life and to cover the pain and the other part being, coming to terms with the predicament I was in. Every morning was a new day to get used to the fact I was momentarily disabled. After I was medicated, washed, dressed, pooped and pee'd I felt a lot better, and was ready to face the day ahead. Livvi's arriving tomorrow night had been planned some weeks ago. It was not just to be a holiday. Rea, Daisy, Livvi and I had business to sort out. We had become a partnership six months ago, a decision we had come to whilst on one of our breaks together when the conversation throughout the four days always came back to the same subject, CRIME. We had already put some of our plans in place and this weekend we were originally going to set more intentions in place. This subject was not to be talked about until my body was able to conform again.

Phil spent an hour with me, holding my hand and gently rubbing my back. He handed me my stress ball, which I was to use several times a day to strengthen my healing fingers. Daisy was going to an antique fare in Anglesey and Phil and Ben were going to do a five mile walk on the Snowdonia mountains that I lived at the bottom of. They could not go to far as it would leave me on my own for too long.

CHAPTER FOUR

O h dear, I was reading the case of an account that Daisy had mentioned that she had seen on the news the day I came home. Obviously, you don't get the full account through the television.

Malcolm Freeman aged thirty-two, single with five children to four different mothers, lives in a shared flat with a friend Jonathan Platt whom had the same substance misuse problem as Malcolm, this being primarily alcohol. Neither men worked, so were receiving benefits. Mr Freeman often begged for money from shoppers in the local city centre and has been known to be quite rude to the people who refused him. He was a blight on society.

On the morning of the thirtieth of November, Malcolm Freeman headed out towards the nearest supermarket to obtain a two-litre size bottle of cider. Before he got to his destination, he saw what he termed, "A fit Girl with a kid in a trolly." He crossed over the road to ask her if she could give him some money so he could get a bus pass, because he needed to go and see his nan that was dying in hospital. I would assume the young woman; Jolie Mackay aged twenty-nine knew the reason he was giving was an untruth but may have felt intimidated or already knew of Malcolm. Maybe she had given money to him previously. When Jolie had opened her purse to take out some cash, Malcolm noticed several twenty-pound notes. Not only was he attracted to Mrs Mackay, he also found the notes enticing.

Jolie was returning home after dropping her eldest child, a five-year-old little girl called Carla off at school. After walking away from the beggar, she had not noticed him following her home. As she entered her property, and immediately put the kettle on, she then had taken her baby, James upstairs to put him in his cot. Freeman broke the small window in the back door, unfortunately like most home dweller's they keep the key in the lock. He could not believe his luck. He entered the property and took a knife from the cutlery draw. He hid in the first room to his right, where he found a piece of furniture holding several bottles of spirit and wine which he could see through the glass doors. He retrieved a bottle of vodka and drank a third of the drink in one go. He waited till Jolie came passed the living room door to go into the kitchen. He then went on to say, that he did not intend to do the pretty young woman any harm. If this was the case, why did he take the knife when he could have just taken her purse from her bag whilst she was busy with her child and left.

He then went on to say that he approached Jolie from behind and put his hand over her mouth. A struggle ensued till he disabled her with a knife wound to her stomach. He took her purse from her bag that was left on the kitchen table and then intended to leave. The vodka he had downed had taken effect and when he realised he had received some scratching to his face, the thought of DNA under her fingernails brought him round to the fact that he would be arrested for what he had done because his deoxyribonucleic acid (DNA) was already on file. He thought if he was going down for this, he might as well have a bit of fun.

His definition of fun was to rape Jolie as she lay dying from blood loss. He tore at her clothes with the knife. He put tea towels over her wound, as he found the blood offensive and could not attain an erection. Once he removed her jeans and pants, he then became sexually aroused and went on to penetrate her vagina with his penis whilst biting her breasts. Her flaying arms held no strength so did nothing to discourage him. Once he had ejaculated, he cleaned himself with a dish cloth that was placed on the side of the sink. His actions then "hit him like a hammer," he reported. The fact that there was evidence of his atrocious attack all over the kitchen area, gave him the idea that he should set the house on fire. He stabbed Jolie in the heart to make sure she was dead but thought nothing of the baby upstairs asleep. He built up a small bonfire in the kitchen and the living room and turned on the gas fire without lighting it. Again, he could not believe his luck when he found that the oven was also gas. Before he had done this, he had taken a hoodie that was hanging on the back of a chair so he could disguise himself when he made his quick getaway. No one saw or heard anything, not even Malcolm entering or exiting the premises.

By the time a neighbour called the emergency services, it was too late to save baby James. He lost his little life from smoke inhalation. Jolie had died instantly after she was stabbed the second time. The fire had not destroyed everything in the house due to the swiftness off the fire services. Malcolm Freeman's fingerprints were recovered from all the items he had touched, especially the dresser that held the family's alcohol. The freak of nature had taken the contents of the cupboard, along with some jewellery that Jolie was wearing. His semen was collected from the victim's vagina, tea towels and the dish cloth he had used to wipe his privates after the rape, and on several fingerprints on the drink's cupboard. He would not have any remorse for his actions, he most likely at the time thought, that if it was what he wanted to do, then it was his right.

I studied Malcolm's previous form. He had been institutionalised most of his life through committing trivial to serious crime, he should never have been let back into society, as his crimes were escalating regarding violent acts. My initial diagnosis would be Mr Freeman was a sociopath. He had absolutely no conscience, this is missing from his genetic make-up. He does not feel love, he would never care for anyone, including his own mother or for the women that had conceived his children. He is a charmer that finds it easy to entertain then seduce people. He was of average intelligence but knew that his actions were wrong. He was an attractive man, so it would be easy for him to claim friends and charm women. Would he be able to gain an emotional attachment to these people? No.

When you're trying to understand the 'why' of someone like Malcolm Freeman and his actions, it should bring expectations of empathy, understanding and maybe forgiveness, however vile the act they commit. I do not feel like this anymore in my work, I show it, however I do not care in reality. I do this job to my highest standard, what I am paid to do, but it does not necessarily mean I agree with what I report. My interviews with perpetrators of crime work well because of my manipulation techniques and the lack of intimidation from anyone.

Malcolm did not need to be interviewed by my stand-in psychologist. My report was enough to cover what was needed in court. I just hope that this monster stays in prison for the rest of his life. My wish would be for him to be beaten to death in prison.

I would love to be able to put this depraved bastard on our hit list. My partnership with my wonderful friends was on hold for the moment due to my disability. Our next subjects were already chosen.

This depraved individual came from what seems like a loving family, only he was known not to return any emotion. That's as much as I can say about his childhood. He had two younger sisters, both had five children each. One sister, Charlie had escaped the family norm and was happily married with both parents working. The youngest sister, Amy followed in her Mummies footsteps and relied on benefits since leaving school and getting pregnant. She had never even applied for a job, never mind worked but carried on having children. Then there's Malcolm who doesn't have to earn a wage because he was getting one from people like me whom pays fucking taxes. Then there's his begging and thieving to feed his habit. Pisses me off to no end when you have the role model of the family, in this case the mother condoning the life that her family have chosen. No signs of her having ever worked. A family of takers. I remember a young girl telling me once how much she had spent on her daughter for her birthday. I answered, "Surely you mean people like me whom pay our taxes through working hard, that has bought your daughter her presents?" She did not take it kindly and neither did the mother who was an acquaintance I had just bumped into whilst shopping. Like I give a fuck. I work hard for my money, just to have lazy bastards like these keep taking, keeping our tax rates high. Driving around in cars, holidays abroad, where was the justice in this? I took my stress ball off the table and did what

I was able to do with it to take my mind off these thieves. It was so bloody unjust.

Ben and Phil had arrived back from their walk whilst I was still focused on my work. Phil just called into see me with a chocolate drink, a kiss and my meds. He could see the disgust on my face, but it was something I could not share with him, it was obviously confidential. I just thought, what an absolute fucking evil bastard. I had spent three hours which is usual for doing my report and learning about the person. My heart went out to Mr Mackay, their daughter, family and friends. What horrors they must live with. I was a definite advocate for bringing the death penalty back.

CHAPTER FIVE

Daisy arrived thirty minutes after the boys and brought with her items from the village bakery, Bitch. It was intolerable, but I couldn't say anything, they were already giving up enough for me. It just made me feel so miserable. The doctor had told me that even when the wires were removed from my mouth, it would still be some weeks before I could eat anything that needed chewing. I should be rejoicing in the fact that I am still alive, and my disabilities are ones that can be overcome with time. I had been approached by therapists in case the torture I had received had affected my mental state. I did not feel at this time that counselling was warranted, but who knows with time. I would not deny it if I thought I needed it.

How did I feel about Alex Dunne? I felt like he was still punishing me, leaving me in this state of relying on loved ones to live. Do I want to rip his fucking face off? Yes. Do I want to do it slowly and torture him like he did me? Yes. If I had that chance, would I do it? Yes. No one brought up his name, everybody knew the extent of my injuries but did not want to know how and why I received them. I have not made any rules that include not talking about my abduction. Were they frightened by the events of those days or did they think that not talking about it was what I wanted? I did not want to impose Alex's actions on the people that care so much for me. Maybe they were waiting until I could talk. They would most certainly learn the truth when it got to court. I should be able to talk by then. I think the photographs of my injuries and the medical records say a lot. Phil had already said he didn't think he could face Alex. His anger was immense.

After my guests had had their lunch, the three of them came into my temporary bedroom. It was hard to socialise when I was so incapacitated, and I felt that it was hard for them to do anything but chat between themselves. All three gave me cuddles and kisses and Daisy had bought me another three books by the same author of the one I had read last night. I was pleased and used one of the books as an excuse to let them leave the room. I wrote "I don't want to be a party pooper, but I think I will read a few pages then probably fall asleep, I feel tired. Meds again I suppose." There was only a couple of hours of light left so the three of them went over to the beach for a walk. Daisy was very creative and had started doing some craft work with items she found each day brought in with the tide. Driftwood excited her, the bigger the piece the better. I got through ten pages before I succumbed to sleep.

I was pleased to be woken from my nightmare by the lovely Sian. I felt a little edgy and the usual grogginess. I did not mention what I was dreaming about, but it was apparent to the people in the room that I was struggling in my sleep. My report on Freeman was accepted as was, and there was to be no follow up interview. If I had interviewed him, I would have nothing to add to what I had already written.

Sian brought me a file on another case knowing I would have it done and sent back to her by tomorrow afternoon. I would look at it in the morning as I had no intention of staying up all night reading tonight. Daisy offered Sian some dinner and I was happy that she accepted. It was lovely to see her and for her to make the long drive here to see me. Daisy must have warned her beforehand that they would eat together in the dining room as I was offended by the aroma of good food. I had tomato soup.

Ben was happy in the company of Sian whom he always commented on. He thought her fit for an older woman, "it's a pity she's married," his words. Phil had gone home to catch up on some post and bills, he also needed some more clothes. Tomorrow night he was going out with Ben and Livvi to eat and maybe a drink. It was by my order. Daisy did not want to go. We were going to play cards. By the time Sian went home it was close to ten o'clock. Phil had come back.

Ben was showing us some card tricks before we all ended up playing rummy. After my last meds Ben and Daisy went their own ways. Phil had decided he was sleeping in the conservatory with me. He brought the sofa up to the side of my bed, added the cushions from the living room sofa, lowered my bed, now it was like a double bed and it felt wonderful. He whispered and I wrote sweet nothings and as much as we could do sexually, we did. I fell asleep purring with Phil's arms around me and Pud lying with her little engine going, on my stomach. I was as content as one could be in my situation and I thanked God for the people around me.

CHAPTER SIX

I had woken with the usual feeling of dread. Phil had left early due to an employee's complaint he had received last night about his company's manager. He wanted to be there when this person arrived into his office this morning. The time was nearly seven o clock and my body and mind were screaming out for its morning medication. I already had empathy for those people that used substances as a kind of escape from their reality, their past, I was even more empathic if not sympathetic to their needs now that I was in a similar position. I lay there and could do fuck all for myself. I needed my drugs to change the thoughts that were going on in my head. It did not take Sherlock Holmes to investigate my line of thought.

Not only did Alex damage my body, he ended my life for now, in many ways. I could not do my job to its full extent. My role in the partnership with my best three friends had come to an end whilst I was lying here like a corpse. This could cause some suspicion regarding our work. How many people had this bastard let down? I'm sure everyone was tiptoeing round me, making sure my self-esteem did not fail me. I will always remember the role Tom Hardy played in my time in that cottage, dethatching from my pain, waiting for that moment my nightmare would end. I believed his words towards the end and coped how he told me I would.

My thoughts then went to the mother that had in effect rejected me at birth. I had not escaped her wrath till I moved to Wales. At least weekly I heard evilness that had come via another, about myself, from her mouth. Lies that were born, upon her waking towards me, when she discovered that I still had a place on this earth. A sister that carried her seed, was as dysfunctional and like Malcolm Freeman she was a sociopath and hated me with all her might. I had stayed away from my Daddy, whom I loved with every part of me, for several years because of the violence that went on in his house, that he shared with a drunk, my brother who was vicious towards everyone whom entered the premises. My children listened to his filth, sexual and aggressive. He stole from my extremely hard-working father all his life and I'm talking about thousands of pounds at a time. Thousands spent on chat lines that he could not pay himself. He attacked my father more times than I could count. I stayed away from this hurtful situation for numerous reasons, the primary one being safety for myself, my children and the constant worries for my Daddy.

The neglect my brother suffered from infancy was the result of his behaviour till the day he died. As far as I was concerned, the high amount of monies he received from the government for his disabilities through his addiction, caused his death. Manslaughter at the hands of those that fed his substance misuse. I was sorry for Simon even though we all suffered at his hands, either mentally or physically. He chose the wrong path. He never took any offers of help for his addiction and there was only me trying to encourage him to do so, but that was seen as interfering. I grew up knowing I had to make a difference and my sister grew up evil, to say the least. The guilt from leaving my father for so long at the hands of the lost souls, I will carry to my grave. No amount of counselling would emit this from me.

Most of the guilt stems from what I found when I reconnected with my father. Daddy knew I was arriving on this particular Saturday; I was so desperate to see him. On entering his property and seeing an old infirm gentleman sitting on a chair I assumed my father had company. It was a second glance that brought recognition. I collapsed onto the living room floor. The tiny bent over figure who was trying his hardest to keep his eyes open was my beautiful Pop's. I crawled the couple of feet to his chair whilst finding it hard to talk due to shock. The most courageous, proud man in my life was a crumbling mess and four stone lighter. He was caked in his own faeces and soaked in urine. I took him in my arms, I was howling, begging for forgiveness and I was now soaked through to my skin with my father's waste. I knew the carpet was also soaked as it had left yellow saturation on my jeans.

What had I done? I had left my Daddy to end up like this whilst supposedly under my sister's care. I could go on and on about the two years that were to follow but the tears were then streaming down my face as if it had all happened yesterday. I was told by the doctor at the hospital, that I immediately got him into, that he would die within the week. This did not happen because the daughter who would give her own life for his, loved and cared for him so much, was back to look after him, as he had done, so well and willingly for me as I grew into an adult. He was a fantastic grandfather to my children. I gave a list of medication I wanted Dad to be put on, to the consultant, it was agreed, and he got better. My Pops didn't remember the previous two years, as he spent it in a haze of alcohol. The only way he said that he could put up with his son.

Dad got slowly better. He had severe infections in sores above his hips and probably from the rats that were breeding in the sofa that he was sitting on, my God this was also covered in my father's waste. The house was unliveable, and maggots lived in many places around his home. His mattress was dripping with watery faeces, urine and whiskey. I got him a new bed immediately and Steve and his friend carried the old one out, it dripped all the way through the house down the step to where it was left up against a wall. I will never be rid of these visions and nor should I be able to.

The reason behind all this was money. Whilst under the influence, Dad had made a will that he knew nothing about, and when he was shown the papers, now sober, he denied he had signed it. He so obviously had but had no memory of it, and he was disgusted. Leaving his estate to my sister with a corresponding letter. The letter was stating my children's, brothers and my names. We were not to contest this will. When I spoke to my father's faithful GP, whom I knew well, he told me that if I had not got to Dad when I did, he would not be alive now.

For the next two years I lived with my Daddy and loved my life twenty-four/seven. The accusations and what I can only call vileness carried on daily. My father's neighbour even let me listen to a voicemail that my so-called mother had left, saying I had spoilt everything by coming back. In many people's eyes it had become obvious that his death was what his ex-wife and youngest daughter wanted. I had what I wanted.

Sharing the same sense of sarcasm and humour, my Daddy and I had a wonderful, funny, loving life together interrupted by many welcome friend's. He loved having visitors. Dad's body remained weak, but he suffered no pain and lived a full life, exactly how he wanted it. Unfortunately, he had to have a short stay in hospital due to a water infection and caught hospital acquired pneumonia which ended his life. I find this whole damned fucking nightmare hard to talk about and eventually will seek counselling for this. Half my heart travelled to my Daddy's resting place and the other half thinks of him every day.

How angry I had become that morning with something I cope with every hour of every day without anger, acceptance, no. I believe that karma will hit those that inflicted such humiliation on my father. This was my line of thought because the lack of drugs and my anger towards Alex was making me feel so hateful. I could not carry on like this and knew I needed help as soon as was able. The thought of another day never mind weeks lying here was driving me mad, literally. I just wanted to seek oblivion.

Ben was to be my med's and breakfast man today, giving Daisy a lie in. I tried my hardest not to show him my low mood. He already knew the seriousness of both the situations I live with. You could not talk to him about these circumstances.

Twenty minutes later my mind-set was already changing.

CHAPTER SEVEN

Ben took himself out for a walk on the mountains with a backpack holding drinks, lunch and a book. Steph had been on time as usual. Phil phoned to say he was staying at work till he had put some plans in place. I told him to take a day off from me to do something for himself. Daisy appeared at ten o clock just as I was about to get the next case Sian had given me out of the way before Livvi's arrival. "Morning Flower, did you sleep well?" I asked my non biological sister. "I slept like a log; I can't believe what time it is. Do you want a latte?" She replied whilst planting a kiss on my head. "Daisy, I cannot thank you enough, I love you with all of my heart. I just hope you don't think you have to keep looking after me? I'm worried you will get so fed up that you will want to see the back of me?" A tear fell onto my cheek as I looked at her with real concern. "Laura, it's me that should be thanking you for letting me stay here. What I do for you is nothing compared to what you are doing for me. I can't be at home whilst I'm going through all this crap with my fucking hormones. I'm not depressed here, I feel relaxed, welcomed and loved and this is what I need right now. I love you very much too." She also shed a tear or two whilst her voice quivered with her answer. Daisy took a book from my bookshelf and sat at the side of me whilst I started on my reading of the new case. For fucks sake. The buzzer went. After Daisy had answered the gate, she walked back in with Joseph. I managed a slight smile which he commented on. Daisy left to make him a brew then took her book and left us alone.

"I don't think she likes my company." Joseph says seriously. "I hope you're kidding. How can she not and what makes you say that?" I asked of him. "Let's just say it's my suspicious mind. Not only does she seem nervous in my presence, she also disappears when I'm around. Did Daisy know this area before you moved here?" He asks as if suggesting something untoward. I made the sound of a giggle then I wrote. "Daisy is in the middle of the menopause and is suffering somewhat. Primarily she is depressed. She feels more relaxed here than at home where she lives with an uncaring husband. She also lives with her two lovely sons, which she still treats as children and does everything for them. Daisy would not have it any other way but its draining. She runs her own veterinary practice, that she cannot cope with at the moment. I would say she has her hands full. I have known her for nearly thirty years, and she is one of the most inoffensive people I know. I would trust her with my life. She does not want to listen to anymore news that includes Alex fucking Dunne. Why would you ask if she knew the area before I moved here?" I was not liking what he was inferring but I would just remain calm. "Like I said, just my suspicious mind. I understand her predicament now you have explained but I was sure I had seen her before you introduced me to her." He was sarcastic in his manner and he was definitely insinuating something. "Daisy helped me move in, along with Livvi and Rae. Maybe you had seen her then and if so, it was probably in the village chippy or bakery." I laughed as well as I could, as I wrote this.

The conversation about Daisy finished there without an apology for his misjudgement of her. I would not tell her of his questioning. Out of the four of us Daisy, although she was in total agreement of our partnership, she was the nervous one of us. If she knew what Joseph was asking about her, I think she would go home when she needed to be here for her own health and safety and worry even more so.

Joseph then went on to say that my court case date should be imminent and asked how I was coping. I told him in short, but I think my swearing gave him the full extent of how I felt.

Hell, I wish he would piss off as he was pissing me off. The next item on his agenda was the 'Vigilante Murders' I didn't need any catch up regarding this subject. He told me that Brian Ward's death was now counted as the fourth of the killings by this same perpetrator. He also said they were no more the wiser on the culprit, or maybe culprits, he added. "It is nearly two months since the last killing, do you think that this is the end of the spree?" He enquired of me. "Have you checked on all the arrests of other criminals as to whether, he, she or them could be locked up? Even looking at suicide victims or even crims that have died of anything else? I have Livvi arriving tonight and I have a report on a new case that I was just about to start when you arrived. I want to get it done and sent off before my friend arrives, but on Monday I will try and get something regarding the 'Vigilante Murders' on paper, that's if you agree?" He accepted my offer with thanks. What I couldn't write was that, I had killed Michael Gorley, (the first of our victims) in Leeds. Daisy had taken Robert Graham's life in the house in the Lane opposite my own home, but adjacent to Joseph. Rae had murdered Miles Taylor in Sheffield, the night she went under the pretence of going to a funeral. The last was Livvi, her scheduled victim was put on hold whilst we changed our decision last minute to Eric Ward, who was incarcerated at Manchester prison. We had yet to go through our slaughters as a team.

I asked him about Rosie and the girls, and he expressed his pride at the girl's school and nursery parent's evenings. Rosie was a great mum and wife and they were all happy ever after. I let him know how happy I was for him and his lovely family. Just before he was ready to go, Daisy entered the conservatory and just placed herself next to him on the sofa. I grinned out of his eyeline. She asked him whether we had finished talking shop and after he replied, she asked him about his family. Good girl Daisy, right on cue. I wondered if she had heard him earlier, on the subject of herself and she had come in to show him that she had nothing to hide. Apparently not because after he left, she didn't say anything except how nice and considerate he was.

Time had gone so quickly; I hadn't realised it was meds and lunch time. As Daisy walked out of my makeshift bedroom, she farted a bloody big fart then said, at least you won't get the aroma of my cheese on toast now that I have left you with my own fumes to distract you. If you could speak, I know you would thank me. I motioned her to read what I was writing. "I'm sure you followed through then. You're a filthy cow and you stink. You are rancid in more ways than two Daisy. Good job I have anti-vomiting tablets. Fuck off in the kitchen and wash your hands before you prepare my smoothie and med's, I'm sure you've been picking your nose as well whilst you were reading your book, ya always doing it." She left me with the finger sign then proceeded to stick it up her nose. Dirty bitch.

Joseph's body language and demeanour whilst he was talking about Daisy gave away the fact that he knew something of her involvement in the killing of Robert Graham. He was stopping himself from either questioning me further about her or telling me what he knew. If he was sure or even suspected anything, why had he not said so before. He knew that the perp who had slaughtered Graham was also guilty of the other three 'Vigilante Murders'. He had suggested that HE thought there might be more than one assailant. He was lying when he told me that the investigation team were considering the killings to be the act of more than just one individual. His behaviour was suspicious to say the least.

The only reason for not coming forward with the information he held was, if he was involved himself in some way. There was no doubt in my mind, he could not have seen Daisy on that night. She had entered and exited through the back of the premises and there was absolutely no evidence at the scene. Forensics would have shared the knowledge if there was any and not just with Joseph. If he did know that Daisy was guilty, then he must have been on the grounds of the Graham's property himself. He must have felt outrage when Robert was paroled to his parents address. His girls were under threat and who would want a fucking nonce living across the road from them. He would leave it some time, in this case six months before he would make a move. How ironic he would choose the same night to kill the Bastard as per our plans.

I remembered the conversation I had had with him when we first spoke of Graham's death. He had referred to him as a nonce whilst speaking in a professional manner. I thought this odd at the time. If it was just friends talking then the term would almost definitely have been used, but we were new to each other's company and he did not use any other profanities except that. God, if I was right, this meant he knew of my involvement in the case he was working on. I had to know if all my summations were fact, if so, I would come clean with Joseph. If he knew who the culprits were, then he might as well know why we chose who we did. Fuck, I wish I could speak, hard to have a serious conversation when you are using a laptop as your voice. I would wait until my court case was over and I can speak then I, in my way will interrogate him. It would have to be left there for now and I will keep this to myself. I wasn't worried. Joseph got away with having to commit murder. Daisy did it for him.

CHAPTER EIGHT

Rae was next to ring, just as I opened the file, I had been doing a lot of texting with my fabulous friend but now I could hear Daisy repeating what I had text or emailed her anyway. Rae was coming on Tuesday. How many times can I say how lucky I am.

I was reading a domestic violence case, same old, same old. The victim, the wife had given her extremely abusive husband the address of the safe house she had been living in for only a month. He was denying he had ever been in that area but there was too much evidence against him which showed that he was the culprit. Not only was there witnesses as to seeing him in the area and placing him at the house, there was multiple forensic evidence. How many times would the Domestic Violence team have told her; he would kill her one day. The report took me no more than an hour to ascertain this Pricks state of mind. The reason I had this report was because of the vicious way he had tortured and then killed his wife of seven years and the mother of his two children. He would claim, unemployment, substance misuse, anything he could as part of his defence after he eventually realised there was no getting away with crying innocence. Daisy came in with a latte, we sat together drinking then we both nodded off.

Daisy always complained to me that when she was at her home in Manchester she could not sleep, here she slept like a log. "Must be the sea air" she says. Well it was her bloody snoring that woke me up and the fact that we had had no lunch and I hadn't had my meds. My back was killing me and that morose part of me was making its way back to the surface. I must have a word with the doctor, I don't think the medication to make me less agitated was helping my mind-set.

I didn't want to wake Daisy, but she was snoring so bloody loud, it was adding to my agitation. I didn't want to prod her and make her jump she might just be in the middle of the throws with George Clooney. I made grunting noises and that woke her up. "Ya miserable cow, I had just got my mojo back and was just about to shag George Clooney." God, I was perceptive. "I had to wake you, ya were driving me mad, it's like lying next to a baboon snoring, but now I know George was in the picture, which I had guessed by the way, I can imagine the noises you make in the bedroom, and you were calling me some weeks ago."

More meds followed by a chocolate shake and the arrival of Phil. Now that I realised, I was in love, my body ached for the man I have eventually given my heart to. Our closeness last night was amazing but only made me want him more. He echoed those thoughts into my ear as he nibbled at it. The shock waves shot up my damaged spine, must be healing then. Daisy walked in with a brew for him and asked for a bucket. Just wait till her hormones balance out and she gets her sexual urges back, I'll give her some shit.

Phil decided to go and have a wander and see if he could meet up with Ben. He had only been gone ten minutes and Livvi arrived. I had seen her at the hospital only last week so there was not much catching up to do.

CHAPTER NINE

fter Livvi had settled and secured her bedroom, she, Daisy and me, got into a discussion that was ultimately out of bounds. We were not to discuss our partnership plans unless all four of us were present. Rae was not here but it would be a few weeks before we could all get together. The only way I can describe the way I felt was 'The vigilante spirit was searing in me'. I was persuaded to hold on till those two weeks arrived and Daisy phoned for a doctor's call out for me instead. Fucking Hell, I was aiming what Alex had done to me at our next victims and I was eager to get started. I would be having a visit from my GP in the morning. I would not take my meds until he had been so he or she could see the extent of my anxiety that was leading to my aggressive thoughts.

Livvi was not over the moon at my decision to send them all except Daisy out to eat. I couldn't give a fuck about being left out of the evening. It was easier than being punished with glorious aromas.

"Livvi, I know you too well, come on out with it, you're dying to ask or tell me something? Your body language

Darling." I write. "I just wanted to ask you whether you still had thoughts of a relationship or any other kind of thoughts regarding Brian? I don't want to cause any animosity, so your answer will help me make a rather awkward decision." Livvi says somewhat nervously. "Absolutely not Babe, it was a one-off occurrence. I'm in love with Phil and what happened between Brian and myself was a mistake and at the time Phil and I were not what you call an item. I can't deny it though Livvi it was fucking electric mate. Go for it and enjoy." I meant it. "The only niggling thing is, he keeps asking about you and I know he came to see you a few times in hospital. I'm not sure whether he wants something long term because were both single or, just a shag. I still think it's you he wants but you know me, I'll soon turn him." We talked further on the subject and I did not deny that he was gorgeous but looks aren't everything. The boys had got dressed for the evening meal and the three left. Daisy and I were left alone. We played cards till I lost fifteen games of rummy. Just shows my mindset. Steph had played a couple of hands with us after she had put me in my night ware.

-

CHAPTER TEN

I woke when I felt Phil cuddling up to me and I just snuggled into his arms in my hazy state and muttered the three words then off I went.

I had woken early but wandered back off to sleep listening to Phil and Pud's purring. I needed to go back to sleep before my aggressive mindset kicked in and I could sleep for England at the moment.

Daisy had just come downstairs to open the gate to Sarah's arrival. She was a small plump giddy lady with the strength of a horse. I didn't have anything to write to anyone being in the awful mood I was in. Phil explained and gave my apologies which I was glad of later but at that precise moment I was a twat and ready to kill verbally. I did as I had said the previous day and held off on my meds and porridge till the doctor had been. I was sick of the shit in the bottle anyway.

The doc was brilliant and summed me up in one. Antidepressants and a higher dose of diazepam. "It will take some time to kick in so take the higher amount of diazepam till the antidepressants take hold." He said. Fucking great.

Life continued, if that's what you can call it, for the next few weeks in a similar vein. I had plenty of visitors including Brian, who came once on his own and once for an evening with Livvi, which he made quite awkward, but helped with the passing of time. I grieved for my Daddy, and Phil and I became even closer, which is pretty-weird under the circumstances. My friends told me "He's obsessed with you." Maybc so, but it didn't feel strange in any way. The girls had decided that our partnership would not be talked about until I could talk. It wouldn't do me any favours having evidence on my laptop, my voice for now.

CHAPTER ELEVEN

The moroseness did not ease until a few days before Christmas when I got my court date and found my attitude towards it quite emotional. I stayed in a more emotional state than usual, but it was better than the suffering. The second day in the new year would see me at the hospital for tests, x-rays and the removal of the metal from my teeth. The day after that, which was the third of January, I would be going to court. It might sound crazy, but I was just looking forward to both of those days. My new mindset would work better for me in court. The antidepressants had taken my mojo away and I looked and felt sad.

I had everyone around me on Christmas day. Rae, Forrest, Daisy, Livvi, Phil and my wonderful son. I watched them play several acting games and Forrest had a whale of a time because I could not be arsed answering him back. He made me laugh along with everyone else. The phone rang, just after Christmas dinner and right in the middle of the Queens speech, only Ben was playing the part of our Monarch. We were pissing our sides until Rae walked in, after she had answered the phone. "Livvi, your phone is on answer machine and Colin Burrows has been trying to contact you. Just stay there Honey, I have some rather bad news for all of us but mainly you Liv. Brian was found dead this morning in his home. He had not turned in for work nor was he answering his phone, so Colin sent one of the PCSO's round to his house. The front door was unlocked, and when the officer found him, he had been dead for some hours. That is all Colin could tell me, so Liv Darling you are going to have to phone him back when you've had a strong drink and maybe one of Laura's sedatives. Come here." Rae delivered the news like a pro and she was calming Livvi down. I had tears running down my face and I cried till there were no tears left. Everyone shed a tear. I was overwrought. My emotions were all over the place now. My God could things get any worse.

Rae escorted Livvi out of the conservatory and into the living room whilst she made her return call to Colin, a police sergeant from Manchester that Livvi had worked with many times. Daisy made her way into the kitchen with Phil following to help her with making some brews. Forrest then excused himself, but I was not listening to what he was saying he was doing. This left Ben and I alone. "Mum, this may not be the right time to say what I'm going to say, but I'm going to say it anyway. Since you moved here, there has been nothing but trouble around you. Well it's worse than trouble, its fucking death mum. You nearly fucking died yourself and don't look at me like that, as if swearing matters at this time. What the fuck, who breaks into a copper's house and murders him? Even if its someone he knows, what the fuck?"

I didn't have anything to say. I felt numb. It was not as bad as Ben thought. It was Daisy who had slaughtered

Robert Graham and I hope to God that Ben nor anyone, but my three friends ever found out what 'Our partnership' had executed. I stroked the head of my son as it lay on my chest, he cried, I cried. Daisy entered with our drinks and my meds. "Phil's gone to see Joseph, I'm sure he will know what's happened regarding Brian, but he's also going to thank him for our gifts." She said.

Rae came in to tell us that she was driving Livvi to Manchester and Forrest was going along so he could visit his daughter. It was unexpected but she was happy that her dad would be visiting. "Brian's car was in the drive and the curtains were still closed so she tried the door and it was unlocked. She phoned the station after getting no answer when she called Brian's name. Two police officers entered Brian's property and found him dead on the living room floor. They didn't try CPR because it was obvious, he had been dead for some time, rigor mortis was already present. The coroner said he thought the death was caused by blunt force trauma. He had two head wounds, but we will know more about this by the time we get to Manchester. The coroner's report will be back by then. Colin said the arrival of the details of his death was imminent. Oh God Laura, first you and now Brian. Are you okay Ben love?" Ben nodded his head in answer as he cuddled up closer to me. "Fucking Hell, what's going on lately? I'll go and pack a bag because I think we'll be there all night." Rae said as she left the room. "Come on Ben, have your brew and pass your mum her drink. Just when you think things are looking up eh?" Said Daisy. Nothing more was said till Livvi, Forrest and Rae entered my, for now bedroom. We said our goodbye's very solemnly.

Christmas day and the first day that I didn't feel like the devil's spawn and it ends up like this. Phil came back after the three had left. I didn't even remember how long he had been away because my mind was fighting, trying to find answers. What was he working on beside the 'Vigilante Murders? Even that case was going cold so who would want him dead? Was the door forced? Was he asleep and woke to find the culprit or culprits in his home? I knew he was working till seven o clock on Christmas eve and he was not going out or could not come here because he had the early morning shift today. "I know what you're doing Laura and stop it, you've got enough on your plate without trying to find answers. Joseph didn't know and because they've become friends he's extremely upset. Has Livvi told you where their up to at the station? Because Joseph phoned Colin to get the details." We all nodded to Phil's question, and he was right. Going over it was going to get me nowhere.

We played scrabble to keep our minds off today's events until Sarah turned up to sort me out. She was aware we had had bad news by our demeanours and our lack of conversation. She was thanked and left uncomfortably as no one wanted to enlighten her as to our sadness. Daisy was yawning that much she nearly swallowed her own head. She took her leave after giving us all a cuddle and took a book from the shelves in the living room. Ben was going up to his room to play on his PlayStation as he had a few new games that he was dying to play on all day. He would stay up all night on the fucking thing. Phil changed into his jimmies and crawled in next to me. We just cuddled up and he chatted about his feelings. I was not in a position (literally) to answer him, so I just made acknowledgement noises.

CHAPTER TWELVE

knew my new meds were not helping me cope with the day's news. I felt an emotional wreck. Both my bed partners were purring with contentment and I was wide awake but with not being able to converse verbally, it was no use waking Phil. At least my agitation and anger had subsided whilst on my antidepressants otherwise I would be going off my tree. Livvi had been seeing Brian on a regular basis for the last few weeks and the fact he was a working colleague and in the police force, made his murder a hundred times worse. My heart went out to her and his family.

I started to think of the murder that I had committed nearly three months ago.

Michael Gorley, aged forty-eight, living in Wakefield. He was paroled to a sister's address, (only the sister did not live on the premises, unbeknown to the parole board). It was a two-bed terraced house that she usually rented out but had kept it vacant ready for Michaels release.

I had called to this address earlier in the evening acting as an officer of the law. I had fake identification just for this purpose. It had been burnt the next day. I did not need any trophies for my evil act. I was wearing a disguise, from a wig to facial changes with stage putty and make-up. I looked nothing like myself. I also had a limp.

I had asked My victim to be, to make us both a brew, only so I could add the small amount of liquid that would render him unable to move any part of his body but would allow him to see and feel everything that would happen to him. To get him to leave the small living room space so I could put in the muscle relaxant, I apologised and asked could I possibly have some more sugar. If he had noticed I had not yet tasted the drink, he did not say.

Within ten minutes he was totally motionless, and his eyes screamed out fright, just like the children he had abused when he was younger and the young man he had tortured then killed before he went to prison this last time.

My intention was to leave and go back when it was dark but what the hell, it was already getting that way and by the time I had finished it would be black outside.

I informed the Bastard why I was there and told him it was his turn to suffer. I got started and had to keep myself informed why I had chosen to do this. It was the right idea not to have eaten this day. I cut him up as we had rehearsed in our partnership and the blood oozed out of every deep slash. I looked him in his dying eyes but could find nothing that would warrant me to feel repulsed at what I was doing. This vile creature had taken innocent lives by sexually abusing his victims, young children. I was in some ways as bad as he was, committing this act in a similar way that he had committed his last, that saw him incarcerated for murder. He murdered the last victim because this one was older, stronger and fought back. Did I enjoy killing him? Yes and no. I had a strange thought, one that worried me, about my mental stability. A question. Do you think God feels good when he kills? WOW. That puts a whole new perspective on what I do and do not believe in.

The girls and I had spent many hours studying our techniques so that it would look like one individual had committed these first four murders. We were like heroes to the public for ridding the world of its scum. Was this not proof that the death penalty should be sought for the worst acts to man, or a greater alternative to what there was now. It was our way of giving some justice to the victims and compensating the family in some minor way. Was this not showing the CJS (criminal justice system) that their efforts in punishing these degenerates was not working. How could they be rehabilitated when their brain/mindset/sexual urges were only confined to one specific age, toddlers, children and whether they be male or female. Is it not time the public had a choice as to how these perverse Bastards were dealt with? Don't let them out of prison again so they can reoffend. Like rapists, it is more likely they will come out of their sentence to commit the same offence. The girls and myself had not been able to go through the events of our murdering spree's, so we really didn't know how each one of us had got on and how it felt to us because of the incidents with Alex, but as soon as I was better we will rush to get together, to compare notes if you like, that's how much these scum meant to me. We didn't want to be heroes', we wanted justice.

Paedophiles are the only criminals that I choose not to work with. I tried twice, not that it was something I wanted to do but in my line of work you must not be judgemental, and I had to try. After the first interview I did with one of these offenders, I was sickened beyond belief but the one thing that I accepted was the absolute revulsion the culprit felt about himself. He had tried to commit suicide after his first rape of a child and for this I admired him for his choice. He eventually did get it right and they found him dead in his cell, not a suspicious death, but a welcome one. Life would be easier if they all did the same.

The second however was very different and if I could have killed him right there and then I would have. He carried the smirk on his face throughout the interview, had no remorse and even asked me if I had children, and if so, could I sneak him in a picture, so he had something to pleasure himself with whilst in the God forsaken place, he found himself. I walked out before the interview was over and never got that smirking revolting face out of my mind. I feigned upset when I came out of that room rather than anger and swore never to work with one again. I had certainly gone to work on Michael Gorley, and I did not feel one iota of guilt. I had obviously cleaned up well enough behind me and left no trace as of yet, the investigation was no further on today as it was when our partnership had taken its first four victims. I fell asleep with the thoughts of Brian's death coming to the fore again.

CHAPTER THIRTEEN

P hil was stirring, which woke me. I didn't yet want him to know I was conscious. I felt like my stomach was still reacting from the previous night's thoughts. I needed time to think. Who would break into an officer of the laws house, to take his life? It must have been someone he knew surely, and an issue had escalated. As far as I knew he did not have any matters of contention in his life. Livvi being the closest to him at this time would have discussed it with the most important people besides her children in her life and she had not revealed anything. I needed to speak to her. I know Rae and Forrest were returning today but I wasn't sure about Liv.

We had decided yesterday that our boxing day celebrations would go ahead, more for Bens benefit really. He had not had a good time of it since I had moved here, each holiday he had taken to spend in the idyllic surroundings of his mummies new home had been a disaster or to put another way, there has been a disaster. Brian had become a good friend of us all and he had a hand in saving my life when I had been abducted by Alex Dunne. Today, Sian and her family along with Joseph and his were coming for the day's festivities. I just hoped for Ben's sake that we would get our summations out of the way then be able to have some happy social time.

I must have fallen asleep again because when I woke Phil came into the conservatory with Steph carrying my meds and breakfast. Steph bless her was quite concerned about Brian's demise as she had met him and had a bit of banter with him on a couple of occasions. My weepy meds brought tears again. Any unhappy news set me off in tears, happy news did the same. My emotional state on the medication I was on. The way I chose to dress everyday dictated either my mood or the activity I was to be partaking in or it would be my work clothes. Today I wanted to wear black out of respect.

After Steph had left, Daisy, Phil and Ben brought their breakfasts into my bedroom of the moment as requested by myself. The smell of bacon and eggs didn't affect me today. I hadn't even finished my porridge. Sian rang to say she would not be visiting after all she was down and didn't feel like leaving the house. The last few months of 2018 had finally taken its toll on her. I understood.

Still gathered in the conservatory Daisy asked Ben if he remembered the time that both Daisy and I had taken our kids when they were younger to a park that covered several acres? Besides Phil the three of us burst out laughing, knowing what she was about to talk about. She was aiming the story at Phil who obviously was unaware of the antics we used to get up to.

Daisy went through the boat trip, the funfair, park and then we went onto a sizeable field to join other families enjoying their picnics. Mark, Daisy's youngest had taken his very expensive professional walkie talkies and the kids were heading off using them as if they were part of the FBI and spying on some of the families that were about. Daisy and Ben chatted about the events until my best buddy decided to put the blame on me for what happened next. "Laura came up with the idea of attaching one of the walkie talkies to the collar of our dog Chance. He was a great big hairy, human like animal with a great character but took his time doing anything, quite lazy bless him. Once I took him off the lead he just started to wander. He wasn't the running type that absconded as soon as he was let loose. He headed over to a family that were approximately a hundred yards away, just to see if they would offer him any of their goodies. Suddenly, the lady who seemed to be the mother, you could see her nearly jump out of her skin. Chance had just commented her on her lovely pink top. With Chance being so big and hairy you could not see the small walkie talkie attached to him. The woman jumped from her seating position and her children were laughing so loud we could hear them clearly. Chance thanked them for his treat and wandered off to the next family who had heard the commotion and probably wondered what was going on. The kids were stroking him, and the male of the group held out something edible to Chance, he ate it then said thank you. Again, there was the same reaction as the previous family, and we were wetting ourselves with stomachs aching hurting from laughing. We were watching families trying to fathom out what was going on and Chance carried on in the same vein with each group he encountered. He must have been full, from his scrounging expedition and headed back to us. Lots of kids and parents were pointing at Chance and we were lying on the field floor in hysterics. Laura was doing the talking in what she thought was a voice that fitted Chance.

We then decided to take my talking animal onto the

bottom park that was full of crazed kids fighting for each apparatus. Chance was let free and he made his way around the area just minding his own business. We were sat on the railings that went around the play area. Chance spotted an Asian family with ice-creams and headed towards them. "Can I have a lick of your ice-cream" he said via Laura and one of the males of the group dropped his cone and jumped over the railing he was leaning on. The rest of his group burst out with laughter and Laura and I fell off the railing laughing so hard. Fucking hell that was one of the funniest days I've ever had, and it still gets brought up every now and then." Ben and I were laughing so hard now remembering it and Phil who was imagining the scenario was joining in with us. it was one of those situations where you had to be there to get the full extent of the comedy value.

I typed. "Daisy tell Phil about the time Damien tried to get his pet rat out of the speaker. Ben agreed with her and egged her on.

"Damien, you've met him, haven't you?" Says Daisy to Phil. "Yeah, course I have several times." Phil said. Daisy started with the tale.

"Laura, Saul and I were sitting in my living room having a brew and chat when Mark came downstairs popped his head in the room, said hello and then headed into the kitchen. After hearing some clattering, I went into the kitchen to find him emptying the washing-up bowl. I asked him what he was doing, and he said Damien needed it. No explanations so I left him to it. We carried on chatting in the living room then heard some commotion upstairs and when I went to the bottom of the stairs Mark was going across the top towards Damien's room with the same washing-up bowl and steadying himself, I guessed it was full of water. I shouted Mark to come downstairs when he had finished what he was doing. He complied and within a minute he was stood in front of us. I asked him what the hell he was doing, he replied "nothing" and went upstairs again. Two minutes later we heard the sod doing the same thing. I shouted Mark downstairs again and said he wasn't going back up until he told me what was going on. He said he wasn't allowed to tell us that he had promised Damien. He saw the look of malice on my face and decided to spill, well he didn't have an option really. Damien's rat had got into one of his big speakers and it had decided it wasn't coming out. My eejit of a son sprayed his Lynx deodorant into the hole in the speaker and then lit his lighter to see if he could see it. The thick bastard got the full brunt of the flame that came out along with the hairless but otherwise okay pet. Damien was missing his eyebrows, eye lashes, goatee, most of his hairline and two layers of his skin. He was so embarrassed especially with Laura there that he wanted to just keep his face in a bowl of water till she left. In fact, it was so bad that an ambulance had to be called. I know I'm his mother, but I joined in with Laura and Saul with their hysterics." We were all laughing at Daisy's account of that day, but I wrote. "Phil, she has neglected to tell you that she was more concerned about the new mattress she had bought Damien being ruined with the water, than her son's injuries at the beginning. She was heartless. Hahaha."

Ben asked a very surprising question which had me worried. "Does anyone want a brew or any scran?" What was he after? We all accepted. He also answered the buzzer and came into the conservatory with Joseph and the drinks. My neighbour had declined Ben's offer of a beverage. "Mum, I'm going to go for a walk." "Okay Ben I said." Then looked at Joseph and said. "Do you think that's a good idea with what's been going on the last few months and particularly what happened yesterday?" I had to be sure. "Laura, there is nothing to connect what happened to you with what has happened to Brian. I'm sorry you've lost a good friend. I rather liked the guy myself. I feel his loss, and I am sorry for yours. Ben you will be fine, go ahead. I just thought I would come around and give you our apologies, but Rosie and I think it would be better if we arranged a get together for another day. Every time Rosie hears of one of ours being killed, she gets on my back about the dangerous job I have, and all the reasons she hates my work goes with it and this will carry on for a few days. I've just heard Rae and Olivia have left the station and they're on their way back here so I won't fill you in on the latest details, I'm sure Olivia would rather do that." Joseph said, rather sadly. Phil had got used to answering for me and doing the usual small talk when someone visited because he knew that my conversations on my laptop were getting more than annoying to me and showed the extent of my disability. Phil told Joseph about my hospital visit in a week's time. My neighbour was pleased and said he would be coming over again to go through the court proceedings with me. Joseph was a witness at the end of the day. I didn't need to be rehearsed in the events of what goes on in court, I had spent a quarter of my life in them. The defence team would make me out to be some kind of horror. I wasn't going to worry about that now anyway.

Daisy went with Ben for a walk just to clear the cobwebs and not, to make sure he was safe. They often went for walks together and sometimes Phil went along. My adorable boyfriend wanted to spend an hour with me getting even more frustrated. My antidepressants had quashed my ardour somewhat although it was still there once my man started with his wandering hands. My pain killers had been cut down due to my bones healing well. Our sexual playing was a bit further along than it was since that Bastard had put his hands on me. I just hope that when the court case was over, I would be able to forget he ever existed. I've always been good at detachment, well let's see how well I do regarding him.

CHAPTER FOURTEEN

Everyone came back at the same time. My head was all over the place. I felt that I needed space away from people today however much I loved them. It seemed the nearer I was getting to have the steel removed from my mouth and the pleasure of being able to get this contraption off my back, the further away it was. There's just no way of pleasing some people.

Rae came into the conservatory by herself. Livvi had gone straight to her room, to sleep, gather her thoughts, who knew but who could blame her. We obviously felt the same and I would have loved at this moment to have been able to join her, to comfort her in the way she needed and then I would fuck off somewhere on my own to get some peace and quiet.

"They believe Brian was killed between the hours of eight o clock and ten o clock Christmas eve. He took two hits to the head after what seems like a bit of a scuffle. Brian might have wanted to subdue the culprit, but the bastard had other ideas and hit him first to the back of the head with a heavy metal door stop that Brian owned. It was the second knock to the front of the head that killed him, and this weapon has not been found. The coroner seems to think it was a hammer and the investigation team whom have worked right through since Brian was found are assuming the perp brought it with him. It looks like premeditated murder. There was no sign of a break in and it has been suggested it had to be a man to have overpowered Brian. Someone called on the pretence of being his friend but had the intention of killing him." Rae informed me. I was fucked off with using the laptop as it seemed so impersonal at this time. Through my wired teeth I found a resemblance of a voice, horrible as it sounded. "What about DNA evidence from the ensuing struggle?" I asked Rae. "Up to now nothing, but its early days. The bastard must have been there sometime after, cleaning up, even to the extent of cutting and bleaching Brian's nails. Being Christmas eve, it seems there was no one around the area but again, it's still early days. Not everyone will have heard about the murder yet because it's also holiday time. Some neighbours left on the afternoon of that day to spend the festivities with their families. I went in with Liv to see him." At this point Rae burst into tears and I followed suit and we held each other till our sobs subsided.

"Do you mind if I stay a little longer? Forrest is going to head off, I don't think he's coping well with all this. It's been nothing but doom and gloom in his eye's for months, I can understand his wanting to leave. Oh God Laura, what the fuck is going on?" Rae finished with. I told her I wanted to have a nap and she left me to it. Ben came in for ten minutes just to make sure I was okay, held me, kissed me and left me to sleep. Apart from waking for meds and a little of my shakes I spent the whole day drifting in and out of sleep. At least I was left alone, and my body was accepting of the napping.

Whilst I had been asleep, the police investigating this latest wicked deed had been to ask questions as to the whereabouts of Livvi on that evening. They didn't need me as I had enough guests to testify that she had been here amongst us. I was pleased to hear that Livvi was still in her room when the investigators arrived. I would have hated for her to go through that.

CHAPTER FIFTEEN

The last few days had passed in a daze for all of us, mostly the girls and I. Phil had gone back to work and Ben had gone along with him and earned himself a few quid which he and I were grateful for. Rae had stayed as she wanted to come to today's hospital visit. In fact, we were all going. I guess this was understandable. I was extremely excited as can be imagined. Liv had gone back home to be with her visiting children, and she was as good as could be expected but unhappy that she was not allowed to work on the investigation involving her boyfriend's death.

The ambulance picked me up at nine thirty in the morning and Phil and Daisy followed in both their cars with the expectance of me returning in either one of their vehicles. Everyone had their fingers crossed. I felt it likely that I would be out of the back brace as I was not now suffering from any pain. A few little pangs as I was being moved into the ambulance but that was only to be expected.

I was ecstatic, I was free of my wires first and although I would not yet be able to chew and my jaw was a little stiff, I could talk. I got a few funny remarks from my friends as I was wheeled out of the surgical room, regarding my capability of speech.

I had an hour's wait between appointment's, but the x-rays had been done. I was agitated with impatience. It was like a new lease of life. I spoke a few times and I couldn't help giggling along with my loved ones at the rough gravel sound of my voice. When my name was eventually called, and I was taken into the doctor I suddenly became terrified. What if my healing was slow and I had had my hopes up for nothing?

I was happy to see the same consultant that had performed my surgery and had been very hands on with my rehabilitation whilst I was in hospital.

"Well I am happy to tell you Laura that you can go home without all this. Your bones have healed nicely in your back and in your arm. That doesn't mean to say you are going to be running about or going back to work for some months yet. I would say that after several months of physiotherapy you will be able to manage without the wheelchair and another several weeks on crutches. How does that sound?" Mr Smether's asks. As well as I could I replied. "Absolutely fantastic." He went on to check my jaw then I was carried onto his bed whilst he prodded the whole of my back legs and arms. A wheelchair was brought in and I was good to go. Fandabibloodydozi, I was free. I was in a little bit of pain with not being used to a sitting up position for such a long time. I was grinning from ear to ear when I came out of his office and so were my buddies when they saw me. We left the wheelchair in the bay and we drove towards home where I had my own rented wheelchair waiting.

Before Ben, who had been insured on Phil's car could drive off, I tapped him on the shoulder and said. "Please can you stop at a MacDonald's so I can have a Mcflurry?"

I just wanted to be able to have one in the normal way, just like everyone else albeit still having to sit in a car and not the actual restaurant. Wow am I going to make up for what I've missed. It was only natural for my jaw to still feel so stiff and I was dribbling when I was trying to talk.

My ice-cream was delicious and now we were heading home so I could meet with Joseph and my lawyer regarding tomorrow. It still looked like I was going to have to answer the questions and tell my story via laptop, this mouth of mine was still in no shape. In fact, I was a bit stiff all over. One thing for sure though, I'm going to sleep in my own bed. With Ben and Phil's help I was going to get up those stairs and get behind my bedroom doors. Fucking privacy, fucking brilliant. In fact, I couldn't wait till bedtime. Tonight, I can return the sexy messages that have been whispered into my ears for the last few months.

I often thought since my abduction how bloody lucky I was to have found Phil when I did. I would never in all my wildest dreams expect anyone to shoulder what he has had to since meeting me. He was a God send.

Joseph arrived after my lawyer had been with us for thirty minutes. They agreed between them that I would not yet be able to give any evidence verbally. Like I said, we didn't have to go through too much because of my knowledge of this type of case regardless of my role in it. Phil came out with what I first thought of as shocking news but when he explained further as to why he could not sit in the court room, I came around to his way of thinking, not without being upset about his revelation. He became extremely emotional as he had harboured this sadness for months. I felt guilty towards the end of our meeting to have expected him not to break down after he had stayed strong for me.

We were still waiting for news as to when Brian's funeral would be. I am sure the judge in my case would adjourn the case for that day as not just myself needed to be present, also most of the witnesses. Poor Brian was meant to be one of those.

CHAPTER SIXTEEN

Maybe it was my time for some good luck. Alex Dunne had decided to plead guilty to all counts against him. He had agreed that all the witness statements and my own were precise, dating from the actual meeting on that day in the supermarket. There was phone call evidence. My injuries read like a person whom had marginally escaped death with photograph's and video footage. I was gobsmacked to say the least. All concerned were in court to hear the guilty plea and that was without being given any kind of deal. I couldn't look at him and didn't. Hearing his voice made me feel nauseous, so thank fuck he had decided to hold his hands up. Forgiveness is a virtue of the brave, which makes me a coward because his actions will never be forgiven, just hopefully forgotten with time. Alex would have to attend court at a further date whilst the judge read him his sentence. I would not be appearing for that, I just hoped it was for a fucking long time.

Phil didn't even come into the court room to hear the guilty verdict, it pissed me off a little. His anger towards Alex was that bad that he was frightened what his reactions would be. Okay, I have to accept that.

We all went to a lovely café and I felt good. I still had to have soup but what the hell, I was as mobile as could be and eating out with my son and loved ones with a spoon and not a fucking bottle. After that Phil drove Daisy, Ben and I around Wales whilst Rae and Livvi made their way home. Liv had had a call from one of her superiors to say that the results of the evidence that was found at the scene where Brian was murdered, had come back from forensics. I still didn't get how Brian had succumbed to the bastard that murdered him. He had to know the person to have been unaware as to what was about to happen. If the culprit's DNA was in the system, then he was fucked. This means we may get a date for Brian's funeral now. I was not going to think or talk about Brian's demise for what's left of Ben's stay, I think he had gone through more than enough. We stopped a few times whilst I took pics of the mesmeric scenery. Today I was a happy bunny, just a little in pain and quite tired.

Daisy had also decided to go home. She had stayed there a night or two over the last few weeks, but I felt that she knew I needed her to be with me until the court case was over. It was only a couple of days ago that Daisy finally got the strength to go over her experience with Robert Graham. Now she had spoken about her feelings, which she couldn't describe entirely, she seemed much better. We had decided between the four of us that we would take a break away somewhere hot so we could put our next plans in place. Of course, it had to be somewhere abroad so we could be away from people and buildings and enjoy the cocktails and the heat. I couldn't wait, although Phil had pulled his face a little when we mentioned it to him. Like Rae said. "I had been through a hell of an ordeal and the weeks holiday would do me good." Rae was rightly a little annoyed at his face pulling and told him that we had planned to go away before Christmas and he had better get used to us having several breaks together over the coming years as we have always done, even when our children were young.

Phil had mentioned it to me before he left to call into work and spend a night at home now the court case was not going ahead. His excuse was that he, wanted to take me away and he felt that I should have talked it over with him first. I don't fucking think so. I didn't explain it in that way to him though. I'm a woman, I know how to charm or in this case creep. I wasn't happy about his objections. I was in my fifties for God's sake, I'm not going to start with all that obsessive jealous crap, I'd rather be on my own.

It was lovely just to be home with Ben so we could spend some quality time together, even though he would have to help me get around a little. I wasn't going to be moving much and thank goodness I had a downstairs bathroom.

"Has Phil been married?" Asked Ben. "Yes, but he's been divorced for two years. Why do you ask?" I answered. I was actually having a latte in a cup, dribbling but enjoying it. Ben wiped my chin and added. "He asks a lot of questions about you and your relationships with men. Not all the time but then he will just come out with, for instance. How many men has your mum actually lived with? What was her marriage like? Have you got on with all her boyfriends? Why has he not asked you these questions or is he just trying to confirm what you have told him? He actually bloody asked me, if you had had an affair and is that why your marriage broke up? I told him a couple of times that it was your business and he should ask you himself. It annoyed me mum. I think he's great but there's just a few little oddities about him. I know he's been fantastic with you, there's no doubt there. I think he is a bit insecure." Ben tells me. I agree with his assumption. I was angry but I wasn't going to show Ben I was. I think I will have to have a good chat, now that I can, with Phil and get all his insecurities out of the way because there was no need for any. I was the most easy-going person in a relationship that you could possibly want. Everything equal, what's good for the goose etc…

Ben and I had a lovely chilled evening together. We played cards, then watched a couple of DVDs'. I phoned everyone to make sure they got home safely and to thank them again. Ben helped me to my bedroom, then went back downstairs to watch some more television. I felt so relieved with the court case not going ahead. In a way, I did feel like it was all over now. Before I fell asleep, I shed a tear for Brian and wondered, who the hell had killed him.

CHAPTER SEVENTEEN

en brought me up a lovely cup of tea. I had to do my
jaw exercises I'd been told to do, to actually be able to
move my mouth. They worked and I enjoyed slurping
my brew. I was looking forward to having cornflakes with
hot milk, oh what joy.

Ben was going to the retail park to spend some of his
Christmas money and now he was insured on my car, I
decided to go with him. I would sit in my jeep and enjoy
another McFlurry. It was just great to be out.

Phil rang whilst I was sat comfortably waiting for Ben
and listening to some Bowie. It was decided that Ben and I
would go to his house for our dinner. He was actually across
the road from where I was sat, in the superstore where I had
met Alex and not been to since. I opted for seafood with
some salmon, as Ben doesn't like sea food, salad and some
tiger loaf. If I cut it up small, I could get it into my mouth,
play around with the luxurious tastes without chewing and
then swallow. Oh my God, I couldn't wait. He obviously
understood my need to get out, after being confined for
so long. I rang Luke Jervis at Top Notch tattoo's as I have

decided whose portrait would go in the only place I had left
on the shin of my right leg amongst my heroes'. It had to be
James Kazia Delaney from the series Taboo. After all, he did
play a part in my survival. I may have a few remarks aimed
at my decision but only I know what that character did for
me. It's my fucking leg anyway. I got a date for March as
Luke was always fully booked for months. I would keep it
to myself, but I suppose it would not really be a surprise to
anyone.

Ben arrived back after an hours shopping spree and a
spree it was. Approximately seven bags went into the back
of my car. "Where now." I asked. "Where do you want to
go, lunch?" Ben asks. "Yeah, but nothing heavy because
we're going to Phil's for dinner." I tell him. "Really mum,
do we have to?" He says. "Yes, we do. I can't go on my own,
I can't drive. Did you have something else planned son?" I
say, feeling a little sorry that I didn't ask him first. I had just
taken him for granted. "It's not that I don't like him mum.
I thought he was going to give us some time together. I feel
like, well he has been at yours constantly and it looks like he
doesn't want you out of his sight. I'm telling you mum, he's
obsessive. I'm a little bit shocked that you can't see it. I think
because you have been on your own so long, you are happy
with all the attention he shows you, but you're getting back
on your feet now and Phil seems the type to want to stop you
from living your own life. I'm sorry mum but you're such a
stickler for your own space and time out with the girls and
I don't think he's going to want you to do it. You've been ill
through nearly all your relationship and he seems to thrive
on having you all to himself and you relying on him. Look
how he reacted when Rae said you were all going away, I
saw his face, he was angry. Okay, we will go but don't make
arrangements with him that include me again, please."

I knew everything he said seemed to look like the truth, but it was so hard for me to see it as we had only been together a short time before the first murder attempt by Alex, and it had been great then, but I was seeing security. "Okay son, I understand I shouldn't make a decision like that without asking you first. I'm sorry I took you for granted and I promise we won't stay too long because I know you have probably bought some PS4 games and DVD's and you can't wait to get started on them. We will just see how the relationship goes in the next few weeks, because you're right, I need my friends and my space. Okay?" I say truthfully.

"Okay mum. Where are we going to eat? What do you feel like?" I was thinking what I could eat and came up with, anywhere that does pasta or noodles. "Home it is son, I just fancy some noodles. Is that okay with you? You can pick up anything you want, and you could have it at ours." I was looking forward to tonight's tea as seafood and salad was one of my faves. Chinese and Indian will have to wait a couple of weeks whilst my gobs healing.

Ben went into Manny's bakery in our village, for some goodies along with a few pastries for me. I will eat them later if I'm watching a film with my boy. My stomach had shrunk a little, so I wasn't able to eat much at once. I will soon change that. I need a little nap, which I will take after I have eaten. We had four hours to spare before we set off to Phil's.

Rae rang as soon as I had settled on the sofa for my nap. "Are you okay Laura?" She said in a worried tone. " Yes, I'm fine. You sound worried, what's the matter?" I didn't like it when Rae made these kinds of calls. She somehow picked up on bad karma and I have never known her be wrong. "I just had a bad feeling and you came to mind, but your home and okay?" She says. "Fucking hell buddy, I hate it when you do this. I just know now somethings going to go wrong coz when have you ever got it wrong? Bens had a word with me earlier regarding Phil and him being obsessive. He's not going to poison us is he, coz we're going to his for dinner tonight." I say. "I just think he is very protective after what's happened to you, you can't blame him in some ways. The guy loves you, that goes without saying. I doubt he has it in him to kill a fly." Rae says but without sincerity. "Oh, just great Rae, you know what they say about butter wouldn't melt? You forget what I do as a job, the one's that won't kill a fly, end up killing people instead. Thanks very much. Ha-ha. I got Big Ben with me anyway." We both end up laughing. We then went on to talk about Livvi and her call, neither of us had heard a thing. "Maybe you should check on her now, you've got me worried?" I say. "I will get onto her now and you just take it easy. Ben idolises you; he is going to be protective even more so than Phil because of what his mum has gone through. Have a lovely meal and I may speak to you later. Ring me if you need anything and take it easy, I know you." She says. "Ya a bit far away if I need any help Rae." I laughingly say.

I felt well refreshed after my nap. Ben was fast asleep on the adjacent sofa. I woke him with my dulcet tones, and he helped me up and to the loo. We were both ready half an hour later to set off to Phil's. We sang along to Hunky Dory by Mr Bowie and the CD just finished as Ben drove onto Phil's drive.

We were speechless and just looked at each other. Phil was stood at his front door with two plain clothes officers of the law. You can tell them a mile off, even though we recognised one from my case with Alex. They were about to leave so we stayed sat in the car till they came to my car door, which was now open.

"Laura, good to see you. How are you?" I gave him a

quick update. I did not like the way he was looking at me as I was talking, and he then introduced me to his partner. I wouldn't allow myself to ask why they were here even though they knew I was in the business, you might say. BUT what the fuck were they doing here. I decided I didn't like today. I just wanted to go home. I had Rae's bad vibes.

After they had left, Phil and Ben made sure I was comfy in his house before Phil said he had just got in when the cops called so he had not brought in some items from his car that he needed to go with the meal. Ben went out with him and they both returned with a bottle of champagne, Belgian chocolates and an enormous bouquet of the most glorious flowers. Not such a bad day after all.

Whilst Phil went into his kitchen after declining Ben's help. My son looked at me with a real warning look. I saw him mess about with something at the side of the chair he chose to sit on, and I was now not at ease. I knew something was going on in Ben's head. I was unsure now whether or not to ask Phil about the officers, but it would be silly not to, anyone would. I will wait till were seated.

We were now at the table, and our plates were full. Ben was cringing at the prawns on his plate, but I would relieve him of them on the quiet if I could. He didn't want to say he didn't like them, sometimes he was too well mannered. "Well are you going to tell us why the old bill was here?" I asked Phil, and definitely not in any kind of insinuating manner. "There was an assault on an elderly lady further up this road over last weekend, and as I was staying at your house, I wasn't here when the police knocked on my door to see if I could help with any enquiries, so they turned up today, literally as I pulled into my drive. Obviously, I couldn't help them, and I don't know the lady whom they were asking about." Phil said. Every word was a lie. Shit. What the fuck was happening. At least I managed to take Ben's pet hate from his plate. He ate everything but seafood, yet he loved fish. Pudding was ice-cream with fruit, but without fruit for me. The meal was lovely, and the conversation flowed.

We were still sat at his dining room table when my phone which was still in my bag, started ringing. I told Ben to leave it after he stood up about to get it. After it had gone quiet, we heard the voicemail message alert. Good, I don't want to be on my phone whilst I'm here and at this moment wishing I wasn't. I was sure Ben felt the same. Phil was such a sweetheart and a big softie; I couldn't imagine what trouble he had got himself into? Perhaps when we were alone, he would tell me. Within five minutes my phone starts ringing again. It was probably Livvi and Daisy wanting to know how I am, and I was looking forward to finding out what news Livvi had from her meeting today. This time the voicemail that was left must have been at least two minutes long before we heard the alert tone.

"Don't you like photos Phil." Ben asks. Where did that come from? I had actually wondered why he had no pics of any of his family on any walls, but with some people they choose that they don't fit into the décor. "Why are you asking? Does it bother you Ben?" Hell, where did that come from. To say there was a change in Phil's demeanour would be an understatement. I had never seen this guy before, cocky and arrogant with an awkward glare. "No, it doesn't Phil mate, it was just an observational question. Why is that a problem? It so obviously is by your attitude. Perhaps we should go mum, I don't think Phil is in the mood for company after all tonight. Thank you for the lovely meal Phil and I hope this little episode isn't going to affect our future friendship? We all have bad days mate. Come on mum, I'll help you." Ben says whilst I'm about to have a breakdown and then my fucking phone goes off again. "Fucking hell, I can't be doing with this. We're going Phil and I will speak to you later." I say, bloody annoyed. I wouldn't be coming back. I have just fallen out of like with the prick. Ben or I had done nothing wrong and I wasn't going to stay here treading on eggshells.

I carefully stood whilst Ben went to get our coats.

CHAPTER EIGHTEEN

Before I had chance to straighten up, I felt something cold at the front of my neck. I would never forget the look on Ben's face as he entered the room and realisation hit me. Phil was stood immediately behind me with what I assumed was a knife at my throat. "Move that fucking thing away from my mum's throat before I rip your fucking head off you fucked up piece of shit." Ben literally screamed. "Shut the fuck up and sit on that chair before I tell you why I've got no other option but to do this." Says Phil angrily. "You only have one option, let my mum go now." Ben screams again. I was speechless. "Please Phil let Ben go home, whatever I've done it doesn't include my child. Please, I'm begging you." I said calmly. "Shut the fuck up both of you and sit-down Ben before I use this fucking knife." I was taught in self-defence, and if my body wasn't just recovering from being broken, I would have got Phil right in his balls.

"Right, I'm sitting down Phil. Do you want to tell us what's going on?" Said Ben, calmer now. I could read him he had a plan of some sort because he seemed less frightened now.

"The detectives were here earlier because they had retrieved my phone number off Brian's phone twice on the day he was murdered. They wanted to know why I had rang him. I have been caught out coz when all the forensic evidence comes back, the cops will be breaking through my front door. The night Livvi arrived at your house before Christmas, Ben, Livvi and I went out for a meal whilst Daisy stayed with you. You were asleep when I got back, and I wondered what you had been up to and because you were using the laptop, I thought I would have a gander. Livvi was asking your permission to get Brian in bed because she's a slut, just like you are Laura. The reason she was asking your mum for her consent Ben, was because your mum was fucking him. Isn't that right Laura? It nearly killed me, but I thought it was all over between her and him now because she was so kindly handing him over to her friend. But fuckin numb nuts here was wrong. You could sense it when he came to your house Laura, it would carry on after you got better.

I didn't go home on that Christmas eve to get my presents for all your fucking friends, I went to Brian's. I didn't go there intending to kill him. It got out of hand, it seemed he thought I was being a fucking idiot. I hit him with the hammer I had taken in. I had it up my sleeve just in case he turned on me. He did, so I don't blame myself for killing him, but I am sorry I have ruined mine and your mum's life together. When Alex and I first saw your mum at the supermarket, it was me that was going to approach her with help, but my so-called fucking friend jumped in there first. You see I met him five years ago when we were both doing the same anger management classes. We both have a record for domestic violence, and we were ordered to go as part of our parole. We got on and were good friends ever since, but we didn't fuck each other's girlfriends. We didn't share like this whore does. I didn't think I left any evidence at the scene but I'm no fucking expert like you Laura, and I so obviously did. So, they've got me, bang to rights. I wasn't going to let you get away with what you caused Laura, it's just unfortunate I will have to kill your son as well." I screamed at the top of my voice, felt my hair being pulled down and then seeing blood and hearing Ben shout. "I fucking hate prawns you bastard and you don't get away with treating my mum like that, I'll fucking kill you." My son was now hitting Phil with a fucking hammer, what the hell. "Stop Ben, stop, stop. He's unconscious." Ben let the hammer fall as I took him in my arms.

Ben and I had cried in each other's arms for at least ten minutes before I phoned the police and ambulance. It wasn't until we let go of each other that Ben realised I was bleeding from my neck. Fortunately, there was nothing vital that was cut, this time I was only left with a flesh wound. Phil's head was a different story. Ben not knowing what he was doing had just kept on hitting him.

Ben had taken the hammer from Phil's boot when they had gone out earlier for the items from the car. He thought it weird that a hammer would just be lying there under the flowers on its own in the middle of the cars boot. That was what he was fidgeting with when I saw him after he sat on the living room chair. Ben hadn't thought at the time that it could be related to Brian's death, but thank God he had the presence of mind to stash it under his coat.

Phil was dead and it was my son who had killed him. How was this going to affect his life? Life for us would now get much, much better. I felt closure of the recent episodes and was positive that Ben and I could get through it without too much damage. I now know how Alex got all his information! Once we had our statements out of the way and appointments with psychologists in our diaries, my son and I spent a few days coming to terms with the week's events. We will work closely together. The only good to come out of it as far as Ben was concerned, he had saved his mummies and his own life. I always thought our bond couldn't be any stronger, but I think this horrendous incident has added more icing to the cake. I'm sure there will still be some surprises and lessons learnt about Alex and Phil in the weeks to come. No one except a few members of my family have tried to repair me but Ben is too much like me to conform into someone he is a testament that the apple doesn't fall far from the tree.

Next month my three best friends and I are going on that trip. My body was healing well, the cut on my neck had hardly left a scar and all that it warranted was a fucking big plaster. I looked a right knob.

THE END

THE VIGILANTE
SPIRIT SEERS!!

"**B**en, wake up sweetheart, you're having a nightmare, it's okay I'm here, Ben, Ben" I whisper to my son, and stroke his arm as he's struggling in his sleep and making curious whining noises. Oh God, and who can blame him for all he's gone through in the last few months. "MOTHER...BUGAR OFF. I was dreaming that I was with Sasha you mentalist. Go away, goodbye."

What's with me and losing my body language skills lately. "Sorry son".

Phil had been dead for two weeks' his funeral was held this morning. For no other reason than his own, Ben wanted to see the guy off. I just hope its closure for him in some way. I must say I am quite surprised at how well he's dealing with the fact that he's taken a man's life, and in such horrific way. After the events of that day had died down a little, Ben and I got to spend this last week alone. I just feel like saying "Ben, you've put his misery." Not really an acceptable statement when this situation is so undeniably very serious, and not good psychologically. I cannot let Ben feel it's okay and what he has done is justified, it isn't, is that not what I fight for 'JUSTICE.' Not considering 'THE PARTNERSHIP'

We've been to the movies, several walks on the beach and mountains, (as much as I could manage in my still fragile state) whatever the weather. Watched what seems like hundreds of DVD's. Obviously, we talk about the evening at Phil's, but that's only normal, in fact there's no use ignoring what we went through. At least we are getting on top of it (no more tears or venom) and I do feel a little sad that Phil died, he like Alex plainly had Psychological issues and were in trauma. For my own reasons I don't seem to hold any grudges now. Age and experience I suppose, and the reality is, I'm still alive.

Lightning Source UK Ltd.
Milton Keynes UK
UKHW010935280919
350593UK00001B/10/P